STONE KILLER

STONE KILLER

Sally Spencer

severn
House

This first world edition published in Great Britain 2005 by
SEVERN HOUSE PUBLISHERS LTD of
9–15 High Street, Sutton, Surrey SM1 1DF.
This first world edition published in the USA 2006 by
SEVERN HOUSE PUBLISHERS INC of
595 Madison Avenue, New York, N.Y. 10022.

British Library Cataloguing in Publication Data

Spencer, Sally
    Stone killer
    1.   Woodend, Charlie (Fictitious character) - Fiction
    2.   Police - England - Fiction
    3.   Detective and mystery stories
    I.   Title
    823.9'14 [F]

    ISBN-10 : 0-7278-6294-4 (cased)
                0-7278-9156-1 (paper)

Typeset by Palimpsest Book Production Ltd.,
Polmont, Stirlingshire, Scotland.
Printed and bound in Great Britain by
MPG Books Ltd., Bodmin, Cornwall.

Too long a sacrifice
Can make a stone of the heart.

W. B. Yeats

Prologue

The opportunity that Judith Maitland had been waiting for came early one morning in the prison kitchen, and it was presented to her by Mary Parkes, who was known to both inmates and staff alike as *Mad* Mary.

It was Mary's task, that morning, to stir the porridge which was slowly cooking in a large metal cauldron. She had not looked particularly delighted with her assignment from the start, and for the previous few minutes she had been muttering – quietly and desperately – to herself. Then, suddenly, she seemed to have reached her own personal breaking point and, stepping away from the cauldron, she began to wave her ladle wildly in the air and scream at the top of her voice.

There were four female warders on duty in various parts of the kitchen complex, and they quickly converged on the spot where Mary had chosen to create her scene.

The most senior of the warders, a hard-faced woman called Miss Donaldson, took a tentative step closer to the prisoner. 'Put the implement down, Parkes,' she said firmly.

As if poor Mary Parkes had even the slightest idea what an 'implement' was, Judith thought.

'I said, "Put it down",' Miss Donaldson repeated.

'Goblins!' Mad Mary told her. 'Goblins with hobnailed boots on their hairy little feet!'

'What?' the warder asked.

'Walkin' around in me head!' Mary elucidated. 'Tramplin' on me brain! Turnin' it all to mush!'

Miss Donaldson sighed. 'I don't care about what's going on in your head,' she said to the deranged woman with the ladle. 'I have given you an order, and I expect you to obey it.'

Mary seemed undecided about how to respond, Judith thought. On the one hand, she clearly wanted to do as she'd been instructed. On the other, she had an almost overwhelming

1

urge to express herself in one of the few ways still left open to her.

'Last chance,' Miss Donaldson said heavily.

Last chance for what? Judith wondered. If Mary refused to obey, what would they do? *Lock her up in prison?*

Mad Mary dropped the ladle, but instead of going limp – as she had been known to do after similar outbursts in the past – she immediately swung round, and turned her attention to the shelf on her left. The shelf in question was loaded down with tins of baked beans, large jars of jam and sacks of flour. For Mary, it presented just too much of a temptation, and using both hands, she swept the entire contents on to the floor.

The tins bounced, the bags burst open, the jars shattered – and the warders moved in. Two of the officers carried out a rapid flanking movement, and, once in position, pinned Mad Mary's arms behind her back. Now the prisoner was helpless, Miss Donaldson stepped forward and slapped Mary hard – several times – across her face.

She should never have done that, Judith thought sadly. Poor, demented Mary needed care and understanding, not cruelty.

The two officers who had a grip on Mary Parkes bundled her out of the room and into the corridor. Mary started screaming again, but the further she and her escort moved away from the kitchen, the fainter those desperate screams became.

Miss Donaldson ran her eyes quickly over the destruction. 'Well, don't just stand there like bloody dummies, clear up this mess!' she said in a tone which suggested she thought the remaining prisoners were almost as responsible for it as Mary had been.

Still in shock, none of the inmates moved.

'Didn't any of you hear me?' Miss Donaldson bellowed. 'Did *you* hear me, Maitland?'

Judith nodded her head numbly.

'Then answer me, you stupid bitch!' the warder demanded.

'Yes, Miss Donaldson, I heard you,' Judith said.

'So why are you still standing there as if you've got a broom handle stuck up your arse? You're supposed to know something about catering! Let's see you prove it.'

I *do* know about catering, Judith thought. In those far-off days of her other life – a life which now seemed to have belonged to someone else entirely – she had catered society weddings and municipal banquets. She had been so good at it that she'd been the most requested caterer in the whole North West. But her role had never included cleaning up a mess like the one which faced her now – a mess she would have felt diffident about asking her humblest employee to clear away.

'Am I talking to myself?' the warder asked.

'No, Miss Donaldson.'

'Then get on with it, Maitland. And do it quickly – before I decide to report you for insolence.'

Maitland! No one had ever called her that name before she entered this prison. It had been 'Judith' or 'Ma'am' or even 'Mrs Maitland', but never just plain 'Maitland'. Yet this was only one of the indignities – and a very minor one, at that – which she'd had to endure since those heavy steel gates had clanked irrevocably closed behind her.

Judith reached for a brush and large dustpan, and knelt down. With a professional eye, she examined the slicks of jam which floated in a sea of flour on the kitchen floor, and noted the occasional shard of glass which glinted in the overhead lights.

'Be careful,' Miss Donaldson ordered from behind her head. 'Don't go deliberately cutting yourself, Maitland, just so you can have a few lazy days in the infirmary.'

Judith began to brush the powdery-sticky mixture into the dustpan. Then, changing position slightly, so that Miss Donaldson could not see what she was doing, she picked up one of the smaller shards of glass and slipped it quickly into her overall pocket.

It seemed to be her lucky day – if lucky was the right word for it. First she had found what she had been looking so long for, and now the woman she shared her cell with had been called to the governor's office.

Sitting on her narrow bed, Judith examined the tiny sliver of glass which had once been a small part of the big institutional jam jar.

Who would ever have thought that this would be the answer to my prayers? she asked herself.

3

Though she tried to do so, she could not now exactly pin down the moment when vague thoughts of killing herself had transformed themselves into a firm determination to actually perform the act.

Perhaps it had happened in court. Standing in the dock – flanked by two mute and emotionless police officers, and listening to the judge pronounce his harsh sentence – she had certainly experienced a deep feeling of despair hitherto unknown to her.

Perhaps though, it had been when she first stepped from the prison van into the yard, and looked up at the imposing grey walls behind which she was to be detained for the greater part of her remaining years.

It could even have been later than that, she told herself.

She may not have decided to take her own life until she had truly understood how the weight of the prison regime – the monotony, the indignity – was slowly crushing her will.

Or maybe it had been her husband who, all unwittingly, had finally pushed her over the edge. Maybe it was the look in his eyes the last time he had visited her. They had been lively eyes before her arrest – sparkling eyes, eyes which showed how much he enjoyed life. But as he had gazed at her through the metal grille, she had seen only a hopelessness which had torn at her soul – and perhaps it was then she had decided to release both him and herself.

But it didn't really matter *when* it occurred, did it? The only significant thing was that it *had*.

She would leave no note behind, she had already decided. Suicide notes were for those who wanted to explain *why* they had chosen to take their own lives. The people who still had faith in her would clearly understand her reasons. And as for the rest – the police and the jurors, the journalists and the general public – who thought she was guilty as charged, well, they wouldn't believe her whatever words she left for them to read.

The time had come. There was no point in putting it off any longer. Judith took a deep breath, clenched her teeth, and drew the sliver of glass across a prominent vein in her wrist.

The Siege: Day One

One

For as long as anyone in the town could remember, the Friday street market had been the high point of the Whitebridge shopping week. From the moment the traders finished erecting their tubular metal stalls, to the point at which the dismantled stalls were slid back into the traders' vans, the High Street was as loud as a carnival and as busy as a port-side brothel.

Housewives – having confiscated most of their husbands' pay-packets the previous evening – could be seen flitting from stall to stall, the brown envelopes which contained the week's wages nestling in the tight security of their firmly held plastic handbags. Market traders – who worked six days a week, but never as profitably as on this day – could be heard screaming out the virtues of their sometimes-dubious wares. Gnarled hill-farmers – free for one morning from scratching out a living on the cruel and unrelenting moors – ambled up and down the road, and wondered if it wasn't perhaps time to pay a visit to the nearest pub. That was how it was, and how it had always been.

But not on this particular Friday in December 1964 – a Friday so close to Christmas that everyone should have been doing record business. On this Friday, the stalls, though weighed down with their merchandise, stood unattended and unscrutinized, and the only people who seemed to have any use for them at all were the dozen or so police officers who had their eyes firmly fixed on the Lancaster Cotton Credit Bank and were using them for protection.

Heavy iron police barriers had been hastily placed at both ends of the High Street half an hour earlier. Behind them – and straining against them – stood the crowd of people who were somewhat aggrieved that their normal daily business had been disrupted, yet were also bubbling with anticipation over the sudden and unexpectedly dramatic turn of events.

The arrival at the police barrier of a Wolseley, with its best years of service already far behind it, excited little interest at first. Then the crowd noticed that it was being driven by a big man in a scruffy tweed jacket – a man whose photograph appeared in the papers far more regularly than he would have liked – and a collective sigh of expectation ran through the throng.

Chief Inspector Woodend had arrived, people told each other. *Now* there would be fireworks.

Woodend stepped out from the driver's side of the car. His assistant, Sergeant Monika Paniatowski – blonde hair, intelligent blue eyes and an Eastern European nose which some of the onlookers considered a little too large for their own snub-nosed taste – emerged from the passenger side. The spectators attempted to surge forward, but the line of constables, their arms linked, held firm.

A uniformed sergeant approached the two detectives. 'Would you like me to remove the barrier, sir?' he asked Woodend.

The Chief Inspector looked mystified. 'Whatever for?'

'So you can drive closer to the crime scene, sir. It'll be a bit of a squeeze, what with the stalls an' everythin' in the middle of the road, but you should be all right if you're careful.'

Woodend looked first at the crowd pressing against the barrier, and then up the High Street towards the bank.

'Just how far would you estimate it is to the Cotton Credit, Sergeant?' he asked.

'About a hundred yards, sir.'

'So you'd go to all the trouble of removin' the barrier just to save me walkin' a hundred yards, would you?'

'Well, yes, sir.'

Woodend shook his head. 'It's a very kind thought, lad, but me an' Detective Sergeant Paniatowski here have both been blessed with legs, so we might as well use them.'

The Chief Inspector stepped around the barrier, and his assistant followed him. They walked up the street, passing Williams' High Class Furniture Emporium, Clark's Chemist's, and Deyton's Family Butcher's – all of them festooned with coloured lights to celebrate the coming holiday.

Some of these businesses had been there since he was a

boy, Woodend thought. Some even before that. But though they all still looked out on to the same street, they now looked out on to a very different world – a world in which strange and violent things were happening which they'd never have dreamed of thirty or forty years earlier.

'What I don't understand, Monika, is why we're here at all,' Woodend said to his sergeant. 'It's always been our job to catch murderers – an' I like to think we're rather good at it.'

'We're *very* good at it,' Monika Paniatowski said.

'Aye, you're right, this is no time for false modesty,' Woodend agreed. 'But if we are so good at it, why are we gettin' mixed up in an armed bank robbery? I admit – given that such things are almost as rare as a sunny day in Whitebridge – that nobody on the force has got a great deal of experience with them, but even so, I'd have thought there were half a dozen fellers better equipped to handle it than I am.'

They were thirty yards from the bank when the uniformed superintendent came up to them.

'According to the witnesses we've spoken to so far, there are three of them in there, Charlie,' he said, without preamble. 'They came out of that van.' He pointed to a dilapidated blue vehicle which looked very like the dozen or so market-traders' vans parked close by it. 'They're dressed in army fatigues and ski masks. They're heavily armed, and they're carrying huge rucksacks containing God-alone-knows what. The whole thing's a complete bloody mess.'

'I can see that, sir, but—' Woodend began.

'Do you *know* how few officers there are in Central Lancashire who are licensed to carry firearms, and trained to handle this kind of thing?' the superintendent ploughed on. 'I've been drafting men in from all over the place – Bolton, Bury, Preston—'

'It must be a difficult job for you, sir – I can well appreciate that – but what the bloody hell am I doin' here?' Woodend interrupted. 'As far as I can tell, I'll only be in the way.'

'You haven't been told, have you?' the superintendent asked.

'Told what?'

The superintendent raised his right hand, and wiped the

9

sweat from his brow with the back of it. 'One of the first things we did was to establish a dedicated phone link with the bank. I rang it, and one of the robbers answered. But he didn't want to listen to what I had to say. In fact, he demanded to talk to you.'

'To me?' Woodend said, astounded. 'To me *personally*?'

'That's right. He was quite explicit.'

Woodend turned to his sergeant. 'Well, what do you think of that, Monika?' he asked. 'Fame at last, eh?' He returned his attention to the superintendent. 'I'd better get on the blower to him, then, hadn't I?'

'He . . . er . . . doesn't want to talk to you over the phone,' the superintendent said awkwardly. 'He insists on a face-to-face meeting.'

'My place or his?' Woodend asked.

'Pardon?'

'Is he comin' out – or does he want me to go in?'

'He made it pretty clear he wants you to go in,' the superintendent said grimly. 'Look, Charlie, I can't *order* you to go in there. In fact, I'd quite understand if you refused.'

Woodend lit up a Capstan Full Strength, and noted as he did so that his hand was shaking slightly. 'How many people are this feller an' his gang holdin' hostage?' he asked.

'It's impossible to say with any degree of accuracy,' the superintendent admitted. 'We know there are seven bank employees, for certain, but as to the number of customers . . . well, on a busy day like this there could have been anything up to a couple of dozen of them there when the robbers burst in.'

Woodend took a deep drag of his cigarette. 'I'd better go an' talk to him then, hadn't I?' he said.

'Are you sure?' the superintendent asked.

Woodend forced a grin to his face. 'Of course I'm sure,' he said. 'Why wouldn't I be?'

'Well, the gang are armed and dangerous and—'

'Don't worry about it, sir,' Woodend said, maintaining his grin with some difficulty. 'This kind of thing happens over in America all the time. Heaven knows, I've seen it in enough Hollywood films. An' the thing about those films is that whatever else happens, the hero – which in this case appears to be me – never, *ever*, gets killed.'

10

Two

The Lancaster Cotton Credit Bank was one of the older banking houses in Whitebridge. And that showed in its layout, for whereas the newer, more 'modern' banks had a warren of small offices in which to conduct their affairs with discretion, the LCCB devoted most of its floor space to one large room in which business could be transacted and seen to be transacted.

Standing in the doorway – still not sure how to proceed – Woodend studied that room. It was square, and lined with second-grade – but still respectable enough – black granite. A long counter, with elaborate scrollwork grilles, separated the third of it in which the clerks worked from the two-thirds where the customers waited to be dealt with. On the wall, an enormous nineteenth-century clock loudly ticked away the seconds, as if to remind those who heard it that time was money – and money didn't like to be kept waiting.

The room was empty, though the discarded morning newspapers on the floor and the smell of cigarette smoke which still hung in the air were evidence enough that it had been recently occupied.

This was just like the bloody *Marie Celeste*, Woodend thought.

'Come out, come out, wherever you are!' he said aloud.

It was then that he noticed the camera. It was crudely mounted on the wall close to the counter – there was evidence of plaster dust on the floor beneath it – and was pointing at the door to the street.

Closed-circuit television! Woodend told himself.

Jesus!

Equipment like that was being used, as an experiment, at a few of the underground railway stations in London, but as far as he knew, it wasn't operating anywhere else in the whole bloody country.

11

So whatever else these bank robbers were, they certainly weren't run-of-the-mill.

A door behind the counter swung open, and a man stepped through the gap. He was tall and broad. He was wearing camouflage uniform and a ski mask. And in his hands he was holding what Woodend recognized to be a submachine gun.

'Come closer,' he ordered.

Woodend began to walk slowly towards the counter. When he was half-way between it and the door, the man snapped, 'That's far enough.'

The Chief Inspector came to an abrupt and complete halt. 'Whatever you say. You're the boss.'

'Have you come alone?' the man with the machine gun asked.

Woodend glanced over his shoulder. 'Seem to have,' he said. 'To tell you the truth, this wasn't exactly a popular assignment.'

'Do you think this is funny, Chief Inspector?' the other man demanded aggressively.

'Not at all,' Woodend replied. 'To be honest with you, I'm findin' it so *un*funny that I'm almost shittin' myself.'

'I'm pleased to hear that. It's certainly the frame of mind I want you to be in,' the man said, and though the ski mask made it difficult to know for sure, Woodend was almost certain that he was smiling.

'You seem to know who I am,' the Chief Inspector said. 'Would you care to tell me who *you* are?'

'You can call me Apollo,' the man answered.

'Apollo,' Woodend mused. 'Funny name to choose. Wasn't he the Roman god of the sun or summat?'

'Amongst other things,' the man replied. Then, as if he had lost interest in the subject and felt it was time to move on, he said, 'But you seem to have got hold of the wrong end of the stick, Chief Inspector. I'm the one with the gun, so I'm the one who gets to ask the questions.'

'Fair enough,' Woodend agreed. 'Ask away.'

'Did you see active service in the war?'

'Yes.'

'So you must have had guns pointed at you before.'

'Aye, I have. Plenty of 'em. But, in my experience, at least, it's not somethin' you ever get used to.'

'Were you decorated for your war service?' the man calling himself Apollo asked.

'Whether I was or whether I wasn't, it's not really any of your business, is it?' Woodend countered.

'You're wrong about that,' Apollo told him. 'It *is* my business, because I have the gun and I *want* to know. And it's your business to answer, because I have twenty hostages back there, and if you refuse to co-operate, I just might make them suffer.'

'I got a couple of medals,' Woodend said reluctantly.

'The Victoria Cross?'

Despite the situation he found himself in, Woodend couldn't help chuckling. 'No, not the VC,' he said. 'I never did anythin' anywhere near impressive enough to merit that.' He paused for just a moment. 'Now, about these hostages of yours,' he continued.

'What about them?'

'Are any of them hurt?'

'No. Not *yet.*'

'Then it seems to me you should let them all go, before one of them *does* get hurt.'

'And what if I don't?'

Woodend sighed. 'Then that complicates matters. An' I don't see there's any point in makin' things complicated when there's a simple solution to hand,' he said. 'Let 'em go. You'll feel better once you have.'

'If I don't release them, you'll try to storm the place, won't you?' Apollo said.

'I don't know about that,' Woodend replied.

'Don't lie to me!' Apollo said harshly.

'Honestly, I really don't know,' Woodend protested. 'I'm no expert in such matters. The only reason I'm here at all is because *you* wanted me here.' He paused for a second time. 'Why *did* you want me here?'

'Would you like to know what would happen if you *did* storm the place?' Apollo asked.

'Like I said, I'd rather discuss other ways of resolvin' the situation,' Woodend told him.

'All the hostages are wired up to explosives,' Apollo said. 'The second I get the feeling you're even *thinking* of going on the offensive, I'll blow them all to Kingdom Come.'

'Dear God!' Woodend breathed softly – and to himself.

13

Aloud, he said, 'But if you did that, you'd go straight to Kingdom Come with them.'

'So what?'

'So I always thought that the main point of pullin' a bank robbery was to get away with the money, an' spend the rest of your life on some nice secluded beach surrounded by dusky maidens.'

'That might be true if this were a real bank robbery,' Apollo told him. 'But, you see, it isn't.'

'Then what the bloody hell are you doin' inside a bank an' armed to the teeth?'

'If a man chooses to make his stand, he should always select the most defensible position he can from which to make it,' Apollo said. 'And what more defensive position could there be than a bank – especially a bank with a vault in which to hold his hostages?'

'Just because you've given yourself a fancy bloody name doesn't mean you have to talk in riddles,' Woodend said. 'Why don't you spell out for me exactly what it *is* you want?'

'Very well,' Apollo agreed. 'I want justice.'

'Justice?'

'I have tried to find it through the conventional means, but that has been a dismal failure, so now I have been forced to take more drastic action.'

'You're still soundin' a bit airy-fairy to me,' Woodend said. 'What, *exactly*, do you want?'

'I want an innocent woman released from prison.'

Woodend shook his head slowly from side to side. 'You're livin' in cloud cuckoo land, lad,' he said regretfully.

'Am I?'

'You most certainly are. The powers that be are never goin' to give in to your demands, however many hostages you're holdin' – and whatever you threaten to do to them.'

'You misunderstand me,' Apollo said. 'I don't *just* want her released – I want her innocence proved. And I want *you* to prove it.'

'An' if I can't?'

Apollo glanced for a moment at the door behind him. 'If you can't, then the blood of those people down in the vault will be as much on your hands as it is on mine,' he said.

14

Three

What he was having to do at that moment was nothing more than a waste of time, Woodend told himself, as he knocked on the Chief Constable's office door, less than an hour after he had left the Cotton Credit Bank.

No, it was *worse* than that, he amended, taking a last drag on his cigarette before grinding it under his heel. A waste of time merely prevented him doing something useful – whereas this meeting could do actual *harm*.

The problem, of course, was Henry Marlowe himself. In Woodend's opinion – and in the opinion of the majority of hard-working bobbies in Central Lancashire – Marlowe was the worst possible kind of chief constable. Where he should have used his intelligence, he usually relied on his cunning. Where he should have been even-handed, he was selectively vindictive. The main function of the Lancashire Constabulary, as far as Henry-Bloody-Marlowe saw it, was to maintain him in his cushy sinecure, so that rather than looking ahead – which was what the job called for – he was perpetually glancing over his shoulder, in order to be best able to guard his own back.

'Enter,' said a deep, practised voice from inside the office.

Woodend opened the door. Marlowe had recently acquired a conference table – he must have read in some management magazine or other that it was the right thing to do – and he was sitting at it now, flanked by four other men.

Woodend already knew the two seated closest to the Chief Constable. The one on Marlowe's right was Chief Superintendent Cunningham, who was – in theory – his own immediate boss, but – in fact – served as nothing more than Henry Marlowe's mouthpiece. To Marlowe's left was Cedric Townsend, the local Member of Parliament, a man who – even for a politician – seemed to be dangerously short of scruples.

But it was the other two men in whom Woodend was more interested. One was tall and thin, and wore his tweed suit as if it were a heavily starched uniform. The other was shorter, and dressed in a pin-striped suit, the waistcoat of which was clearly straining against his rounded belly. Neither of them had the air of local men about them. Both, instead, exuded the smell of outside trouble.

'Take a seat, Chief Inspector,' Marlowe said, somehow managing to make even this simple invitation seem both unwilling and ungracious.

'Thank you, sir.'

'You won't have met these gentlemen before,' Marlowe continued. 'This – ' he indicated the tall, thin man – 'is Colonel Danvers of the Lancashire Fusiliers, and this – ' pointing to the smaller, pin-striped man – 'is Mr Slater-Burnes, from the Home Office.'

Woodend nodded to both of them, and, after a slight pause, they half-nodded back.

'The reason I have convened this extraordinary meeting is that we are facing an extraordinary situation,' Marlowe intoned impressively. 'Cases of hostage-taking are not at all common in Central Lancashire. Indeed, with the exception of seeing such occurrences in the American talking pictures, I personally have never come across one before.'

The same thought had occurred to Woodend earlier, and had probably crossed the minds of scores of other folk as well. But of all the people who might have shared the thought, only Henry Marlowe would ever have dreamed of referring to films as 'talking pictures'.

It was a pure affectation, the Chief Inspector thought, aimed at reinforcing the impression of those listening to him that Marlowe was an old-fashioned bobby with old-fashioned values. But all it really showed, he decided, was that the Chief Constable stood head and shoulders above anybody else when it came to talking a load of old bollocks.

'Perhaps we had better begin with a briefing from Mr Woodend,' the Chief Constable said. He leant back expectantly. 'Chief Inspector?'

'What the man in the bank seems to want me to do, is to find—' Woodend began.

'Never mind what he *wants*!' Colonel Danvers interrupted. 'I don't give a damn what he does – or does not – want from

16

you. What I need – what we all need – is to be briefed on the security situation!'

'I'm no expert on such matters,' Woodend warned.

'Of course you're not,' Colonel Danvers said scornfully. 'But you'll just have to do the best you can, won't you?'

'As far as we know, there are three armed men an' around a score of hostages in the bank,' Woodend said, slowly and carefully.

'Three of them. Well, that shouldn't present *too* much of a problem for my lads,' Danvers said.

'The man I talked to – he called himself Apollo, by the way – was at pains to inform me that all the hostages are bein' held in the vault,' Woodend said. 'Now I've done some checkin' on that, an' it seems that back in the old days – when local banks backed the paper money they issued with actual *gold* – the Cotton Credit was the place where most of the other banks in the area chose to keep their bullion. Which means, I would suggest, that it's a very secure vault indeed.'

'Even so—' Danvers began.

'In addition,' Woodend interrupted, 'Apollo claims to have wired up all the hostages to explosives – an' I'm rather more than inclined to believe him.'

'That's ridiculous!' Danvers said dismissively.

'Is it?'

'Of course it is. Handling explosives is a tricky and dangerous business. To have organized anything like that without creating an explosion, the man would have to have had military training.'

'I believe that he has,' Woodend said. 'In fact, I believe that I know who he is.'

'Then why didn't you tell us right away?' Marlowe asked.

'I was goin' to, sir – before your friend over there interrupted me,' Woodend said mildly.

Marlowe shot him a look of pure hatred, then said, 'Tell us about it in your own way, if that's what makes you happier, Chief Inspector. And try not to keep us here all day.'

'Thank you, sir,' Woodend said, pretending not to notice the sarcasm. 'Apollo's main – and as far as I can see, his *only* – concern, is the current situation of a woman called Judith Maitland.'

'Current situation?'

'She's servin' a life sentence, with a recommended twenty-five years minimum, in Skipley Prison.'

'For what?'

'For murder.'

'Should we have heard of her?' Marlowe asked.

Yes, you most certainly should have, Woodend thought. And *would* have – if you ever read anything in the newspapers besides the golfing reports.

But he contented himself with saying, 'Possibly. Her trial made quite a stir, a few months ago.'

'Ah yes, I think I remember it now,' Marlowe said, unconvincingly. 'Just fill me in on the details.'

'She's a Whitebridge woman, but since the murder she was accused of took place in Dunethorpe, we weren't directly involved in the investigation,' Woodend said. 'Anyway, as I said, she was convicted of this murder an' sent to prison. Then, three days ago, she tried to commit suicide by slittin' open her veins. The prison authorities got to her in time, and she'll recover – but it was a damn close-run thing.'

'I still don't see what all this has got to do with this Apollo chap?' Colonel Danvers said impatiently.

'I was just comin' to that,' Woodend told him. 'Apollo's not only the Roman god of light, which is what I'd always thought of him as, but he's also their god of truth. I know that for a fact, because I looked it up.'

'I'm so pleased that you feel you have so much free time on your hands you can afford to chase up classical references,' the Chief Constable said, his sarcasm thicker than ever.

'I think it's relevant,' Woodend said. 'An' so will you, if you give me time to get to the end of my story.'

'Take all the time you need, by all means,' Marlowe said.

'Judith Maitland was a successful local caterer before her arrest,' Woodend explained. 'She did jobs all over Lancashire. But she's also married – an' her husband is a Major Thomas Maitland.'

'You're surely not trying to drag the Army into the middle of all this, are you?' Colonel Danvers asked, outraged.

'No, sir, it seems to be comin' in of its own accord,' Woodend said. 'Major Maitland went missin' two days ago.'

'I thought you said that there were three armed men in the bank,' Danvers said.

'An' so there are,' Woodend agreed. 'Maitland's regiment's just returned from an overseas postin', an' a lot of the men are on leave. We're tryin' to trace them all, but I'd be willin' to bet there'll be two who we *can't* contact – because they'll be in the Cotton Credit with their boss. In other words, what we're dealin' with here are three battle-hardened soldiers.'

'You're quite sure that Major Maitland and this man who calls himself Apollo are one and the same, are you?' Colonel Danvers asked.

'It'd be a bit of a coincidence if they weren't, now wouldn't it, sir?' Woodend replied.

'And what exactly does he want?' Marlowe asked. 'Did you say it's his wife's release he's after?'

'Yes, but it's not quite as simple as that. He also wants me to prove that she should never have been locked up in the first place.'

'He wants *you* to prove it?' Marlowe asked sceptically.

'Me – an' nobody else,' Woodend said. 'He says he's been followin' my career for years. Apparently he's a big fan of mine.'

The Chief Constable winced at his subordinate's choice of words. 'But the woman's been found guilty of the crime,' he said. 'So she must have done it, mustn't she?'

'Not necessarily,' Woodend disagreed.

'Are you saying that she's innocent?'

'I'm sayin' that there have been miscarriages of justice before, an' no doubt there will be again.'

'And you think this Judith Maitland might be a victim of a miscarriage of justice?'

Woodend sighed. 'I won't know till I've looked into the case, will I, sir? But her husband plainly doesn't believe she did it – an' he's the one callin' the shots right now.'

'How long has he given you to investigate this case?' Slater-Burnes – the Home Office man – asked.

Woodend shrugged. 'To tell you the truth, he didn't seem overly concerned about the timescale – it's the right result he's after.'

'But doesn't he appreciate the situation he's in?' the Chief Constable demanded.

'Oh yes,' Woodend said. 'From what I could see, he's got a *very* clear appreciation of it.'

'But . . . but . . . he can't possibly hope to hold out for much more than a day, can he?'

'I don't know,' Woodend admitted. He turned to Colonel Danvers. 'What's your opinion, sir?'

The military man thought about it for a moment. 'Where has Major Maitland served?' he said finally.

'In Palestine, Malaya, Aden and Cyprus.'

'And you think the other two might have been with him on those tours of duty?'

'I wouldn't be at all surprised if they had.'

'And what's your reasoning behind that conclusion?'

'The only reason I can see for them bein' so willin' to put their lives on the line for him in the bank is that he's done somethin' similar for them, sometime in the past.'

Danvers shook his head gravely. 'In that case, I would have to say that – provided they've got adequate supplies in there – they could probably hold out for a week or more.'

'We can't have that!' the Chief Constable said, mopping his brow with an Irish linen handkerchief. 'We can't have that at all. The press would crucify us if we let it run on for a week. We'll have to go in.'

'I really wouldn't advise it,' Woodend told him. 'He says he'll blow up the hostages if we try anything, and I believe him.'

Marlowe looked around the table for support for his plan for an assault, but both Danvers and Slater-Burnes were refusing to meet his eye.

'If that's true – if he really would blow them up – then we have no alternative but to simply tell him what he wants to hear,' the Chief Constable said.

'Tell him what he wants to hear?' Woodend repeated.

'That's what I said.'

'But what did you *mean*?'

'Do I have to spell everything out for you, Chief Inspector?' Marlowe asked irritably. 'We'll tell him that we've released his wife, and arrested the real murderer.'

20

'He's not a fool,' Woodend said. 'He isn't goin' to swallow any old cock-an'-bull story you feed him.'

'Then we'll just have to come up with a story that doesn't *sound* like it's cock-and-bull,' the Chief Constable said, as if doing that were the easiest thing in the world.

'I said earlier that I'm no military man,' Woodend told him. 'Well, I'm no actor, either. If I try lyin' to him, he'll see right through me.'

'So we'll just have to get *someone else* to lie to him, won't we?' the Chief Constable said, exasperatedly.

'He won't talk to anyone else,' Woodend said firmly. 'He made that quite clear.'

'That's probably because he thinks you're the best he can get,' Marlowe said. 'When he realizes that a superintendent, or even a chief superintendent, is willing to speak to him—'

'It'll make no bloody difference at all!' Woodend cut in, no longer able to hide his anger. 'This man's a professional soldier. He's been in the Army long enough to realize that rank isn't necessarily any guide to ability.'

'What did you just say?' the Chief Constable demanded.

'Look, sir, he's thought all this through,' Woodend said, trying to sound more reasonable. 'He knows *what* he wants doin' – an' he knows *who* he wants to do it. He's simply not goin' to accept any alternative.'

'Your arrogance seems to know no bounds,' the Chief Constable said, with disgust.

'It wasn't me who decided I should become involved,' Woodend pointed out. 'It was Apollo. Or Major Maitland. Or whatever else you want to call him. An' he doesn't just want me to investigate the case – he wants me to report my findings to him on a regular basis.'

'That's outrageous!' the Chief Constable exploded. 'Who does he think he is?'

'He thinks he's a man holdin' twenty hostages at gunpoint,' Woodend replied.

'May I intervene here?' Slater-Burnes asked diffidently.

'Of course,' Marlowe replied, hardly able to hide his relief.

'There might be something to be said for listening to your chief inspector, Mr Marlowe,' the man from the Home Office advised. 'After all, if storming the bank would result in all the

21

hostages being killed – and Colonel Danvers seems to think that might well be the case – then it is certainly a strategy you should adopt only as a last resort. So what is your alternative? Why, to allow Mr Woodend to do what he wants to do!'

'I never said I *wanted* to do it at all,' Woodend pointed out.

'Then to allow Mr Woodend to do what he feels *needs* to be done,' Slater-Burnes said, shifting his ground with all the speed and elegance of a professional ballroom dancer.

'You're saying I should allow Woodend to re-open the case?' Marlowe asked, like a drowning man grasping at a lifeline.

Slater-Burnes laughed lightly. 'Good heavens, no, Chief Constable.'

'No?'

'Certainly not. You're the man on the ground – the man who is ultimately responsible. I'd be the last person on earth to try and steal any of the credit which will be rightfully due to you when this whole terrible affair is brought to a successful conclusion. All I was doing – although I readily admit I may not have made myself completely clear – is suggesting an option which is open to you.'

The Chief Constable had been dodging responsibility his whole career, and now – in what was undoubtedly the biggest challenge he would ever have to face – he could dodge it no longer. Under normal circumstances, Woodend would gladly have *paid* to see Henry Marlowe in such an uncomfortable situation. But these were *not* normal circumstances. Innocent lives were at risk, and he simply could not stand by and watch as the Chief Constable put them in further jeopardy.

'You have no choice, sir,' he heard himself say. 'There's only a slim chance I can prove Judith Maitland didn't do what she was sentenced for, but it's the only chance we've got.'

The lifeline had presented itself at the last possible moment. Marlowe grabbed it with both hands.

'That's your considered opinion, is it, Chief Inspector?' he asked.

'Yes, sir.'

'Let us be quite clear about this – you'd advise me to take no further action at the moment, other than allowing you and your team to re-investigate the Judith Maitland case?'

'That's correct.'

Marlowe could not resist taking in a gulp of air. 'Very well,' he said. 'If that's your considered opinion, I'll let you play it your way. You have three days to produce some sort of result. But I warn you now, Chief Inspector, that if any of the hostages are killed in those three days, I will hold you personally responsible.'

Oh, I've no doubts about that, Woodend thought. No doubt at all, you slippery bastard!

Four

The office which Woodend shared with his sergeant was thick with smoke when the Chief Inspector entered it – and it didn't take a detective to work out why. At least a dozen dead cigarettes were already crammed into Monika's small ashtray, and two more – rapidly burning themselves down – were balanced precariously on the edge of her already-burn-scarred desk.

Monika herself had the phone jammed between her chin and shoulder, and was making copious notes on the pad in front of her. When she saw Woodend, she gave him as much of a nod as was consistent with keeping the phone in place, then returned her full attention to listening and writing.

The Chief Inspector walked over to the window. Below it was the car park, and in two of the visitors' spots stood an Army jeep and Rover 2000.

The vehicles were a perfect match to their owners, he thought. Colonel Danvers' jeep declared unequivocally what he was – blunt, straightforward and perhaps a little crude. Slater-Burnes' Rover, on the other hand, was powerful without being ostentatious – the sort of vehicle which could manoeuvre around you without you even realizing it had happened.

Woodend's thoughts shifted from the unwelcome visitors' cars to his seated sergeant.

The poor lass had had a really rough time over the past couple of years, he reminded himself.

First there had been the revelations about her childhood –

revelations under which a lesser woman would have sunk without trace. Then, even before she'd had time to come to terms with them – or perhaps, on reflection, it was *instead of* coming to terms with them – she'd begun her love affair with Inspector Bob Rutter, Woodend's protégé, whom he'd brought with him from his days in Scotland Yard. The Rutter–Paniatowski affair had ended disastrously, of course – as it was always bound to. And worse was to follow. With her own life still lying in pieces around her, Monika had found herself investigating the murder of Bob Rutter's blind wife, Maria – a murder which a few people, at the very least, had probably initially believed she had had a hand in. And as the final icing on the bloody cake, Rutter had suffered a – not entirely unexpected – nervous collapse, and gone away on sick leave.

Woodend turned away from the window. Monika Paniatowski had put down the phone, and was looking at him expectantly.

Aye, it had been a lot for her to handle, Woodend thought, and it was a miracle that she'd coped with it as well as she had.

'Would you like to hear what I've got so far, sir?' the sergeant asked her boss.

'Why not?' Woodend replied. 'Since I'm here anyway, I suppose I might as well solve yet another mystery which has baffled the criminal experts on five continents.'

Paniatowski grinned – almost as naturally as she would have done before her downward spiral had begun.

'Judith Maitland,' she began, reading from her notes. 'Twenty-nine years old. Until recently, she ran a very successful catering company in partnership with a man called Stanley Keene.'

'In *partnership*?' Woodend said quizzically.

'It's not what you might think,' Paniatowski said. 'There was nothing going on between them.'

'You're sure of that, are you?'

'Absolutely. Nobody's come flat out and said it in so many words, but everyone I've talked to has left me with the distinct impression that when Keene gets in the horizontal position, he'd much rather it was a man lying under him than a woman.'

'You're so tactful you could almost be a chief constable,' Woodend said. 'Tell me more.'

'Keene was essentially the officer manager. He did the ordering, balanced the accounts, that kind of thing. Judith was what you might call the field operative. Whenever the company catered an event, she was there on the spot, supervising it. All of which meant that though the company was based in Whitebridge, she didn't actually spend much of her time here.'

'How does her husband, the Major, fit into all this?' Woodend wondered.

'Judith met him two years ago, at a function for the Territorial Army that she was catering in Bolton. Maitland was the guest of honour. It appears to have been something of a whirlwind romance. They were married just two months after that first meeting. They had a brief honeymoon touring in France, then he was posted overseas, and she carried on running the business.'

'Tell me about the man she's supposed to have murdered,' Woodend said.

'His name was Clive Burroughs,' Paniatowski said, consulting her notes again. 'He was a couple of years older than Judith Maitland. He lived in Dunethorpe, where he ran a builders' merchant's business which he'd inherited from his father. He was killed in his own office – his head smashed in with a hammer. According to the officers who investigated the crime, Judith did it.'

'Motive?' Woodend asked.

'If we're to accept the word of the Dunethorpe Police, it was one of the oldest – and most boring – in the book. He was a married man with two children, and he was having an affair with Judith. They had a disagreement of some kind – the police think he'd probably told her he'd decided to end their relationship – she lost her temper, and killed him.'

'How long had this affair been going on?'

'Judith claims there *was* no affair—'

'Well, she would, wouldn't she,' Woodend said dryly.

'But the general consensus seems to be that they were seeing each other for nearly a year before Burroughs was killed.'

'How did they first meet?'

25

'In the same way she met her husband. Judith was catering a party for the Dunethorpe Chamber of Commerce. It was a family occasion. Burroughs was there – and so was his wife.'

'She *knew* he was married, then, did she?'

'I assume so.'

'So he couldn't have lied to her – said that he was unattached. Which means that if she *did* have an affair with him, she must have known exactly what she was gettin' herself into, doesn't it?'

'Ah, now I see where you're going with this!' Paniatowski said, an angry note suddenly apparent in her voice.

'I'm sorry?' Woodend said, mystified.

'You mean, you're wondering whether she *set out* to be a home-breaker? You're wondering if she embarked on the affair already knowing full well that someone was bound to get badly hurt? In other words, you're asking yourself if she was a heartless bitch—'

'Monika!'

'. . . like me!'

'That's not right, and it's not *fair*, Monika!' Woodend said sternly. 'In this job, as you well know, you have to learn to divorce your personal life from your professional life.'

'Divorce! Now that's an interesting choice of word to use,' Monika Paniatowski said.

'Separate it, then,' Woodend said impatiently. 'Anyway, you see what I'm talkin' about, don't you? When we're discussin' a case, we have to be able to do it fully an' openly. I can't go pussyfootin' around the issues – wondering whether you'll think that when I talk about a suspect I'm secretly talkin' about you. We'd never get anywhere if we did that.'

'You're right,' Monika Paniatowski said contritely.

But the problem was, he wasn't entirely sure himself that he *was* right, Woodend thought. He had always tried his best to understand human failing rather than condemn it, and he often told himself that he certainly wasn't going to condemn Monika and Bob for their affair. Yet at the same time, he was forced to admit, there was a small corner of him which *did* blame – and found it very difficult to forgive – them.

'The reason I asked if she knew whether or not he had a

26

family is because that could have had an effect on her behaviour,' he said, feeling he was still not *quite* being entirely honest with either her or himself.

'Her behaviour,' Paniatowski repeated dully. 'For example?'

'For example, if she'd believed they had a future together, and then suddenly found out he would never leave the kids that she didn't even know he had. That sort of revelation would be enough to make most people furious – and *more* than enough to make some people turn that fury into violence. If, on the other hand, she already did know about the kids, then she must also have known that there was at least a *good* chance she'd never have him for herself.'

'And so she'd be less likely to suddenly lose control of herself?'

'Exactly.'

You've no idea what it's like to be the *other* woman, have you, sir? Monika Paniatowski thought. Even if that other woman goes into it with both eyes open, there are still times when she feels so much rage at the situation that she wants to kill her lover, his wife – or herself.

She took another cigarette out of the packet, and lit it from the stub of one of those burning a new scar into her desk.

'How did we ever get to this point?' she asked.

'What point?' Woodend wondered.

'The point at which we're asking ourselves whether or not she had sufficient motive to kill her lover.'

'Come again?'

'We don't even know yet if she even *had* a lover. Maybe the Dunethorpe bobbies were completely wrong about that, and Judith Maitland was actually telling the truth.'

She was right, Woodend thought. Without noticing it, he had fallen into the same trap as the Chief Constable had – the trap of assuming that everything the Dunethorpe Police said was unquestionably accurate, and that if Judith Maitland had been convicted, then she was probably guilty.

Himself and Marlowe of one mind! Now there was a terrifying thought if ever there was one!

'We need to go right back to the start of the case,' he said. 'We have to look at this murder as if it had just happened – as if the blood on the floor of Burroughs' office hadn't even

27

dried yet. In other words, we need to approach it with open minds an' a completely clean sheet.'

'And we need to *investigate* the people concerned – not judge them,' Monika Paniatowski said.

'Aye, that an' all,' Woodend agreed, starting to feel slightly uncomfortable again.

Five

Like so many of the other businesses which had sprung up in Whitebridge since the end of the war, Élite Catering was situated on the industrial estate three miles from the old town centre. It was not a very prepossessing building from the outside. Indeed, there was very little – apart from the sign on the wall bearing its name – to distinguish it from the depressingly barrack-like industrial units which flanked it, one of which produced pet baskets and the other proudly proclaimed itself to be 'surgical tape suppliers to the world'.

Inside, the building showed a warmer, more personal self. The walls of the reception area were painted in relaxing pastel shades, and one of them was dominated by a large painting – in what Woodend considered garish colours – of two naked men, one standing behind a shower curtain and the other beside it.

'That's a David Hockney,' said Paniatowski – who knew something about modern art.

'Is it, indeed?' asked Woodend – who didn't.

'But it's only a copy, of course.'

'An' how can you be sure about that?'

Paniatowski snorted at her boss's obvious ignorance. 'Because the original's probably worth more than this entire building,' she said.

'I believe you,' Woodend said. 'It's a funny old world we live in, when you think about it.'

He walked over to the reception desk. The smart young woman sitting behind it seemed surprised when he produced his warrant card, and even more astonished when he asked to speak to the owner.

'This isn't about what's happening down at the Cotton Credit Bank, is it?' she asked, in the kind of discreet whisper that some people resort to when they think they're about to learn something confidential.

Jesus Christ! Woodend thought.

He knew from experience that the Chief Constable's lips were usually about as tightly sealed as a tap with no washer, but surely even *Marlowe* couldn't have started shooting off his mouth about the case already.

'The Cotton Credit Bank?' Woodend repeated. 'An' why ever should you even think your boss might be involved in that?'

The girl looked suddenly flustered.

'I don't,' she said. 'I can't think of a more unlikely bank robber than Mr Keene. But since the bank robbery's all that anybody's talking about at the moment, I naturally thought . . .'

'This has nothing to do with the Cotton Credit Bank,' Woodend lied. 'But we would still like to see your boss.'

'Of course,' the girl said, reaching for the intercom button.

Keene was a slight, dapper man, of around forty. His blond hair was wispy at best, he had almost no chin to speak of – and he looked very unhappy indeed about being unexpectedly visited by the police.

'Have there been complaints?' he asked, the moment Woodend and Paniatowski walked into his office.

'Complaints?' Woodend echoed.

'The Corporation Park is a public space,' Keene said, with a voice which sounded surprisingly firm. 'I've as much right to walk around it as anyone else – at any time of day *or* night. And as for deliberately hanging about outside the men's toilets, well, that's simply not true!'

'We're not here to ask you questions about your personal life, sir,' Woodend told him.

For a moment, the relief was evident on Keene's face. Then his expression became troubled again.

'If it's not about me, then it has to be about Judith,' he said heavily.

'That's right, it is,' Woodend agreed.

Keene waved to them to sit down on the visitors' chairs, and then sank back into his own as if he wished it would swallow him up.

'I've experienced some terrible things in my life,' he said, sounding as if he really meant it, 'but what happened to Judith was about the worst. It was so . . . so . . . unjust.'

'I take it that means you don't think she did kill this Burroughs feller,' Woodend said.

'Of course that's what it means. Judith wouldn't hurt a fly.' Keene giggled, unexpectedly. 'Well, *maybe* a fly,' he conceded. 'She was fanatical about cleanliness in the kitchen. But kill another person? Never!' He paused for a moment. 'Why are you asking all these questions? Are you going to re-open the case?'

'We're thinkin' about it,' Woodend said guardedly.

'Then there really is a God after all,' Keene said. 'I was beginning to have my doubts.'

'How long were you and Judith Maitland partners?' Monika Paniatowski asked.

'We still *are* partners,' Keene said fiercely.

'But I would have thought that—'

'Judith might be in gaol, but this is still just as much her business as it is mine. I'm putting half the profits aside, and when she comes out of prison – however long that may be, and hopefully it won't be *much* longer now – the money will be waiting for her.'

'And there'll be plenty of it, will there?' Woodend asked, as if he were genuinely interested.

'I beg your pardon?'

'There'll be plenty of money to hand over to her? The business is going well, is it?'

'Even without Judith, we're still the pre-eminent catering company in Central Lancashire, if that's what you mean,' Keene said, a little waspishly. 'But that's mainly due to the hard work she put into building up the company in the first place.'

'Surely you played some part in that yourself?' Woodend said.

'Me?' Keene asked, as if that were a novel idea he'd never even considered before. 'I was a senior clerk at Ruddlestone's

Bakery when Judith offered me a partnership, and that's what I'd still be today if I hadn't had the good sense to take up her offer.'

'I'm sure you're just bein' modest, sir,' Woodend said.

'Don't you believe it,' Keene said emphatically. 'Oh, I can keep a neat set of books, and I never make the mistake of ordering chocolate macaroons when what we really need is lady's fingers, but I can think of half a dozen people who could do my job as well as I can. It's Judith who was the key to our success. The girl's a positive catering genius. She has taste. She has flair and elegance. It breaks my heart to see her in that drab prison uniform.'

'So you go and visit her in gaol, do you?' Paniatowski said.

'Naturally I do.'

'Often?'

'Once a month. Without fail.' Keene sighed. 'Not that it's easy.'

'Do you find the travelling a strain?'

'No, I don't. Far from it, in fact. I quite enjoy the drive. It's once I get there that the problems start. You see, when we were working together, we always had oodles to talk about, but the longer she's in that dreadful place, the more strained our conversation becomes. I don't want to tell her about the business, because that will only remind her of what she's missing. And she certainly doesn't want to talk about *her* life.'

'So what do you talk about?' Paniatowski asked.

'Anything I can think of at the time,' Keene confessed. 'Sometimes I tell her about my mother – they used to get on well together. Sometimes I'll tell her about a new friend I've met. I'm not sure she's even *listening* some of the time, but I prattle on anyway. I tell myself my presence makes her time in there a little more bearable, but I've no idea if it really does.'

'Tell me about the man who she's supposed to have killed,' Woodend suggested.

'There's not much I *can* tell you about him. They say he was her lover, but I don't believe that.'

'Did she mention him to you?'

'Once or twice.'

'An' what did she have to say about him?'

31

'Not a great deal. Certainly no more than she'd said about any of our other clients.'

'So he was a client?'

'That's right. He was impressed with the spread that she did for the Dunethorpe Chamber of Commerce, so after that he hired us whenever he needed a caterer.'

'An' how often would that have been?'

'I'd have to look it up in the ledger to give you a definite answer.'

'A rough estimate will do.'

'I'd guess it was five or six times.'

'In little more than a year?'

'Yes, I suppose so.'

'I know Mr Burroughs was in business, but it's hard to imagine even a businessman needing the services of a caterer once every couple of months,' Monika Paniatowski said.

Keene laughed. 'I can tell you don't know a great deal about the social climbers of Central Lancashire, Sergeant,' he said. 'You'd be surprised how many of them think they can bribe their way up the ladder of acceptability with a few canapés and salmon vol-au-vents.'

The phone rang, and Keene picked it up. He listened for a moment, then said, 'Yes, I have heard about it . . . There's no *need* to worry . . . Yes, we do use that bank, but even I wouldn't be stupid enough to go near it until this horrible business is all over . . . Yes, I *do* promise, and I *will* be home at the usual time . . . And *of course* I love you.'

Keene replaced the phone on its cradle, and looked across at Woodend. 'It's almost a cliché, isn't it?' he asked.

'What is?'

'That a man like me should still be living with his mother. But she is an old dear, and she *does* need me.'

'I'm sure she does,' Woodend said. 'But to get back to the point, did Judith Maitland ever discuss her private life with you, Mr Keene?'

'Yes, she did,' the caterer replied. He gave a smile which was almost a smirk. 'I was like a big sister to her.'

'So she'll have told you about her lovers?'

'Naughty!' Keene said, wagging his finger in rebuke.

'Sorry?'

32

'Judith hasn't *had* any lovers – at least, not for as long as I've known her. Before she was married, there was never any time, because all her energy went into building up the business.'

'An' after she was married?'

'She'd never have thought of betraying her Tom. She absolutely adored the man.'

'People make mistakes, however much they love their spouses,' Woodend said, avoiding looking at Monika Paniatowski. 'The spirit may be willing, but the flesh is weak.'

'You don't need to tell me – of all people – about that,' Keene said, almost flirtatiously. 'But I'm sure that if Judith had been having an affair, she wouldn't have been able to keep it from me,' he continued, growing serious again.

'Why didn't she live with her husband?' Monika Paniatowski asked.

'He's in the Army.'

'I understand that. But he's an officer, isn't he? Surely she could have moved into some quite pleasant married quarters if she'd been of a mind to?'

'She did think about doing that, the last time Tom was posted back to Britain,' Keene admitted. 'She considered it quite seriously, as a matter of fact. She even talked about selling her half of the business. Then she suddenly changed her mind.'

'An' why do you think that was?'

'She said she'd never really be happy living anywhere but Lancashire, and that Tom understood that. So they came up with a new plan between them. She'd stay where she was, and when Tom had served out his time in the Army, he'd come and join her.'

'When did she have this sudden an' unexpected change of heart of hers?' Woodend asked.

Keene thought about it. 'I think it must have been about a year ago,' he said finally.

'Just around the time she met Burroughs?'

'Yes, I suppose it was,' Keene said. Then the import of Woodend's words struck home. 'Have you talked to Judith yourself?' he asked, sounding disappointed and possibly betrayed.

'Not yet,' Woodend confessed.

'You should,' Keene told him earnestly. 'And if, after having talked to her, you can still believe she's guilty of this terrible crime, then you're simply not the judge of character I took you to be.'

Six

Dunethorpe, where the Burroughs murder had taken place, lay just the other side of the Lancashire–Yorkshire border, in a lush rolling dale. The town itself was pleasant enough, too, with an old, stone-built centre ringed by new brick-built housing estates, but Woodend began to scowl immediately he had driven past the town's welcome sign.

'Something the matter, sir?' Monika Paniatowski asked.

'It's all a bit too pretty-pretty for my likin',' Woodend grumbled. 'Where are all the dark satanic cotton mills an' decayin' canals?'

'True,' Paniatowski agreed. 'Yorkshire really does seem to have missed out when it comes to blots on the landscape, doesn't it?'

'Besides,' Woodend continued, 'you should know by now that I never feel happy on enemy territory.'

Paniatowski grinned to herself. She was all too well aware of her boss's half-mock, half-serious antipathy to Yorkshire.

It wasn't the Wars of the Roses – when the House of Lancaster had battled with the House of York for the English crown – that made him suspicious of tykes, he had once explained to her. It wasn't even that Yorkshire would self-ishly insist on winning the County Cricket Championship every year – which meant her neighbours never even got a look-in. It was the Yorkshiremen themselves. They were dour, they were tight with their money – and if they did have a sense of humour, then it was certainly not one which would be recognized as such anywhere else in the civilized world.

Paniatowski took it all with a pinch of salt, having heard

34

Yorkshiremen make pretty much the same complaints about Lancastrians.

Anyway, she told herself, if there was one thing that you had to say about Charlie Woodend, it was that he always took people as he found them, and that their accident of birth, position in society or previous history was of no interest to him. He was, in other words, the most tolerant and open of men – whether he was willing to admit it or not.

Except in the case of adulterers, she thought, as they pulled up on the forecourt of Dunethorpe Central Police Station. She wasn't sure that he was so tolerant of adulterers any more.

The policeman who'd been in charge of the Clive Burroughs murder case was Chief Inspector Baxter. He was a big, pipe-smoking man with wild grey hair, and his office looked just as chaotic as Woodend's own.

'Cards on the table?' he asked, the moment that his two visitors had sat down.

Woodend nodded. 'Cards on the table.'

'There's a lot of bobbies who'd really resent some bugger coming in from the outside with the sole purpose of worrying over the bones of one of their old investigations,' Baxter said.

'True,' Woodend agreed, guardedly.

'But I'm not one of them,' Baxter continued. 'If I've made a mistake, I want it uncovered.' He paused to light his pipe, and the room was suddenly filled with wispy blue smoke. 'Of course, if you do happen to prove me wrong in this particular case,' he added, 'then it certainly won't do my prospects of promotion any bloody good.'

'No, it won't,' Woodend confirmed.

'But I'm not sure I'm interested in promotion any more,' Baxter said. 'After twenty long hard years of studying superintendents as a breed, I think, on the whole, that I'd rather not become one of them.'

'Amen to that,' Woodend replied, with feeling.

'Having said that – and bearing in mind how important it is for the situation in Whitebridge that you *do* prove me wrong – I have to admit that I'm not over-optimistic about your chances of success.'

'That's Yorkshire for, "You've no chance at all,"' Woodend explained to Paniatowski.

Baxter smiled. 'I wouldn't put it as strongly as that,' he said. 'But I do have to tell you that this was not one of those cases I ever lost sleep over. Judith Maitland may not have deserved twenty years for something she did in the heat of the moment, but there's no doubt in my mind that she actually did do it.'

'Can you fill us in on the details?' Woodend asked.

'Be glad to,' Baxter replied.

It was just after midnight when the young constable on the night-shift patrol noticed that the gate to the builders' merchant's yard was slightly open. Looking beyond it, he saw the office door was also a little ajar, and his first thought was that he'd come across a burglary in progress. He resisted the impulse to call for back-up – why share the credit when you don't have to? – and instead he unsheathed his truncheon and strode, with all the confidence of youth and inexperience, towards the office door.

The place was in darkness, but by groping along the wall with his hand, he located the light switch. He flicked it on – and soon wished he hadn't.

Clive Burroughs was lying on the floor, in what looked at first to be a large puddle of red paint. It took the constable's brain no more than a second or two to work out that the paint was, in fact, blood, and it took his body only slightly longer than that to react to the news by heaving up the contents of his stomach on to the office floor.

'The moment I saw the corpse, I was almost certain it was a crime of passion,' Chief Inspector Baxter said.

'An' why was that?' Woodend asked.

'It was so messy. Burroughs would have been down – and probably dead – after the first blow, but his assailant kept on striking the top of his skull until there was nothing left but mush and bone splinters. Whoever had hit him didn't just want him out of action – there was real hatred behind the attack.'

'It's a tough thing, the human skull,' Woodend mused. 'Could a woman really have had the strength to reduce Burroughs' skull to a pulp?'

'There are cases on record of women who lifted up the front end of cars to rescue their trapped children,' Baxter said. 'Most women are capable of great feats of strength when they're very worked up.'

That was true enough, Woodend thought.

'What happened next?' he asked.

'That was when the witness turned up,' DCI Baxter said.

The witness was the night-watchman from the garden centre opposite Burroughs' Builders' Merchant. He had not only seen Burroughs himself drive up, but also the arrival of a white Vauxhall van with the words 'Élite Caterers' painted on the side of it.

The van had been parked in front of Burroughs' for fifteen minutes, the watchman claimed, then a woman had rushed out of the building, climbed into it, and driven away at some speed. The next vehicle to appear on the scene had been the police patrol car, about half an hour later.

Baxter did a quick mental calculation. Half an hour between the woman's departure and the body being discovered, plus another forty minutes between that moment and this discussion with the night-watchman. If the woman had been in as much of a hurry as the watchman said she was, she could be as much as fifty miles away by now.

'It's probably a pointless bloody exercise, but alert all patrols to be on the lookout for this white van anyway,' he told his bagman.

'But it wasn't a pointless exercise at all, was it?' Woodend asked.

'No,' Baxter agreed. 'It certainly wasn't.

It was a police car on a routine patrol of the main Dunethorpe–Huddersfield road which spotted the van. It was parked in a lay-by, and all the lights were off. The patrolmen pulled in behind it, and approached the van with caution.

Their caution proved unnecessary. The van contained only one person – a woman – and she was slumped over the wheel.

One of the officers tried the driver's door, and discovered that it wasn't locked. When he opened it, the first thing that hit him was the overpowering smell of whisky.

37

The officer prodded the woman gently on the shoulder. 'Are you all right, love?' he asked.

The woman raised her head slightly. 'He's dead,' she moaned. 'He has to be dead.'

'But she didn't actually say she'd killed Clive Burroughs?' Woodend asked.

Baxter shook his head, then relit his pipe. 'No, she didn't say that. She *never* admitted killing him. Right up until the end of the trial, she insisted that he was already dead when she got there.'

'Did she give you any reason for why she had visited Burroughs so late at night?'

'She claimed it was nothing more than a business meeting.'

'What kind of business meeting?'

'She said Burroughs had called her, and told her he wanted her to cater his daughter's birthday party.'

'Maybe he had.'

'His daughter had had a birthday only three weeks earlier. Besides, she's only four years old, and Élite Catering is far too grand to even consider doing kids' parties.'

'Even for a friend?'

'That's just the point. Judith Maitland insisted throughout that Burroughs wasn't a friend at all – that he really was no more than someone she did business with.'

'I'm going to have to ask you to step out of the van, madam,' the patrol-car driver said.

'Go away!' Judith Maitland said.

'I'm afraid I can't do that, madam. If you require assistance, I will willingly provide it. But with or without assistance, you're still going to have to get out of the van.'

Judith Maitland tried to climb out of her seat several times – and failed. In the end, it was a combination of assistance and manhandling which got her out on to the lay-by, and once she was there it was immediately apparent that she could not stand unaided.

'Have you been drinking, madam?' the constable asked.

Judith did her best to focus her bleary eyes on him. 'Well, of course I've been drinking. Wouldn't you have had a drink, if your whole world had just fallen apart,' she said, slurring her words.

'*What, exactly, is that supposed to mean, madam?'*

'*Why did it have to happen?' Judith asked, addressing her remark more at the dark night which surrounded them than at the constable. 'When everything was going so well – when it was all going to work out – why did* that *have to happen?'*

And then she burst into tears.

'Not quite the admission of guilt you would have liked, though, was it?' Woodend said.

'True,' Baxter agreed. 'There was no "You've got me bang to rights, Officer. Put the cuffs on me." But what she *did* say was certainly enough to convince the jury that she was the one who did it.'

'Did you find any physical evidence to tie her in with the murder?' Woodend asked.

'None.'

'But surely, in a violent attack of that nature, there would have been bloodstains on her clothing?'

'If they'd been the clothes she was wearing when she committed the murder, yes.'

'But you don't think they were?'

'Élite Catering issues all its employees with a uniform. It consists of an overall, a pair of light, washable canvas shoes, and a plastic cap of the sort people use in the shower. Judith Maitland always carried a set of these clothes with her – nobody disagrees about that – but there was no sign of them in the van.'

'So you think that was what she was wearing when she allegedly killed Clive Burroughs?'

'Exactly.'

'And that she dumped the uniform somewhere, shortly after leaving the scene of the crime?'

'Just so.'

'But you never found it?'

'No, we did not.'

'There's something that's rather puzzling me here,' Monika Paniatowski said.

'And what's that?' Baxter wondered.

'I've only skimmed through the transcript of the trial, but I don't remember finding any reference at all in it to her overall.'

'No, you wouldn't have, because there isn't one,' Baxter said.

'And why is that?'

'It wasn't *necessary* to include it in the evidence. We had a strong enough case without it.'

Woodend lit a cigarette and took a thoughtful drag. 'Correct me if I'm wrong, but didn't you start this conversation by sayin' that you were goin' to put all your cards on the table?' he asked.

'Yes, I did,' Baxter agreed. 'And I've done just that.'

But though his voice was still steady enough, he did not look exactly comfortable with the assertion.

'Now that *is* interestin',' Woodend said.

'What is?'

'I've been wrackin' my brains for some other example where the investigatin' officers deliberately excluded some of the evidence from the prosecution's case because they'd decided it wasn't really necessary. An', do you know, I can't come up with a single one. In Whitebridge, we normally throw everything but the kitchen sink into the evidence, just to make sure we've got as watertight a case as we possibly could have.'

'Normally, we'd do that in Dunethorpe, too,' Baxter agreed, his evident discomfort growing by the second.

'So what happened in the Burroughs case?'

Baxter took out a knife and scraped the bowl of his pipe before speaking again.

'I liked Judith Maitland,' he said. 'I really did. I think you would have done, too, in my place.'

'Go on,' Woodend said.

'And I'd done some checking on Clive Burroughs. It wasn't a very edifying task, because Judith Maitland wasn't the first of his little flings – not by a very long chalk.'

'That may be so, but I still don't see where you're goin' with this,' Woodend admitted.

'I felt sorry for the woman,' Baxter admitted. 'I know I shouldn't have, but I did. So I asked the prosecutor if we could present the case as a crime of passion, and he agreed.'

'I understand that, but—'

'In court, the prosecutor argued that Clive Burroughs and Judith Maitland had a blazing row, and that in the midst of it she picked up a hammer and caved in his skull.'

'Yes?'

'But I don't think it happened quite like that. I'm sure the row did actually occur, but I don't believe she was wearing the overall at the time.'

'Why not?'

'Because no woman ever goes to meet her lover wearing her working clothes.'

'So what you're sayin' is that she decides to kill him, then goes out to her van, puts on her overall, and returns to Burroughs' office?'

'Essentially.'

'An' once she's done the deed – once he's lying there dead – she strips off the overall an' disposes of it?'

'Yes.'

'Then I still don't see what made you exclude the overall from the evidence you presented.'

'It's difficult to explain to someone who wasn't there,' Baxter said awkwardly. 'I interrogated Judith for several hours, and at the end of that process I emerged with the view that what had happened had *undoubtedly* been a crime of passion.'

'But . . .?'

'But I could well imagine the court's reaction to hearing about the overall. They would have decided, then and there, that what they were dealing with was a stone killer.'

'A what?' Woodend asked.

'A stone killer,' Baxter repeated. 'I was in America a couple of years ago, working with the FBI. It's a term they use a lot over there.'

'An' what does it mean, *exactly*?'

Baxter frowned. 'It's hard to find an exact English equivalent,' he admitted, struggling to find the right words. 'A "total" killer, I suppose. Someone who almost seems *born* to kill. Someone who'd think no more about killing than you or I would about ordering a pint of bitter just before closing time.'

'In other words, a *cold-blooded* killer?' Woodend suggested.

41

'More or less,' Baxter agreed, gratefully.

'But what's all this got to do with the way you put together your case?' Woodend wondered. 'Your job is just to find out who committed the murder. It's the judge and jury who decide what *kind* of killin' it was. That's what they're there for.'

'But they didn't *know* her. They hadn't *talked* to her, as I had.' Baxter paused, as if garnering his strength for what he knew he had to say next. 'So I used my discretion,' he continued. 'With the agreement of the prosecution, I excluded evidence which I felt might lead the court to reach the wrong conclusion. Judith had to pay for her crime – there was no doubt in my mind about that – but I didn't want her to serve any more time than she had to.'

'She still got life, with a recommendation that she serves a minimum of twenty-five years,' Woodend pointed out.

'Yes, she did,' Baxter agreed, sadly. 'She was unlucky enough to come up against a judge with pure ice in his veins and, despite my best efforts, he imposed a heavy sentence anyway. But I still think I did the right thing.'

'So, cuttin' through all the niceties an' the clever talk, what you're actually sayin' is that you deliberately doctored the evidence?' Woodend asked.

Baxter smiled. 'I'd prefer to stick to the niceties and say that I merely *re-aligned* it,' he told Woodend. 'And just between you, me and the bedpost, Chief Inspector, haven't you done something similar yourself, once or twice?'

Woodend returned his smile. 'I'd never have been able to hold my head up again if I hadn't,' he confessed.

Seven

'Very nice,' Woodend said. 'Very nice indeed, if you can afford it – which, bein' a humble bobby, I couldn't.'

The object of his admiration was a large detached house with a double frontage and an integrated double garage. It was located in one of the best areas of Dunethorpe, and it had once been the home of a murder victim called Clive Burroughs.

Woodend took his cigarettes out of his pocket and lit one up. 'Well, now we're here, I suppose we might as well go an' have a word with the grievin' widow,' he said.

'You sound as if you think it'll just be a waste of time,' Monika Paniatowski commented.

'An' it probably *will* be,' Woodend told her. 'Wives are always the last to know what their husbands are gettin' up to.'

Images of Maria Rutter flashed across both their minds, and as Monika Paniatowski quickly lit up a cigarette of her own, she noticed that her hand was shaking. She wondered if she'd ever be able to put the past behind her, and immediately decided that she probably wouldn't.

The two officers walked up the path, which was flanked on either side by an almost obsessively geometric front garden. When Woodend rang the bell, they both heard a woman's voice say, 'For God's sake, be quiet for once, Timothy. Can't you hear there's somebody at the door?'

There was a sound of footsteps in the hallway, then the front door opened. The woman who appeared in the doorway was probably in her early thirties, Paniatowski guessed. She had undoubtedly been pretty a few years earlier, but now she looked completely washed-out and very, very tired.

'Yes?' she said.

'We're police officers from Whitebridge,' Woodend explained, showing her his warrant card. 'We're sorry to trouble you, Mrs Burroughs, but, if we may, we'd like to ask you a few questions about your husband's murder.'

'Ask me a few questions?' the woman repeated. 'I thought that was all over and done with.'

'There are still a few loose ends to tie up,' Woodend told her. 'I know it can't be easy for you, but—'

'Easy!' the woman echoed, as if she'd caught him using an obscenity. 'Easy? Of course it won't be easy!'

'I appreciate that, but—'

'It wasn't *easy* living with Clive while he was alive, and it's not *easy* living without him now that he's dead.' Mrs Burroughs raised her right hand, made a fist with it, and pressed that fist against her forehead. 'If you want to know the truth, it's bloody hard. Everything's . . . so . . . bloody . . . hard.'

Paniatowski tapped Woodend's arm lightly. 'I don't think we'll be needing you, sir,' she said softly.

'Pardon?'

'I said, I don't think we'll be needing you here. You've a lot of interviews to get through today, so why don't you go off and see someone else on your list, while I talk to Mrs Burroughs. I think that would be simpler all round.'

'Oh, right,' said Woodend, who had no such list. 'We'll . . . er . . . meet up again in the pub next to the police station, shall we?'

'Yes, sir, we'll meet up again in the pub,' Paniatowski agreed.

She waited until Woodend had almost reached his car, then turned to Mrs Burroughs and said, 'Well, at least now we can have a chat without me constantly wondering where his hands are going to wander next.'

'Oh, he's like that, is he?' Mrs Burroughs asked.

'He's so well known for it back in Whitebridge that all the women officers call him the Octopus-Man,' Paniatowski lied. 'Men can be such right proper bastards, can't they?'

'You're telling me,' Mrs Burroughs agreed, with a kind of bitter enthusiasm. 'Would you like to come inside?'

'I'd love to,' Paniatowski replied.

There were two children in the living room. The elder, a boy, was sitting at the table, working on a jigsaw puzzle. The younger, a girl, was sitting on the hearthrug and attacking her colouring book with a dogged determination.

'Why don't you two kids go upstairs for a few minutes?' the mother suggested.

'Don't want to,' the boy said, not even bothering to look up from his self-imposed struggle.

'Maybe you don't. But then we can't always have what we want in this life, can we?' Mrs Burroughs asked.

'Why can't we?' the boy wondered aloud.

Mrs Burroughs sighed. '*If* you go upstairs like I've asked you to, and *if* you can keep your sister quiet for half an hour or so, there'll be a nice surprise waiting for you down here when this lady's gone,' she said coaxingly.

'What kind of surprise?' the boy asked.

44

'Well, if you don't do as I say, you'll never find out, will you?' the mother replied.

The boy thought about it for a moment, then slid off the chair and said, 'Come on, Emma!'

The girl climbed to her feet without any hesitation, and obediently followed her brother out of the room.

'He's always been a bit of a handful, but he's got even worse since his father was killed,' Mrs Burroughs said, half-apologetically. 'Still, I don't suppose I can blame him.'

'Does he know what happened to your husband?'

'No. I've told him his dad's just gone away for a while. But he's a bright boy and I think he may have started to suspect that whatever I might say, Clive's never coming back.' Mrs Burroughs paused for a moment. 'Do you have children yourself?' she asked.

'Two,' Paniatowski lied.

'What are they?'

'A boy and a girl, like yours.'

'And who looks after them while you're out on police business? Your husband?'

'Not him!' Paniatowski said contemptuously. '*He* ran off with his bitch of a secretary, and left me to look after them myself. The swine!'

'So who . . .?'

'My mother! I have to rely on my mother. She doesn't take a penny off me, but she certainly finds other ways to make me pay for it! She never misses an opportunity to remind me of just how much I'm in her debt!'

'At least I'm spared that,' Mrs Burroughs said, sympathetically. 'Clive was a proper bastard, but he left me well provided for.' She hesitated for a moment, then said, 'I don't suppose you're allowed to have a drink while you're on duty, are you, Sergeant Paniatowski?'

Paniatowski laughed. 'Not allowed to drink on duty, Helen? It is Helen, isn't it?'

'Yes, it is,' Mrs Burroughs agreed.

'And you must call me Monika. You're half-right in what you've just said. The uniformed branch *aren't* allowed to drink while they're on duty. In the CID, on the other hand, it's virtually compulsory that we indulge in the odd tipple.'

Mrs Burroughs looked almost relieved. 'In that case, would you like to share the bottle of wine I've got cooling in the fridge, Monika?'

'I'd be delighted, Helen,' Paniatowski replied.

Mrs Burroughs produced the wine, and by the time Monika had taken a sip of hers, the widow had already knocked back a full glass herself. And it wasn't, Paniatowski suspected, her first drink of the day.

'Did it ever occur to you that your husband was playing around with other women?' Mrs Burroughs asked.

'No,' Paniatowski said. 'I thought we had a very happy marriage. It came as a complete shock when he announced that he was abandoning me and the kids. How about you?'

'That Maitland woman wasn't the first – not by any stretch of the imagination,' Mrs Burroughs said bitterly. 'There was a string of other women before her. In the end – and this was about two years ago now – I told him I'd had enough of it, and that I was divorcing him. And do you know what he did?'

'No. Tell me.'

'He begged me not to start proceedings. He actually went down on his knees and *begged* me. He said that he knew he'd done wrong, but that was all over, and he'd be a new man from then on.'

'And you believed him?'

'Yes, fool that I was, I did.' Mrs Burroughs drained her second glass of wine, and filled up the glass again. 'He really *did* seem to have changed after that, you know. He was much more attentive to me. It felt like it used to when we were first married. But he hadn't changed at all. He'd just got sneakier!'

'Sneakier?' Paniatowski repeated. 'How?'

'You won't believe this – I can hardly believe it myself – but he used Timothy, *his own son*, as a cover.'

'I'm not sure I understand what you mean,' Paniatowski confessed.

'The way I always caught him out the other times was that he couldn't account for the time he spent with his women. Well, he learned by his mistakes, didn't he? He suddenly started taking Timothy out for treats – a trip to the zoo, a picnic in the country. I was pleased. More than pleased – I was *delighted*.

46

But, you see, he only took Timothy to fool me – to hide from me the fact that he was seeing the Maitland woman.'

'Good God!' Paniatowski said.

'I told you you'd find it hard to believe,' Mrs Burroughs said, with grim satisfaction.

Worse than hard, Paniatowski thought. Almost impossible.

She tried to imagine her and Bob making love with his child present. They just couldn't have done it. And Bob's child had only been a baby!

If that *was* what had actually happened – if Burroughs and Judith really had used Timothy as a cover – how the hell had they managed it? Had they drugged the child – or merely left him to play with an expensive new toy while they disappeared into some quiet corner and slaked their lust?

'But surely Timothy wasn't actually with your husband on the night he was murdered, was he?' Paniatowski asked.

'No, thank God,' Mrs Burroughs replied. 'Tim had a bad case of the flu that night. The poor little mite was almost burning up with it. So however much Clive wanted to, the lying swine simply couldn't use him as an excuse for being out of the house that time.'

'Are you sure it did actually happen like that?' Paniatowski asked, still finding it hard to accept that any man would use his child as an alibi for his liaisons. 'Have you talked to Timothy about it?'

'A little,' Mrs Burroughs said. 'Enough to get him to admit that when he and his father went out together, they often met a nice lady. Yes, that's what he called her. A nice lady! The selfish whore!'

'But he didn't . . . he didn't see anything going on between his father and this woman?'

'I don't know. I really don't. It's something I *daren't* ask him. Because if he *did* see it, and I *do* ask, he might start to attach more importance to it than he has so far.'

'I can see that,' Paniatowski said sombrely.

Mrs Burroughs filled her glass for the third time. 'My big fear is that when he gets older – when he starts to learn all about sex – he'll think back to what happened then and realize what was *really* going on. God alone knows what that might do to him emotionally.'

'It's too terrible to even think about,' Paniatowski said – and she truly meant it.

'I could kill Clive for it, I really could.' Mrs Burroughs gave a laugh which was bordering on the hysterical. 'But I can't even do that, can I? Because the bastard's *already* dead.'

Paniatowski placed her half-full glass on the table, and stood up. 'I think it's about time I was going, Helen,' she said.

Mrs Burroughs' mood suddenly swung from self-pity to anger. 'What's the matter?' she demanded. 'Can't you take being in the company of the mad woman any longer?'

'No, that's not it at all,' Paniatowski said. 'I'd like to spend more time with you, but my boss . . .'

'Do you ever blame yourself for what happened to you?' Mrs Burroughs demanded.

'I beg your pardon?'

'Do you ever think that it might be your fault that your husband left you for another woman?'

'I—' Paniatowski began.

'Because I do,' Mrs Burroughs interrupted. 'I sometimes lie awake at night wondering if it's all my fault.'

'You mustn't—'

'Because I don't think I ever really satisfied him in bed, you see. But maybe if I'd tried a little harder, he'd never have strayed. Maybe if I'd been a better lover, he'd still be alive!'

Eight

The prison uniform consisted of a plainly cut dress and flat cloth shoes. The dress was dishwater grey in colour, and was an almost perfect match with the complexion of the woman who, just a few days earlier, had tried to take her own life.

It had not been Woodend's intention to visit Judith Maitland so early in the investigation – he'd wanted to fill in more of her background first – but finding he had unexpected free time on his hands, he had come to the prison almost on a whim.

Or perhaps it had not been a whim at all, he suddenly thought. He remembered Stanley Keene's parting words –

'*If, having talked to her, you still believe she's guilty of this terrible crime, then you're simply not the judge of character I took you to be.*'

Maybe, though he hadn't realized it on any conscious level, that was what had motivated him to come to the prison. Maybe, because Keene had seemed so sincere and so sure, he'd felt the need to find out for himself just how good a judge of character the caterer himself was.

The prisoner was still standing uncertainly in the doorway.

'Sit down, Judith,' Woodend said.

The woman hesitated for a moment, and then crossed the room and took the chair at the opposite side of the table from the Chief Inspector.

Woodend studied her face, and thought he could detect, just below the surface, the prettiness and confidence which she must have shown to the world before her arrest.

'Smoke?' he asked.

Judith Maitland glanced down at the packet of Capstan Full Strength he was holding out to her, then shook her head.

'Are these too strong for you?' Woodend asked. 'Would you prefer cork tipped? Because if that's what you want, I'm sure I could soon rustle up a packet from somewhere.'

'I don't smoke anymore,' Judith Maitland said, in a voice which was almost a whisper.

'Probably wise,' Woodend told her. 'Bad for your health. I wish I could give it up myself.'

'If I cared about my health, I wouldn't have slashed my wrists,' Judith Maitland countered.

'You're right,' Woodend said contritely. 'I'm an idiot. I spouted out the first cliché which came into my head, without even thinking about it. I won't make the same mistake again.'

'It doesn't bother me what you choose to say or you don't choose to say,' Judith Maitland told him flatly. 'This whole interview is a complete waste of time because I really have no interest in talking to you at all.'

'Why did you give up smokin'?' Woodend asked.

'Is that just another conversational gambit – words with no purpose but to break the silence?'

'No,' Woodend assured her. 'I'm genuinely curious.'

'I used to think that death was the worst thing that could

49

happen to a person,' Judith Maitland said. 'Now I know that I was wrong. The truly terrible thing is to realize that you've lost your ability to control your own destiny – to understand that you're totally in the power of others.'

'What's that got to do with smokin'?'

'In here, it's the warders who have most of the power. But what little is left over, when they've taken their share, belongs to the inmates who control the tobacco supply. You'd be amazed by what some women will do for a smoke. Well, not me. Not anymore.'

'You'd really like a cigarette, though, wouldn't you, Judith?' the Chief Inspector asked.

'I'd kill for one,' Judith Maitland replied.

What had made her use those particular words? Woodend wondered.

Was it the kind of thing people said without thinking about it – just as he'd said smoking was bad for the health? Or had she done it deliberately – to provoke him?

'Have a cigarette,' he coaxed. 'I promise you, Judith, there's no strings attached.'

'There's *always* strings attached,' Judith Maitland said firmly. 'Can I go now?'

'If you want to. But if you do go now, what would have been the point in holding this interview in the first place?'

'None. I told you, there was never any point.'

'So why did you agree to it?'

'You think there was a choice in the matter?' Judith Maitland asked, incredulously.

'There's always a choice. You're not obliged to talk to me if you don't wish to.'

Judith Maitland laughed. 'Haven't you been listening to a single word that I've said?' she demanded. 'This is a *prison*. There's no such thing as free will in here.'

'I repeat, it's your right not to talk to me, if you do not wish to,' Woodend said.

'Do you have *any* idea at all of how things work in this bloody place?' Judith asked. 'Don't you understand that there are a hundred ways – a thousand ways – that the warders could make my life even more unpleasant than it is already if I refused to co-operate with one of their own?'

'I'm not one of their own,' Woodend pointed out.

'Oh yes, you are. Or, at least, you're close enough for it to make no difference. Because you're certainly not one of *my* own.'

'So you're talkin' to me because that's the lesser of two evils?'

'Essentially.'

'If I were in your situation, I wouldn't see talkin' to me as an evil at all,' Woodend said. 'If I were innocent – as you claim to be – I'd *want* to talk to the man who just might get me off.'

'So that's what you're here for, is it? To get me off?'

'If you are innocent, then I'll certainly do my damnedest to,' Woodend promised her.

'Then listen very carefully,' Judith said. 'I *am* innocent. Clive Burroughs was *not* my lover, and I did *not* kill him.'

'But when you were arrested, you told the officers that you already knew he was dead.'

'Well, of course I knew he was dead. I was there, wasn't I? I'd seen him lying in his office, in a pool of his own blood. I'd have to have been an idiot *not* to know that he was dead.'

'Why did you go to see him that night?'

'We had a business meeting.'

'The local police think otherwise.'

'That's scarcely surprising, now is it? The local police have refused to believe anything I've said from the start.'

'And what about the other times you saw him?'

'They were business meetings, too.'

'Then why did he always seem to have his son with him?'

'I don't know. You'd have to ask him about that. Only you can't, can you? Because he's dead.'

'Once you'd discovered the body, you got straight back into your van, drove to a lay-by which was less than a couple of miles from the scene of the crime, and got drunk.'

'Yes.'

'Why?'

'Why not?'

'Most people's reaction would have been to phone the police immediately. Didn't it even occur to you to do that?'

'No, it didn't.'

51

'So I'll ask you again. Why?'

'I suppose I must have panicked.'

'I don't believe you,' Woodend said.

'I don't care what you believe.'

'Don't you want to get out of here?'

Judith Maitland shuddered. 'The only way that I'll ever leave this terrible place is feet first. They stopped me from ending it all the last time, but they won't the next.'

'I still don't see why you decided to get drunk,' Woodend persisted.

'I should have thought that was obvious, even to a flatfoot like you. I'd just seen a body.'

'Of a man who was no more to you than a business associate?'

'Yes.'

'In your situation, most people I know would probably have got drunk, too. But I doubt they'd have done it alone. They've have wanted someone there to hold their hands.'

Judith Maitland smiled. 'You keep using this phrase, "Most people",' she said. 'I'm not "most people", Chief Inspector. I would have thought you'd have realized that by now.'

'When "most people" *do* choose to get drunk alone,' Woodend said, ignoring her comment, 'they do it either because they can't tell anybody else *why* they're doing it, or because they're afraid of what they might say when they're drunk. Which of those was it in your case?'

'Neither. I'd had a shock. I needed a drink.'

'You had your caterer's overall with you that night, didn't you?'

'I always had it with me. I wasn't the kind of boss who thought it demeaning to work side-by-side with my staff when the need arose.'

'Were you wearing it when you went into Burroughs' office?'

'No. As I said, it was a business meeting, so I was naturally wearing my business suit.'

'Then where was the overall?'

'It was in the back of the van, where I always kept it.'

'And at what point did you put it on?'

'I didn't put it on at all.'

'So what happened to it?'

'Happened to it?'

'You say it was in the back of the van when you got to the builders' merchant's yard, but by the time the police arrested you it had gone missing. Where do you think that it went?'

'I don't know. Maybe the police took it away.'

'They said they didn't.'

'Perhaps they're lying.'

'They think you got rid of it because it was covered with bloodstains,' Woodend said.

'Well, they're wrong.'

'Did you like Clive Burroughs?' Woodend asked.

A look of revulsion appeared on Judith Maitland's face for the briefest of moments, and then was gone. 'I never really thought about it one way or the other,' she said.

'Or did you hate him?' Woodend asked.

'You'd like me to say that – to admit I hated him – wouldn't you?' Judith Maitland demanded. 'Then you could go back and tell your friends – the screws – that they've got the right person in here after all. Well, forget what I said earlier, about not thinking about it. I *did* like Clive Burroughs. I thought he was a wonderful human being.'

'You hated him because he'd robbed you of the power to control your own destiny,' Woodend guessed. 'Exactly what kind of hold *did* Burroughs have over you, Judith?'

Judith Maitland stood up so violently that she sent her chair flying off behind her.

'I want to go back to my cell!' she said, almost hysterically. 'I don't want to talk to you any more.'

'Don't you even want to hear why there's this sudden new interest in your case?' Woodend wondered. 'Wouldn't you like to find out why I'm even here in this prison at all?'

'No,' Judith Maitland said, backing towards the door. 'I don't care. All I want is to be left alone.'

'We've got a real problem on our hands back in Whitebridge,' Woodend told her. 'Three heavily armed men are holdin' twenty innocent people hostage in the Cotton Credit Bank.'

'Then you should be there, rather than here,' Judith said tartly. She had retreated as far as she could, and now had her

53

back pressed against the locked door. 'Didn't you hear me? I said you should be back there – in Whitebridge – rather than wasting your time talking to me.'

Woodend said nothing. It had seemed to him it would be cruel to smoke when she wouldn't, but now he lit up.

'Are there . . . are there any children involved?' Judith asked, in a voice so faint it was little more than a whisper.

'There are no kids actually inside the bank,' Woodend told her.

'Thank God for that, at least.'

'But if it all goes wrong, as it very well might, there are a few who might be orphans by tomorrow.'

'Then *don't* let it go wrong!' Judith pleaded. 'Let the robbers get away with their haul.'

'It's not as simple as that.'

'Of course it's as simple as that! What does money matter, when children's happiness is at stake?'

'You really *don't* know, do you?' Woodend asked.

'Don't know what?'

'I suspected you didn't, but now I'm absolutely sure.'

'You're not making any sense,' Judith said.

'The armed men in the bank aren't robbers,' Woodend explained. 'They don't want money.'

'Then what do they want?'

'They want me to prove that you're innocent.'

For a moment it looked as if Judith Maitland might faint clean away. Then she somehow managed to stagger forward and grab hold of the edge of the table for support.

'Thomas!' she gasped. 'Thomas is one of them, isn't he?'

'It looks that way,' Woodend agreed. 'In fact, I'm pretty sure that your husband is the leader.'

'Tell him to come out,' Judith said in anguish. 'Tell him to give himself up before he does any real harm.'

'I could certainly do that,' Woodend agreed, 'but do you think he'd listen to me?'

Judith Maitland bowed her head. 'No, knowing Thomas, he probably won't,' she said.

'So there's one way to resolve the situation without bloodshed,' Woodend said. 'By giving him what he wants. By proving that you're innocent. And if you're not—'

'I didn't kill Clive Burroughs,' Judith Maitland interrupted. 'I swear to you I didn't.'

'Then help me with my investigation,' Woodend implored her. 'If you won't do it for yourself or your husband, at least do it for the poor buggers trapped in that bank. And for their families.'

'How can I?' Judith Maitland said, in a voice which was almost a croak. 'I don't *know* who killed Clive.'

'Then tell me about things you *do* know,' Woodend pressed. 'If he wasn't your lover, what was he to you?'

'He was . . . he was . . .' Judith Maitland began. She shook her head, and grimaced, as if it were causing her real agony. 'I can't tell you.'

'Why not, in God's name?'

'Because I have responsibilities.'

'You're damn right you do!' Woodend said angrily. 'You have a responsibility to the hostages. They're only there because of you!'

'Are they?'

'You know they are! If you hadn't slit your wrists – if you hadn't shown the full extent of your desperation in the most dramatic way possible – your husband would never have acted as he did.'

'If only I'd succeeded in my attempt,' Judith Maitland wailed.

'But you didn't,' Woodend said bluntly. 'An' now you've got to make amends. You've got to help me in every way you can.'

'I could try again,' Judith said. 'Give me something to kill myself with. A knife! A rope! Anything!'

'Listen—' Woodend began.

'You don't even have to do that. Just turn your back for a couple of minutes, and I'll find some way to finish myself off. And with me dead, Thomas will have no reason to hold on to his hostages.'

'You're bluffin',' Woodend said.

'I'm not. And if you'll just give me the chance, I'll prove it to you.'

'D'you know, I really think you would,' Woodend said. 'But as convenient as it might be, all round, for you to do away with yourself, I simply can't allow it.'

'Then there's nothing more I can do to help you,' Judith Maitland said.

Nine

'Judith Maitland's a complete mystery to me,' Woodend confessed to Monika Paniatowski.

They were sitting at a corner table – Woodend always liked corner tables – in a pub called the Green Man, just a few doors down from Dunethorpe Central Police Station. It was one of those old-fashioned boozers which the bright young designers at the brewery hadn't yet managed to get their hands on, but there was no doubt that *its* days – like those of old-fashioned policemen – were numbered.

'In what way is Judith a mystery?' Monika Paniatowski asked, taking a sip of the neat vodka she habitually drank.

'She doesn't seem to have any real hope of gettin' out of prison before she's served her full sentence,' Woodend replied, reaching for his pint of best bitter. 'Her suicide attempt is proof enough of that.'

'Agreed.'

'So if she *was* havin' an affair with Clive Burroughs, why doesn't she just admit it?'

'It's always possible that whilst she doesn't particularly mind people thinking of her as a murderess, she hates the idea that anybody might also consider her an adulteress,' Paniatowski said tartly.

Jesus, but Monika's bein' hard work today, Woodend thought.

'An' if Judith *wasn't* havin' an affair, why won't she tell me what her relationship with Burroughs actually *was*?' he ploughed on.

'Maybe we should get back to basics,' Paniatowski suggested. 'Is Judith Maitland in prison for a crime she didn't commit?'

'Yes,' Woodend said. 'I rather think she is.'

'And what are you basing this assumption of yours on, sir? Gut feeling?'

'That's part of it,' Woodend admitted.

'So what's the rest?'

'An assessment of Judith Maitland as a person.'

'Go on.'

'I just don't think she's what DCI Baxter would call a "stone killer". When I told her about the hostages, she tried to act as if it didn't bother her at all. But she couldn't keep that up. She was really distressed by the thought that the hostages' kids might lose their parents.'

'In other words, however you might choose to dress it up, it's *all* down to gut feeling,' Paniatowski said.

Why was she doing this? Woodend asked himself.

But he already knew the answer to that. She was attempting to diminish him in her own eyes – because then his opinion of what she and Bob had done would somehow matter less!

'Besides, she's a planner by nature,' he continued. 'She was part of one of the most successful caterin' businesses in Lancashire, an' even her partner admitted she was the real drivin' force behind it.'

'So?' Paniatowski asked sceptically.

'So you don't build up that kind of business without bein' able to think ahead. Just look at the way she decided to kill herself, as an example. She didn't just rush at it – she waited for the right opportunity.'

'She didn't succeed, though, did she?'

'No, but that was only because there was a random cell inspection that nobody could have anticipated.'

'And all this proves . . .?'

'That if she had killed Burroughs, she'd have been much cleverer about it. For a start, she would never have driven her distinctive white van right up to the scene of the crime.'

'Perhaps she didn't intend to kill him,' Paniatowski suggested. 'Perhaps it all happened in the heat of the moment.'

'Even if it had, the woman I talked to wouldn't simply have driven to the nearest lay-by, an' set about gettin' herself thoroughly pissed.'

'No?'

'No! What *that* woman would have done was put as much distance between herself and the scene of the crime as she could, an' then try to establish some kind of halfway-decent alibi.'

57

'Well, if you're so convinced she's innocent, why are you worrying about her relationship with Burroughs at all?' Paniatowski asked.

'You know why I'm worryin' about it, Monika. Because that's the way I operate.'

He shouldn't need to explain this to a woman he'd been working with so closely for so long, he thought. She knew as well as anybody else – *better* than anybody else – that he liked to collect all the information he could, even if much of it was later discarded. And she was fully aware of the fact that an essential part of his methodology was to do all he could to get right inside the heads of the people he was dealing with.

'I don't think you can afford to be quite so leisurely in your approach to this case as you usually are,' Monika Paniatowski told him.

She had said it with the express intention of hurting him – he knew that – but he chose to ignore the remark, and contented himself with saying only, 'Is that because we're workin' against the clock?'

'Of course it's because we're working against the clock!' Paniatowski replied brusquely. 'There are twenty hostages in that bank, and the longer the siege goes on, the greater the danger that some of them will lose their lives. So we have to focus, don't we? And for once that means that you're going to have to learn to cut corners.'

'And what particular corners do you think I should be cuttin', Monika?' Woodend asked.

'Well, for a start, you can stop worrying yourself about the Maitland–Burroughs relationship.'

'All right,' Woodend agreed. 'So we go for a new approach, do we? We abandon the methods we've used so successfully over the years?'

'Exactly.'

'An' what, specifically, will that new approach involve?'

'There are two possible ways of going about the investigation,' Paniatowski said crisply. 'The first is that we can prove that Judith Maitland *didn't* kill Clive Burroughs. The second is that we can prove someone else *did*. And given that it's very hard to *disprove* circumstantial evidence, I suggest that we concentrate most of our efforts on the latter.'

She was lecturing him as if he were a raw recruit, Woodend thought. And the purpose of that lecture was perfectly apparent. It was no more than part of her ongoing campaign to reduce him to a man whose opinion of her didn't really matter a damn.

He should have been angry. He *was* angry. But she was his protégée – he had nurtured and developed her – and there was at least a part of him which was proud that she had found the strength within herself to stand up to him.

'So you're suggestin' that we centre our investigation on Clive Burroughs,' he said.

'Exactly,' Paniatowski agreed. 'Even from what we've learned so far, he seems to have been a particularly nasty piece of work, and I'm sure there are more than enough people around here who've at least *thought* about topping him at one time or another.'

'So if we follow that line of thought through to its logical conclusion, the main thrust of the investigation will have to be concentrated on Dunethorpe, rather than Whitebridge?'

'Precisely.'

'You do realize, don't you, that that pretty much dictates that the major part of the investigation is goin' to be entirely down to you?'

'Me?' Paniatowski said.

'You,' Woodend repeated.

'I don't see why.'

'Then I'll explain it to you. I'm the only person Thomas Maitland will talk to, which means that *when* he wants to talk to me, I have to be near at hand. Which means, in turn, that I can't be far away from the Cotton Credit Bank for too long. So like I said, any investigation in Dunethorpe is largely down to you.'

'This isn't a punishment, is it?' Paniatowski asked.

Woodend didn't ask her what she meant by that, because he knew – and knew that she knew he knew.

'Nay, lass, it's not a punishment,' he replied.

'Then just what *is* it?'

'It's no more than one of them corners that you said we were goin' to have to cut.'

Monika took another sip of her drink. Perhaps she had won

a victory of sorts, she thought – but it certainly didn't feel like it.

'I wish Bob was here,' she said.

Aye, Woodend thought, we *both* wish Bob was here.

Ten

Even during the years when he had been absent from the town, Whitebridge High Street had still formed a part of Woodend's spiritual and emotional life. It was there that he stood as a toddler, watching the victory parade at the end of the Great War, waving his Union Jack at the smiling soldiers with no idea of what hell they had endured. It was there that he had sat with his mother – in what would turn out to be the last year of her life – at a street party to celebrate the coronation of Queen Elizabeth II.

He knew the place on market days when it was bustling with life, and on quiet Sunday afternoons, when there were only a few window-shopping strollers to be seen. He had known it in all its guises, and in all its moods. But he had never seen it as he saw it now – as he observed it through the gap between the big police vans which effectively sealed this end of the street off.

All the market traders' stalls – save for those too close to the bank to be safely approached – had been dismantled and removed, leaving only the odd piece of fruit lying in the gutter as proof that they had ever been there. The traders' tatty vans had been towed or driven away, too, and the only vehicles left on the street were police cars, behind which officers dressed in bullet-proof vests and carrying high-powered rifles were positioned.

The Chief Inspector stepped clear of the barricade, and began to walk up the High Street. Despite all the other clearing up they'd done, none of the officers in charge seemed to have thought to turn off the shop window illumination. That probably wouldn't have been noticed much earlier in the day. But now – as darkness began to fall – the windows took on a cheery appearance quite at odds with the abandoned emptiness of the shops themselves, an effect made even more bizarre by the merry twinkling of the Christmas fairy lights.

It was all a scene that no one in Whitebridge could ever have expected to see, Woodend thought. It was as if an alien way of life had invaded the town – and completely taken it over.

He reached the bank, pushed open the door, and entered. There was no one in evidence, but the single eye of the camera, still pointed at the door, would soon inform those deeper inside the building that he had arrived.

It was perhaps a minute before the door behind the counter opened, and the hooded man with the submachine gun stepped through it.

'Come closer!' he ordered. Then, when Woodend had reached the middle of the room, he barked, 'That's far enough!'

'Whatever you say,' Woodend agreed.

'It's well over an hour since I rang your headquarters and said I wanted to see you,' the man with the gun said angrily.

'Is that right?' Woodend asked.

He reached into his jacket pocket with his right hand. Maitland/Apollo, noticing the move, raised his submachine gun so that it was pointing directly at the Chief Inspector.

'Oh, for Christ's sake, relax! I'm only reaching for my packet of fags!' Woodend said.

'You want a *cigarette*?' Apollo/Maitland asked incredulously.

'Yes.'

'Now?'

'There's no need to sound so surprised about it,' Woodend said. 'I like to smoke when I'm nervous – an', for some strange reason, nervous is what I'm feelin' at the moment.'

'How do I know it's not a trick?' Apollo/Maitland asked.

'A trick?' Woodend repeated. 'Just what do you think I've got down there in my jacket pocket? A knife? A bazooka? A couple of platoons from the Parachute Regiment?'

'You may take out your cigarettes, but you must do it very slowly and carefully,' Apollo said.

'Fair enough,' Woodend agreed.

He extracted the packet of Capstan at a speed which would

have made slow-motion film look hurried, took a single cigarette out of it, and lit up.

'I know what you're doing,' the other man said.

'Is that right?' Woodend asked, puffing on his cigarette and
then blowing out the smoke. 'An' what might that *be*, exactly?'

'You're hoping to avoid answering my question.'

'I wasn't aware you'd asked one.'

'Don't try to be clever with me. I asked why it had taken
you so long to get here.'

'No, you didn't,' Woodend contradicted. 'You *informed* me
that you'd asked for me over an hour ago. But let's assume, for
the sake of argument, that you did mean to ask what took me
so long. The answer's simple – I can either be the investigative
detective you said you wanted me to be, or I can be your little
pal who's always droppin' in for a chat. But I can't be both.'

'A few moments ago, you said you were nervous, but I
don't think that's true,' Apollo said. 'You're not *really* afraid
of me, are you?'

'No, I'm not,' Woodend agreed. 'But I am afraid of what
you might *do* in here. Which is why I'm workin' as hard as
I can to get you what you want. Which is why I went to see
your wife.'

'My wife!' Apollo said, trying – and failing – to make it
sound as if he had no wife, and hence had no idea what
Woodend was talking about.

'You can't have expected to keep your identity secret for
long, Major Maitland,' Woodend said. 'So why bother at all?'

'It's one of the rules of warfare never to reveal more to the
enemy than you absolutely need to at the time,' Maitland said.

'But I'm not the enemy,' Woodend pointed out.

'Yes, you are,' Maitland told him. 'You're not working for
me because you want to – you're doing it because you have
no choice.'

'How about the two lads you've got with you in the back
of the bank?' Woodend wondered. 'Did they have any choice?'

'Yes, they did. I warned them of the risks – but they insisted
on coming with me anyway.'

'Aye, I've served under officers I'd gladly have gone through
hell with,' Woodend said. 'Come to think of it, that's usually
where they took me. But you did wrong to bring them on this

62

particular operation, Major. It's not their fight. So why don't you make amends while you still can?'

'Make amends?'

'You know *exactly* what I'm talkin' about. Those two men of yours are in as much trouble as you are, but if you lift the siege right now, I'll do my level best to see that they get off as lightly as they possibly can.'

'They stay here,' Maitland said firmly. 'We *all* stay here until you've done what I want you to.'

Woodend shrugged. 'Well, at least the powers that be can't say I didn't try,' he said, almost to himself.

'How is my wife?' Maitland asked.

'She asked me to tell you to give up.'

'Answer the question, you bastard! How is she?'

'How do you expect her to be? She's drained physically, but she's still very angry an' bitter inside. An' she's deeply worried about you.' Woodend took another drag on his cigarette. 'You're deeply worried about *each other*,' he continued. 'You must be very much in love.'

'We are.'

'How long have you been married?' Woodend asked.

'Two years.'

'An' is it the first marriage for both of you?'

'You could find that out from the records,' Maitland said.

'Yes, I could,' Woodend agreed. 'But records take time, an' I thought you were in a hurry.'

'I've been married once before,' Maitland said, 'but it's Judith's first marriage.'

'Strange that a woman as attractive as her should have stayed unattached for so long,' Woodend mused.

'Just what exactly are you suggesting by that remark?' Maitland demanded angrily.

'I'm not *suggestin'* anythin',' Woodend said. 'I'm thinkin'. I'm tryin' to build up a picture in my mind. It's the way I work.'

An' that's the truth, he thought.

Because however much Monika told him they needed to cut corners on this one, he couldn't. This was how he investigated, and he felt too old to start learning new tricks now.

'Judith . . . Judith did talk about having one serious relationship before we met,' Maitland said.

63

'An' why did it end?'

'I don't know, exactly. She didn't say much about it. I don't even know the man's name, to tell you the truth. But I do get the impression that he let her down rather badly.'

Posh-speak, Woodend thought. Working-class girls get 'chucked' – officers' ladies get 'let down rather badly'.

'Tell me about your wife's business partner, Stanley Keene,' the Chief Inspector said.

'You surely don't think he's the man she had the serious relationship with, do you?' Maitland asked.

'No, I don't. As far as I can tell from just one meetin', he's as bent as Dickie's Hatband.'

'Then why are we wasting time even talking about him?'

Woodend sighed. 'If you want me on this case, you're goin' to have to learn to trust my judgement, Major Maitland,' he said. 'I'm interested in him because I'm interested in anybody who's played a significant part in Judith's life. An' don't worry about givin' me the wrong impression – I'll form my own opinion of him whatever you say. But I'd still like to hear what you think.'

'We'd never have become close friends – I'm not at ease enough with homosexuals for that to have ever happened – but I like him well enough. And he does have a certain integrity about him. Many men would have distanced themselves from Judith after she was imprisoned, but Stanley's stuck by her like a faithful hound.'

'What's he like as a businessman?' Woodend asked.

'It was Judith's drive and energy which built the business up in the first place, but she was of the opinion that once it *was* set up, a trained monkey could have run it.' Maitland paused. 'She wasn't referring to Stanley, of course. She's always had the greatest respect for Stanley's abilities.'

'Which makes it all the stranger that she didn't leave him to run the business once she got married,' Woodend said.

'Are you playing games with me, you bastard?' Major Maitland demanded, angry again.

'How do you mean?' Woodend asked innocently.

'I'm not a fool, you know,' the Major said. 'I've done some interrogating myself, so I know a thing or two about it. And it's quite a common trick to ask a question about one thing when what you're really after is the answer to quite another one.'

64

'So you think I was askin' questions about Keene because what I really wanted was answers about Judith?'

'Well, weren't you?'

'Perhaps partly,' Woodend admitted. 'But it is rather interestin', don't you think, that when Judith had the opportunity to go an' live in married quarters with you, her husband, she chose instead to continue runnin' her caterin' business in Whitebridge?'

'She told me she didn't want to leave her home town. We decided that when I left the Army, we'd settle here.'

'Aye, Stanley Keene told me as much,' Woodend agreed. 'But at one point she *was* goin' to move, wasn't she?'

'Well, yes, I suppose so.'

'An' then she suddenly changed her mind – an' that was shortly after she'd met Clive Burroughs.'

'Are you saying that you think the Dunethorpe Police were right – that Judith was Clive Burroughs' lover?' Maitland asked hotly. 'Because if you are, then I've no further—'

'No, I'm not sayin' that at all,' Woodend interrupted him. 'I believe, as strongly as you obviously do, that they didn't have any kind of *sexual* relationship at all. But the timin' of her change of mind is too coincidental for me to completely rule out the possibility that Burroughs had some influence on it – that he had some kind of hold on her.'

'I simply can't accept that – and I'd rather that you didn't either,' Maitland said.

'I won't tell you how to fight battles if you don't tell me how to conduct investigations,' Woodend countered. 'An' now we've got all that out of the way, would you like to tell me why I'm here?'

'To brief me, of course,' Maitland said. 'A good commander always ensures that he's well briefed by his men who are out in the field.'

Bollocks! Woodend thought. It wasn't a briefing you wanted, it was reassurance. You're like a doubting kid who constantly needs to be told that Father Christmas does actually exist.

'You really don't need to carry on with this siege any more, you know,' he said aloud. 'I've got my teeth well sunk into this case now, an' I won't give up until I've got a result. So why not let the hostages go? An' while you're at it, why not come out yourself?'

Maitland laughed. 'I was wondering when you'd start to show your true colours,' he said. 'I was wondering when the concerned policeman would recede from view, and the hardened negotiator would rear his ugly head.'

'Oh, for God's sake, grow up!' Woodend said impatiently. 'Stop thinkin' of yourself as some romantic storybook hero, and start seein' yourself for what you really are.'

'And what am I?'

'You're a desperate man who wants to get his wife freed, an' doesn't care who else gets hurts in the process. You're a feller who's either goin' to get shot dead by a police marksman or will spend the next twenty-odd years in gaol. I want to help your wife – I honestly do – but after what you've put those people inside through, I don't give a damn what happens to you.'

Maitland laughed again. 'You certainly speak your mind, don't you?' he asked.

'I'm well known for it around Whitebridge Police Headquarters,' Woodend replied.

'Or is this just another one of your games?' the Major wondered. 'Are you, perhaps, just *playing* the part of the bluff, honest policeman?'

Woodend sighed. 'I don't care what you believe,' he said. 'An' I don't care what you think about me personally. But understand this. If just *one* of your hostages is hurt in *any way*, then I'm off the case.'

'You shouldn't bluff with such a weak hand,' the Major said.

'This is no bluff,' Woodend told him. 'The Chief Constable may order me to continue with the investigation, but I won't do it. He may threaten me with the sack, but I still won't do it.'

'Then he'll put another officer on the case.'

'But you don't *want* another officer on the case. You want *me*. I've told you my terms – an' you take them or leave them.'

'It was never my intention to hurt any of the hostages,' the Major said. 'You believe that, don't you?'

'I believe that you've put twenty innocent people in danger, an' that they'll probably have nightmares about it for the rest of their lives,' Woodend told him. 'So whatever else you do, don't go lookin' for a good conduct medal from me, Major Maitland.'

Woodend turned round, and headed for the door.

'I haven't said you can go yet,' Maitland called after him.

'No, you haven't, have you?' Woodend agreed over his shoulder. 'But then I don't need to wait for orders from you, because I'm not one of your bloody soldiers, am I?'

There were a number of armed officers on the High Street – some hiding behind police vehicles, some standing just beyond the line of fire – but Woodend did not notice any of them. He took in a deep gulp of air, and thought about what had gone on inside the bank.

He had tried his level best to sound in control of the situation, but he wasn't convinced he'd even been close. He had spoken with an air of confidence and assurance which had been far from his true feelings. He had told himself that he was handling the whole bloody mess as well as he could have handled it – as well as *anyone* could have handled it – but now he was far from sure that was the case.

His whole body was trembling, as if he'd been suddenly struck down by the flu. His heart was galloping so fast it was threatening to burst.

It had been a mistake to take quite so much air into his lungs all at one go, he thought.

'Are you all right, sir?' some disembodied voice called from the distance.

Of course I'm not all right! he wanted to call back.

But he never got the words out, because his body, acting with a will of its own at that moment, chose to double over, and his stomach – taking advantage of the position – decided to heave almost its entire contents out on to the street.

Eleven

The Philosophers' Arms was a pretentious name to give to any pub, Monika Paniatowski thought. And the décor – powder-blue, over-stuffed sofas which hunkered beneath gilt-framed portraits of great historical thinkers – chimed with the name's pretensions perfectly.

Apart from the barman – who was standing behind the bar counter and half-heartedly polishing beer glasses – the place was empty.

'Well, what do you expect?' Paniatowski could imagine Woodend saying. 'The Philosophers' Arms! Sofas! Soft lightin'! No drinkin' man worth his salt would be seen *dead* in a poncy dive like this.'

Yes, that's what he would have said if he'd been here.

But he *wasn't* here, was he?

He was back in Whitebridge.

Treating this case just as he'd treated all those he'd successfully solved in the past.

Stubbornly sticking to his old well-tried ways, without even bothering to ask himself if those old ways still worked.

The barman looked up at his one-and-only customer. He had thin, sandy hair, Paniatowski noted, and was probably somewhere in his mid-thirties. His eyes were pale blue and washed out, and his chin, which might once have tried to pass itself off as firm and determined, now seemed to have settled for being only slightly less than weak.

'What can I get you, love?' he asked, favouring her with the typical barman's brief – energy-efficient – smile.

'Are you Hal Greene?' Paniatowski said.

The barman grinned. 'Now that depends, doesn't it?'

'On what?'

'On who's asking. If he owes you money, then I'm definitely not him. On the other hand, if you're looking for Hal because you've been told he can give you a good time, then I'm definitely your man.'

He'd obviously successfully completed the full course in the School of Clumsy Flirting, Paniatowski thought, but though he'd remembered the script perfectly, his heart wasn't really in it.

She reached into her handbag and produced her warrant card. 'My name's Monika,' she said sweetly. 'But if you like, Mr Greene, *you* can call me "Sergeant Paniatowski".'

The barman's grin rapidly faded away, to be replaced by a look of some concern.

'If it's about what happened the other night, you have to understand it's not my fault,' Greene said.

68

'Isn't it?' Paniatowski replied noncommittally.

'These days, kids will do anything to pass themselves off as eighteen,' Greene told her. 'Even though they've more bum fluff than bristle, the lads put sticking plasters on their faces, to make it look as if they've cut themselves shaving. And as for the girls – well, the amount of rolled-up toilet paper they stuff down their bras doesn't bear thinking about. And on a busy night, Sergeant Paniatowski, I simply don't have the time to give all my customers a thorough inspection.'

'I'm not here about under-age drinking,' Paniatowski assured him.

'Then why *are* you here?'

'I'd like to ask you a few questions about Clive Burroughs.'

'What for? Clive's dead and buried. It's all over and done with.'

'Vodka,' Paniatowski said.

'Pardon?'

'When I walked in, you asked me what you could get me. Well, I'll have a vodka.'

Greene went over to the optics and measured out the drink. 'Have this one on the house,' he suggested.

'Not a chance!' Paniatowski replied, slipping her money across the counter. 'So what can you tell me about Clive Burroughs?'

'Not a great deal.'

'Now that is surprising,' Paniatowski mused. 'Because according to the thick file that they have back at Dunethorpe Central, you were one of Burroughs' best friends.'

'Oh, I'm not saying I didn't *know* him,' Greene said.

'Very wise.'

'I *did* know him. But only not really well, if you see what I mean. Just well enough to say hello and ask him how he was getting on.'

Paniatowski looked around her. 'I really like this pub,' she lied. 'It's very classy.'

'Yes, it is, isn't it?' Greene agreed. 'We like to think it's a cut above the average.'

'In fact, I'm getting so fond of it that I just might stay till closing time,' Paniatowski said.

'Pardon?'

69

'Yes, I think I'll stay. It might be interesting to find out if it really is as difficult to spot under-age drinkers as you seem to think it is.'

Greene did not take the announcement well. For several moments he fell silent, then he said, 'All right, Clive Burroughs was my friend. Or at least, I *thought* he was at the time.'

'How often did you see him?'

'He used to come here most nights. When he wasn't out chasing skirt, that is.'

'Yes, I heard he was a bit of a ladies' man,' Paniatowski said. 'Now tell me something I *don't* know.'

'I'm not sure where to start.'

'Did he have any enemies?'

'I suppose you could say that the woman who battered his head in wasn't exactly his friend.'

'Apart from her?'

'There's a few men round here who wouldn't have been too kindly disposed to him if they'd found out what he was getting up to with their wives. But they never *did* find out. He was far too careful for that.'

'Who else?'

'Other than them, nobody comes to mind. He could be a real charmer, could Clive – with men *as well as* women.'

'Did it seem as if there was anything he was particularly worried about just before he died?'

'Not *just* before he died, no.'

'Earlier, then?'

'For the last year or so of his life, he was a bit concerned about how his business was going.'

'A *bit* concerned? What does that mean?'

'You know.'

'No, I don't,' Paniatowski said. 'I'm a *bit* concerned I might get a ladder in my new stockings. I'm a *bit* concerned the cost of vodka may go up. Is that the sort of concerned he was?'

'Well, no.'

'So what kind of concerned was he?'

'All right, he was a worried man,' Greene conceded.

'Worried about what?'

'The business had been going through a very lean patch, and he was finding it difficult to meet all his commitments.

One night, when he was feeling really low, he told me there was a real possibility he might even go bankrupt.'

'But, by the time he died, that had all sorted itself out?'

'Yes.'

'Because business picked up?'

'Not exactly.'

'Because he'd come into some money?'

'Again, not exactly. He said that he'd found somebody – a woman from Whitebridge – who was prepared to give him a loan for as long as he needed one.'

'That would have been Judith Maitland?'

'I assume it was now, though he didn't actually mention any names at the time.'

'Did he give you any indication of *why* she was prepared to lend him the money?'

'Not really. He just smirked, in that way he had, and said she just couldn't resist him.'

'In other words, she was putty in his hands because she was having an affair with him.'

'That's what I took it to mean at the time.'

'But not now?'

Greene shook his head. 'No, not now.'

'And what's caused you to change your mind?'

Greene picked up a pint glass from the counter, and, despite the fact it was already sparkling, began to polish it with vigour.

'I'd much rather not say,' he mumbled.

'And I'd much rather you *did*,' Paniatowski said firmly.

Greene sighed. 'I suppose it can't do much harm to tell you now,' he said, in a dull, defeated voice. 'Most of the people around here already know all about it anyway.'

'Know about what?'

'I was quite upset when I heard that Clive got himself killed,' Greene said. 'I mean, don't get me wrong, I always knew he was a bit of a bastard – he'd never pretended to be anything else, at least not to me – but I still couldn't help liking the feller. And when I was standing over his grave, I just couldn't stop myself from shedding a few tears.'

'Very touching,' Paniatowski said.

'Of course, if I'd known then what I know now,' Greene

71

continued, a sudden violent anger entering his tone, 'I'd have pissed on his coffin instead of weeping over it.'

Though she suspected she'd already worked out just what he was about to tell her, Paniatowski said, 'So what exactly is it that you know now that you didn't know then?'

'My wife, Doreen, left me a couple of months ago,' Greene told Paniatowski, and now the anger transformed itself into self-pity. 'Just packed her bags and went. Said she had no choice. Said she couldn't stand being with me any more, because all the time she was, she was thinking of him.'

'Him? Clive Burroughs?'

'That's right. Clive-bloody-Burroughs. Clive-stab-your-best-friend-in-the-back Burroughs. All those nights she said she was out with her mates, she was really out with him. So, you see, it wasn't Judith Maitland he was having an affair with – it was my Doreen.'

Twelve

There was not a soul to be seen in the car park at Whitebridge Police Headquarters when Woodend drove on to it, but by the time he'd actually climbed out of his old Wolseley, the press was bearing down on him like a pack of hounds that had scented blood.

'I have no comment to make personally concerning this situation,' he told the dozen or so reporters who surrounded him and began baying for news. 'Any statements which are to be issued will come directly from the Chief Constable's office.'

'Have you seen any of the hostages yourself?' one of the reporters on his left called out.

'How long do you expect the Cotton Credit Siege to last?' another asked from his right.

'As I've already said, I've no comment to make,' Woodend repeated firmly. 'So if you wouldn't mind gettin' out of my way, we can all avoid the need for me to book you for obstruction.'

A reluctant gap opened in the tight circle of journalists, and Woodend stepped into it.

'Have you spoken to Major Maitland yourself?' asked a female voice he immediately recognized as belonging to an old enemy.

Woodend, already clear of the circle, stopped in his tracks, and swivelled round.

'What was that you just said, Miss Driver?' he demanded.

Elizabeth Driver smirked, clearly proud of the fact that she had brought him to a halt when all her colleagues had failed.

'I asked you if you'd talked to Major Maitland, Chief Inspector.'

'An' who might he be, when he's at home?' Woodend asked.

Elizabeth Driver's smirk turned itself into a broad smile. 'He's the man who started all this,' she said.

'Somebody's been feedin' you a load of cock-an'-bull, Miss Driver,' Woodend said. 'I've never even heard of this Major Mainfleet—'

'Maitland. His name's Major Maitland.'

' . . . an' I can't imagine where you'd get the idea that an army officer would want to try an' rob a bank.'

'But it's not a robbery at all,' Elizabeth Driver said.

Sounding surprised.

Pretending she really had believed him when he claimed to have no knowledge of Major Maitland.

'Not a robbery?' Woodend said, playing the deception game to the end, even though he knew he'd already lost it.

'All Major Maitland wants is for his wife to be released from gaol,' Elizabeth Driver told him. 'And exactly when is that going to happen?'

Woodend turned again, and strode angrily towards the station entrance. Elizabeth Driver had her own, carefully cultivated, sources in the Force – he suspected the Chief Constable to be among them – so she often learned things she had no right to know. But normally she would keep them to herself until she'd written her story. The fact she was bandying Maitland's name around at this point had to mean that all other reporters also knew it, or soon would – that what he was dealing with was not so much a leak as a bloody flood.

*   *   *

'Who the hell released Major Maitland's name to the bloody press?' Woodend demanded.

The Three Wise Men – the Chief Constable, Colonel Danvers and Mr Slater-Burnes – looked at each other across the table, then Marlowe said, 'That really is no concern of yours, Mr Woodend.'

'Isn't it just? Has nobody thought about what that kind of leak will do to my investigation? Now, when I ask questions, everybody'll know *why* I'm askin' them. It's like releasin' your entire plan of attack to the enemy before the battle's even started,' Woodend said, noting to himself just how much like Major Maitland he was starting to sound.

'You always did have a colourful way of expressing yourself, Chief Inspector,' Marlowe said disapprovingly. 'But my immediate concern is a report I've just recently received.'

'A report?'

'Is it true that you actually *vomited* in the High Street?'

'What?' Woodend said, hardly able to believe he'd heard the Chief Constable's words correctly.

'I asked you if you'd been sick in the High Street.'

'Yes, I was.'

'But – good God, man – whatever can you have been thinking of to put on such a display?'

'I wasn't *thinkin'* at all, sir. I was just lettin' my body do what it needed to do.'

'Are you ill?'

'No.'

'Then what do you think might have brought on this sudden and rather unseemly attack?'

'It think it might have had somethin' to do with the fact that I'd just been talkin' to a man who has the lives of twenty civilians in his hands, an' I was worried about whether what I'd said to him had made their situation better or worse,' Woodend told him.

'Who saw this unfortunate incident?'

'Unfortunate incident?' Woodend said. 'What unfortunate incident?'

'The one I've just been talking about, Chicf Inspector – the one in which you threw up in the street.'

This was bizarre, Woodend thought. 'The only people who saw me were the officers on duty,' he said.

'You're sure none of the press was present?'

'Yes, I am,' Woodend said, wearily. 'The press were being kept well behind the barricade.'

'Well, that's something, at least,' the Chief Constable said. 'Though I have to tell you, that is not the kind of behaviour I expect any of my more senior officers to display.'

'I'd like to hear what the Chief Inspector talked to Major Maitland about,' Colonel Danvers said.

'We talked about what Major Maitland *wanted* us to talk about, of course,' Woodend said.

'Which would have been . . .?'

'Which was his wife.'

'So you didn't discuss his hostages at all?'

'Yes, we discussed them.'

'And what did you actually say?'

'I asked him to let them go.'

Slater-Burnes, the Home Office man, tut-tutted.

'That is not the proper way to go about it at all,' he said. 'As I may have pointed out previously, we haven't had a *great* deal of experience of negotiating with hostage-takers – thank the Lord, it is still a rare enough occurrence in England – but we've certainly had enough to know that it's a mistake to ever make blanket demands on them.'

'Is that right?' Woodend asked.

'It is, indeed. What you should have done was to appear concerned about Maitland's own well-being, and in that way established a bond between the two of you. Next, you should have asked him if there was anything he needed. He would probably have requested chocolate or cigarettes. Once you had done something for him, you could have asked for something in return – a small concession, like releasing one or two of the hostages, for example.'

'Take note of this, Chief Inspector,' Marlowe said.

'Oh, I am,' Woodend promised.

'Having made the first concession, it would have been very difficult for Maitland to refuse a second, and then a third,' Slater-Burnes continued. 'Wearing your man down, Chief Inspector – that's always the key to success in this kind of operation.'

'Do you have any idea of the *kind* of man we're dealing

with here?' Woodend asked, keeping a lid on his fury – but only just.

'I'm aware that he's a soldier—' Slater-Burnes began.

'He's more than just any old soldier – he's a *veteran* soldier with considerable combat experience,' Woodend interrupted. 'Findin' himself in a potentially life-threatenin' situation isn't anythin' new to him, you know, Mr Slater-Burnes. This is a picnic compared to some of the things he's been through.'

'Nonetheless, the techniques I'm suggesting have been tried and tested by our American cousins,' Slater-Burnes persisted.

'You just don't get it, do you?' Woodend asked. 'Offerin' concessions an' tryin' to wear him down is just what Maitland *expects* and is *ready* for. They're old tricks to him – an' they simply won't work.'

'Then what *will* work?' Slater-Burnes asked.

'Provin' that his wife was falsely imprisoned.'

The Home Office man frowned. 'I think we should consider replacing Chief Inspector Woodend with another negotiator with a more positive attitude,' he said to Marlowe.

'You can do what you like, but I'm tellin' you now, he won't talk to anyone but me,' Woodend said.

'Then we must consider the military option,' Slater-Burnes said. 'What's your opinion on the matter, Colonel? Surely Maitland will see the pointlessness of continued resistance, when he's faced with overwhelming force.'

'Bollocks!' Woodend said.

'I beg your pardon?'

'If he can get what he wants – his wife's conviction squashed – then he'll surrender without any fuss, an' serve his prison sentence with no complaints. If he *can't* get what he wants, he'll decide to make this his last stand, an' go out in a blaze of glory. He won't deliberately kill any of the hostages himself – though most of them will probably die anyway, in the crossfire – but he'll certainly be determined to take as many of his attackers with him as he can.'

'Colonel Danvers?' Slater-Burnes asked.

'It's possible that Major Maitland would react as the Chief Inspector has outlined,' the Colonel admitted. 'Men like him – men used to going into extremely sticky situations – sometimes convince themselves that defeat is not an option. They develop what I tend to think of as a samurai mentality.'

'I'm sure this is all very interesting, in its way, but it doesn't do anything to help solve our immediate problems,' the Chief Constable said. 'What I'm looking for from you gentlemen is some specific guidance as to what to do next. I'd like to hear from you first, Mr Slater-Burnes.'

The man from the Ministry had first advocated removing Woodend from the case, then proposed storming the bank. Now, from the conciliatory expression which had suddenly appeared in his features, it looked as if he were ready to do a complete volte-face.

'Mr Woodend has argued his case very persuasively – if a little too forcefully,' he said, smiling to show there were no ill-feelings. 'And he is, after all, the only one who has spoken directly to Major Maitland. Bearing all that in mind – and assuming that his assessment of the situation is correct – then the course of action he suggests would seem to be the only one open to us.'

Smooth! Woodend thought. Very smooth indeed. If the siege was resolved successfully, Slater-Burnes could easily claim that he had given his full backing to the strategy behind it. If, on the other hand, it ended in a bloodbath, he could always say it was not his advice which was at fault, but the assessment on which the advice was based.

'Colonel Danvers?' Marlowe said.

'I agree with Mr Slater-Burnes,' the Colonel said.

'And so do I,' the Chief Constable said.

So that was it, then. Snakes might proverbially be considered to be the slipperiest things around, Woodend thought, but they were rank amateurs when compared to these three.

'I think that concludes our meeting,' the Chief Constable said. 'Thank you, gentlemen. We will reconvene whenever it is deemed appropriate.'

Woodend stood up.

'Not you, Mr Woodend,' the Chief Constable continued. 'I'd like an additional word with you, if you don't mind.'

If he wants to talk about vomit again, I'll show him what it looks like from close to, Woodend thought.

Marlowe waited until the soldier and the bureaucrat had

closed the door behind them, then said, 'You look like you could use a drink, Mr Woodend. What can I get you?'

Now this really *was* bizarre, Woodend thought.

'A drop of whisky would be nice,' he heard himself say.

'Of course.'

Marlowe walked over to his impressively scholarly bookcase, and touched a hidden switch. Woodend had always suspected that most of the leather-backed books had never been read, but now he saw that they weren't even real books at all, but merely a cladding to hide the drinks cupboard.

'I've got a rather special twelve-year-old single malt here that I haven't even got around to trying myself, yet,' Marlowe continued, conversationally. 'I think you'll like it.'

He returned with two drinks, and handed one of them to Woodend. The Chief Inspector took a sip. It was *bloody* good.

'Sorry about going on and on about you being sick in the street, earlier,' Marlowe said convivially. 'I probably wouldn't have even bothered to mention it if it happened to any other officer in my command. But there you are – old habits die hard, you know.'

'Do they?' Woodend asked, half-prepared to wake up in his own bed any second.

'I suppose it's a question of expectation,' Marlowe continued. 'If you *expect* an officer to behave badly, you will inevitably perceive whatever he does in just that light. It becomes, as it were, a self-fulfilling prophesy.'

It becomes, *as it were*, an exercise in talking complete bloody bollocks, Woodend thought.

But he was wise enough to hold his peace.

'I think I may have held completely the wrong opinion of you for quite some time, if truth be told,' Marlowe said. 'I was, if I'm honest, rather put off by your blunt exterior, and it prevented me from fully appreciating what a fine detective you are. But that's all in the past now. The veil has been lifted, and I would truly like to apologize for any injustices I might have done you.'

He wasn't asleep after all, Woodend told himself. He was on bloody *Candid Camera*!

But just in case he wasn't, he said, 'That's really very big of you to say so, sir.'

Marlowe nodded. 'Yes, I like to think I'm a big enough man to acknowledge my faults. My job's not always the easiest in the world, you know. You should try spending half your time dealing with idiots like Slater-Burnes and Danvers yourself. It's a wonder I haven't cracked up long ago.'

Well, you're certainly crackin' up now, Woodend decided.

'They just don't understand the world we live in,' Marlowe said. 'Before you arrived, Danvers was all for storming the bank, and Slater-Burnes for filling it with an army of civil servant negotiators who would have tried to bore Maitland to death. You talked them both out of it, but even if you hadn't, I would never have allowed either course of action to go ahead.'

'You wouldn't?'

'Of course not. Why should I put my faith in their men, when I can put it squarely in my own? And that's what I have – *faith* in you, Charlie.'

He called me Charlie, Woodend thought. Bloody hell fire! Where's the Four Horsemen of the Apocalypse when you need them?

'Would this be a good time to ask for a few extra bodies on the case, sir?' he said.

Marlowe's bonhomie melted away as quickly as ice cream in a furnace. 'Extra bodies?' he repeated.

'Inspector Rutter's been out on sick leave ever since his wife's murder, an' Sergeant Paniatowski's all tied up with the side of the investigation that's based in Dunethorpe,' Woodend explained.

'Yes?'

'So, bearin' all that in mind, I was wonderin' if you could see your way clear to allowing me to draft in a few more detectives.'

Marlowe's frame had gone rigid.

'As you know, I am not one of those chief constables who courts popularity in the eyes of the general public,' he said. 'And so, while it would be easy enough for me to devote most of my available resources to a case which will obviously catch the popular imagination, I feel obliged to resist the temptation to do so.'

'Is that a "no"?' Woodend asked, taking another sip of his whisky, only to discover that it seemed to have turned to ashes.

'I am responsible for a whole county, Chief Inspector, and whilst I have the greatest possible concern for the hostages, I cannot allow myself to forget that little old ladies in sleepy villages also need my protection,' Marlowe told him.

It sounded like part of a speech he might have delivered at some chief constables' boozy junket, Woodend thought – and it probably was.

'Do you mean you can't spare me *any* men?' he asked.

Marlowe looked about to say that that was precisely what he meant, then he suddenly changed his mind.

'I can spare you one extra man,' he said reluctantly, 'but only to do some of the leg-work for you. It certainly can't be anybody from CID.'

Of course not, Woodend thought. The CID were needed to protect the little old ladies in sleepy villages.

'So all that you're offerin' me is one of the uniforms?' he said.

'That's right,' Marlowe agreed. 'Talk to the duty sergeants. See who they can spare.'

Thirteen

Dunethorpe *Central* Police Station exemplified its name, for not only was it the centre of the town, but it was in the centre of a terrace of three-storey buildings. Or at least, it had been in the centre of the row when it was originally opened towards the end of the nineteenth century.

Back then, it was generally believed that respect for the law was so widespread that just a handful of bobbies was all that was needed to keep a lid on crime in the area. As the years rolled by, however, it became plain to everyone that while the police force still held on to a great deal of the moral authority it had once had, it also needed a fairly strong physical presence to back that authority up. Thus, more young men were recruited into the force, and more space was needed in which they could practise law-enforcement.

The county council had toyed with building a completely

new station, but eventually abandoned that idea in favour of expanding sideways. A grocer's shop to the left and solicitor's office to the right had been the first victims of this expansion, but the businesses beyond them had also soon been absorbed by the need for more extensive policing. By the start of the Second World War, only the newsagent's on the very edge of the terrace had not been incorporated into the headquarters' building, and by the end of hostilities, even that had disappeared.

The result of all this ad-hoc expansion was that Flatfoot House – as it was known locally – looked quite a modest building from the outside, but *inside* was a maze of corridors resembling the warren of a territorially ambitious rabbit. New recruits found it took them several months to master the place well enough to move through it with complete confidence, and Monika Paniatowski was well aware that she would soon have become totally lost had she not had Chief Inspector Baxter there to guide her.

'This is it,' Baxter said.

The door in front of which he stopped had nothing written on it, but the patch of paint at eye-level, surrounded as it was by a much darker shade of the same paint, suggested a name-plate might have hung there.

'My old room,' Baxter said, nostalgically. 'The scene of my earliest triumphs.'

The chief inspector opened the door to reveal the office. The desk took up most of the available space, and the top of that desk was piled high with files and documents.

'This is just about everything that we have on the Burroughs case,' Baxter told Paniatowski.

Monika whistled softly to herself. 'You seem to have been very thorough,' she said.

'I was,' Baxter agreed. 'There's a great deal on the crime itself, and on Judith Maitland's background – as you might expect – but I also had my lads go through Clive Burroughs' life history with a fine-toothed comb.'

'Why?' Paniatowski asked.

'Because the essence of good police-work is attention to detail?' the chief inspector asked.

Paniatowski laughed. 'That might well be the approved

81

theory, but we both know it's not the way things actually happen, don't we, sir?' she said.

'Then what does happen?' Baxter wondered, as if testing her.

'In an ideal world, we would – of course – collect every available scrap of possible evidence,' Paniatowski said. 'But since we're permanently undermanned and always pushed for time, we have to concentrate our efforts on what seems most relevant.'

'Sad but true,' Baxter agreed.

'So I would have expected most of the information to have been on the prime suspect, rather than on the victim,' Paniatowski said.

Baxter was starting to look uncomfortable. 'I wanted to be *sure*,' he said awkwardly.

'Sure?'

'You remember that I told your boss there was no doubt in my mind that Judith Maitland was guilty?'

'Yes?'

'And based on the evidence we presented at the trial, I still believe that she was.'

'But . . . ?' Paniatowski prodded.

'But the small part of me which *isn't* a professional policeman – and I assure you it's a *very* small part indeed, Sergeant – found itself believing Judith Maitland, when she said she didn't do it.' Baxter shrugged, as if bewildered by his own reaction to the case. 'There was no logic at all to that, you understand,' he continued. 'It was just a feeling.'

'So you looked for fresh evidence which might back up this feeling of yours?'

'Exactly.'

'And did you find any?'

'Not a sausage. Not even the *smell* of a sausage, nor even the hoof-print of the pig that the sausage first came from. There may have been people who disliked Burroughs – there *were* people who disliked him – but none of them seemed to have either a strong enough motive, or the opportunity, to murder him. So while I'm happy to have you go through all the documentation, I don't hold much hope of you coming up with anything new.'

82

'Did you ever consider Hal Greene a possible suspect?' Paniatowski asked innocently.

'Hal Greene?' Baxter mused. 'That name does sound familiar, but I'm afraid I can't quite—'

'He's the landlord of the Philosophers' Arms.'

'Oh, that's right. Nasty, pretentious little pub, isn't it? All sofas and pastel shades?'

'That's the one,' Paniatowski agreed.

'Why should I have considered him?'

'Because Burroughs was having an affair with his wife.'

'Are you sure of that?'

'I got it straight from the horse's mouth.'

'So you think Greene might have killed Burroughs?'

Paniatowski shook her head. 'No. Greene said he didn't find out about the affair until long after Burroughs' death. And I believe him.'

Baxter took his pipe out of his pocket, and lit up. Clouds of blue smoke filled the tiny office.

'Well, that's certainly put me in my place, hasn't it, Sergeant Paniatowski?' he asked.

Paniatowski felt herself starting to redden. 'I'm sorry, sir. I never meant to suggest—' she began.

'Of course you did,' Baxter interrupted, dismissively but not unkindly. 'You're a cocky, energetic, young sergeant, who wants to prove to the old fellers like me – who are still inexplicably clinging on to the posts of authority – that their day is almost gone. You want to make them aware that you're the new breed and you're the way of the future.'

'I didn't want to—'

'I don't blame you, lass. I did the same in my day. We all did. And one day, when you start feeling aches in your legs that you'd never noticed before, you'll be the butt of those kinds of comments yourself.'

Baxter was perhaps a few years younger than Cloggin'-it Charlie, Paniatowski thought, but talking to him was not unlike talking to Woodend. And perhaps he was right in what he'd said. Perhaps she was cocky. Perhaps she did tend to dismiss the old guard too easily.

She had been glad when Woodend went back to Whitebridge – leaving her on her own, to conduct the case the way she wanted to – but now she began to realize how much she missed him.

Baxter glanced at his watch. 'It's getting late. I expect you'll want to put off making a dent in these files until the morning.'

'No, I think I'll start now,' Paniatowski said.

Baxter nodded his head sagely. 'Of course you will,' he agreed. 'Given what I've just said about you, I shouldn't have expected anything else.'

Constables Colin Beresford and William Pratchett were standing behind the barricade at the southern end of Whitebridge High Street. Earlier on in the evening, they had been fully occupied in keeping the rubber-necking spectators well away from the barrier. But now – as the temperature dropped and the crowd began to thin – they could finally relax a little.

It was Pratchett – or 'News Boy Bill', as he was widely known at the station – who initiated the conversation which the lull in activity allowed.

'Heard the latest?' he asked eagerly.

Beresford found himself grinning. Bill Pratchett combined an eagerness for collecting gossip with an equal thirst for disseminating it, and it was only to be expected that after hours of enforced silence he was just bursting to deliver his latest bulletin.

'Well, have you?' Pratchett demanded.

'There's a rumour that the Rovers are about to sign a new centre-forward,' Beresford said innocently.

'Bugger the Rovers!' Pratchett said, with the contempt of a man who could instinctively distinguish between stale news and news which was hot from the press. 'I'm talking about the siege! And the murder!'

'Oh, that!' Beresford said. 'Has something been happening?'

'*A lot's* been happening! Cloggin'-it Charlie's been over to Dunethorpe – which is where the murder actually took place.'

'And why did he do that?'

Pratchett frowned. The function of his listeners, as he saw it, was to be in awe of what they'd learned. It certainly wasn't their place to ask him questions he didn't know the answer to.

'Maybe they've decided to release Mrs Maitland,' he speculated. 'Maybe Mr Woodend went over to Dunethorpe to square any new investigation which might be started with the local police.'

'If that was the case, I'd have thought they'd send somebody more senior,' Beresford said dubiously.

'And there's something else,' Pratchett said, attempting to reclaim the initiative. '*Before* Woodend went over to Dunethorpe, he paid a call on Stan the Half-Man.'

'Who?' Beresford asked.

'Stanley Keene, Mrs Maitland's business partner.'

'I don't think I know him,' Beresford admitted.

'Of course you know him,' Pratchett insisted. 'If you've ever been on a park duty, you can't have missed him.'

'Can't I?'

'You must have seen him hanging around the public lavatories. Nasty little poof. Couldn't pass himself off as a real man if he was standing on stilts. Bloody hell, he must be nearly forty, and he still lives with his—'

Pratchett swallowed the rest of the sentence. It looked painful.

'Still lives with his . . .?' Beresford prompted.

Pratchett looked desperately around him. 'I think there's some bloody kids at the other end of the barrier,' he said, unconvincingly. 'I'd better go and shoo them off.'

Beresford watched the other constable hurry away.

'So this Stan the Half-Man still lives with his mother,' he said softly to himself. 'Well, he's not the only one, is he?'

He didn't know how Keene felt about living under the matriarchal roof as he slid into middle age, but he was only too well aware of how difficult it was to take yourself seriously when you were a 24-year-old police constable who was doing the same thing.

And even if you could pull off that particular trick, the constable thought – even if you did manage to see yourself as a police officer, first and foremost – it was bloody difficult to persuade the rest of the world to follow suit.

Beresford thought wistfully of the numerous other young officers who'd come to him for advice – because it was obvious to them that he was *bloody* good at his job – but who'd stopped coming the moment they'd learned he was still sleeping in the same bedroom he'd grown up in. It really wasn't easy to be viewed as a mentor one minute, and nothing more than a big kid in a uniform the next, he thought, but he didn't see what he could actually *do* about it.

A car pulled up, and the duty sergeant got out of it. Beresford clicked his heels smartly together, and gave a salute which would not have disgraced a passing-out parade at Police College. But he probably still looked to the sergeant as if he was a lad in fancy dress, he thought gloomily.

'You're relieved, Beresford. Get yourself back to the station,' the sergeant said.

'Is somethin' the matter, Sarge?' the constable asked.

'That depends on how you look at it. Some might regard what's about to happen to you as a golden opportunity. On the other hand, there's others who'd start thinkin' about movin' into another line of work entirely.'

'What *is* happenin' to me?' Beresford asked.

'Didn't I say?'

'No, you didn't.'

The sergeant pulled a comical face. 'It appears that Cloggin'-it Charlie wants you for a sunbeam,' he said.

The documentation on Clive Burroughs was as extensive as Chief Inspector Baxter had promised it would be. There were his discharge papers from the Army at the end of his National Service. There was his application for a driving licence and copies of his marriage certificate, his daughter's birth certificate, and the divorce papers which his wife had once filed, but later withdrawn. And there were bank statements – endless bank statements which stretched all the way back to the day he had first opened an account.

It was, indeed, a daunting task, and for a moment Paniatowski was tempted to leave it all until the morning. Then she thought of the amused smile that Chief Inspector Baxter would wear on his face if he learned that, despite what she'd said to him earlier, she'd gone home – and she felt her resolve suddenly stiffen.

She reached into her handbag, and extracted a packet of

cigarettes and a miniature bottle of vodka. It was going to be a long night, she told herself.

'It's the classic success story,' Woodend said to Constable Beresford. 'So classic, it's almost a cliché in itself. The leadin' lady breaks her leg just before the curtain's about to go up on the first night, the understudy steps into her shoes – an', just like that, a star is born.'

'Pardon, sir?' Beresford said.

'Or, to put it more prosaically,' Woodend said, 'Inspector Rutter's out on sick leave, Sergeant Paniatowski's workin' mainly out of the Dunethorpe nick, an' I need somebody to do some of the legwork for me here in Whitebridge. Are you up to the job?'

'Too bloody right, I am!' Beresford said, before he could stop himself. 'What I mean, sir, is . . . er . . .'

'I think I get the message,' Woodend said. 'But what I'm offerin' you isn't all glamour an' glitz, you know. In fact, there's no bloody glamour an' glitz at all. Until this case is cracked, you'll be workin' sixteen or seventeen hours a day, and most of what you do will turn out to be a complete bloody waste of time.'

'Oh, I quite understand that, sir,' Beresford said, trying to sound grave and serious.

'No, you don't,' Woodend said dryly. 'But when your legs ache like they've never ached before, an' your back feels like it's broken in three places, you might just begin to get some idea of what I'm talkin' about.'

'Can I ask a question, sir?' Beresford asked.

'Aye, if it's a short one, an' I can answer it without puttin' too much pressure on my already-strained brain cells,' Woodend agreed.

'Why me?'

'What exactly are you askin'? Why did I choose to give you the questionable honour of workin' on this case?'

'Yes, sir.'

'Why not you? You're young, you're eager, an' from what I saw of you on the Pamela Rainsford case, you can handle most situations you find yourself faced with.'

Besides, Woodend added mentally, from seeming to be –

surprisingly – his strongest ally, the Chief Constable had done a sudden about-turn when it came to providing extra manpower, and now he was having to make do with what was available.

'Where do you want me to start, sir?' Beresford asked, with an enthusiasm which Woodend could see might soon become exhausting.

'You can start by gettin' yourself out of that uniform,' the Chief Inspector said.

'Pardon, sir?'

'Members of the general public are quite happy to have uniformed officers find their missin' dogs for them, an' tell them what time it is, but when they're bein' questioned about anythin' as important as a murder, they like to talk to a suit. You do *have* a suit, don't you?'

'Oh yes, sir,' Beresford said, adding silently to himself, my mum made sure of that. She even went with me for the fitting.

'So go home an' put your suit on. Then, once you're properly kitted out, I'd like you to do a bit of investigatin' for me,' Woodend continued. 'An' do you have any idea what it is we'll be investigatin'?'

'The Judith Maitland case,' Beresford said, without a second's hesitation. 'Her husband wants you to re-open it.'

'Is that what it said on the news?' Woodend asked.

'No, sir. All it said on the radio was that Major Maitland was behind the siege. The other lads thought he just wanted to get his wife released, but I knew it couldn't be as simple as that.'

'Did you, indeed?' Woodend asked. 'An' what was it brought you to that conclusion?'

'If all he wanted was to free her, he wouldn't have gone about it the way he has.'

'So what *would* he have done?'

'He'd have broken into the gaol and sprung her.'

'That wouldn't have been easy,' Woodend pointed out.

'It would have been a bloody sight easier than what he's decided to do instead.'

'Takin' over a bank? That doesn't seem too difficult.'

'No, sir, but *holding* the bank is. Every police marksman in Lancashire is looking down his sights at that bank at the moment, and by tomorrow, the Army will probably have got in on the act. And what would he have had to deal with if he'd gone for the prison instead? Half a dozen shotguns. At the most.'

'You've got a point,' Woodend agreed.

'So he doesn't just want her freed – he wants her name cleared. And that's why he sent for you.'

'The famous Chief Inspector Woodend,' Woodend said sourly.

'You are famous, sir, at least in Central Lancashire. I know it's not something you like to hear, but it's the truth.'

'Interestin'. You seem to think you know me better than my own mother ever did,' Woodend said. 'So I don't like bein' a celebrity?'

'No, sir.'

'An' what do you base this theory of yours on?'

Beresford shrugged. 'It's hard to say, exactly. I suppose it's the little things – the way you walk, the way you dress, the way you talk to other people.'

Woodend lit up a cigarette. 'Well, Constable Beresford, since you seem to be an expert on all things Woodendian, tell me how I feel about this case?'

'You feel it's difficult, sir. Probably one of the most difficult you've ever handled. And even if Judith Maitland *is* innocent, you're not sure that you can prove it.'

'An' this particular branch of your theory about me is based on what?' Woodend asked.

'On the fact that I saw you puke up your ring all over the High Street,' Beresford said.

Fourteen

If he'd been asked to make a list of those most likely to visit him in his office, late in the evening of the first day of the siege, Woodend would have put Stanley Keene very low down it. Yet there he was. And not dressed, as the Chief Inspector might have expected him to be off-duty – in something camp and flamboyant – but instead wearing a very conservative blue suit, that fitted perfectly with the serious expression he had on his face.

Woodend rose from behind his desk to shake hands – Keene's handshake was remarkably firm, but then he might have been making an effort with that, too – then sat down again.

'Why don't you take a seat yourself, sir?' he suggested.

The caterer shook his head. 'I'm too nervous for that,' he said. 'So if you don't mind, I'd rather stand.'

'I don't mind at all,' Woodend said. 'Would you like to tell me what's on your mind, Mr Keene?'

Keene took a deep breath. 'When you and your sergeant were talking to me about Judith earlier, you never once mentioned the fact that the man in the bank was her husband,' he said accusingly.

'You're right, I didn't,' Woodend agreed.

'Why not?'

'To put it quite simply, I wasn't at liberty to divulge that information to anyone at the time.'

'And even if you had been, you wouldn't have divulged it to an old queen who would immediately have rushed off and blabbered about it to all her slack-wristed little friends,' Keene said bitterly.

'You're way off the mark if you think that – and you're way out of line, an' all!' Woodend said harshly.

Keene flinched under the attack, but gamely stood his ground. '*Am* I off the mark?' he asked defiantly. 'Am I really?'

'Yes, you bloody well are! I was very impressed by how much you seemed to care about Judith Maitland, Mr Keene, and if I'd have been able to tell anyone what was goin' on, I'd have told you.'

Keene looked down at the floor, as if he felt a sudden urge to give his immaculately polished shoes a thorough inspection.

Neither man spoke again for perhaps a full half minute, then the caterer lifted his head again and said, 'Well, I am surprised.'

Woodend grinned. 'I surprise a lot of people,' he said. 'I seem to have a real talent for it. Now if that's settled, I'd be grateful if you'd leave, because – ' he lifted up his notes for Keene to see – 'I really do have quite a lot of work to attend to.'

'I—' Keene began.

'A lot of work,' Woodend repeated.

'I . . . I can understand that,' Keene said, 'but couldn't you spare a minute or two more of your time? Please!'

'All right.'

'I think we got off on the wrong footing, just now. That was my fault, and it's a real tragedy – because the reason I came here was to help.'

'To help? Do you have some new information for me, Mr Keene?'

'No,' Keene admitted. 'I don't. And that's not what I meant.' He paused for a moment, before continuing. 'When do you think you'll be seeing Thomas again, Mr Woodend?'

'That's not up to me, Mr Keene. Maitland's the one who's in control at the moment, so I'll see him when he *asks* to see me. But I really don't see what that's got to do with—'

'Take me with you!' Keene pleaded.

'What?!'

'Take me with you. I know Thomas. I'm not sure that he likes me as much as I like him, but he *does* trust me and he *will* listen to me.'

'An' what is it you'd like to say to him?'

'I'd like to tell him that this isn't what Judith would want at all. That she won't be happy that he's terrifying other people, even if he is doing it for her. That if he hurts even one of the hostages, she'll never be able to live with herself again. I'd tell him I know why he's done it – and that I'd probably have thought about doing it myself if I'd been brave enough – but it still isn't right.'

'An' you really want to do this?' Woodend asked.

Keene gulped. 'I really want to do this.'

'The bank's a dangerous place for anyone to enter right at this minute, you know.'

Keene clamped his hands on the back of the chair on which he had refused to sit earlier, and shuddered. 'You don't need to tell me that. My bowels are turning to water just thinking about it. But I owe Judith so much, and this . . . this is the only way I can repay her.'

'I'm not goin' to give you any promises,' Woodend said, 'but if you make yourself available the next time I'm called to the bank, I'll ask Major Maitland if he's willin' to talk to you. And if he is – and if I judge it to be right at the time – I'll allow you a couple of minutes with him.'

Keene looked down at his long, slim hands. 'Thank you!' he said. 'Do you know, on the way over here, I was hoping – praying almost – that you'd say no. But I'm glad you didn't.'

The Chief Constable had locked himself in his office, and was talking on his private phone – the one which didn't go through the station switchboard – to a number in London.

'Yes, Home Secretary, I agree that Mr Slater-Burnes is a very capable chap, indeed,' he was saying. 'And I can't thank you enough for sending him to us, because there's no doubt that he *did* help us to avoid making some very serious errors in the initial stages of the operation.'

'Good, good,' the Home Secretary said, almost complacently. 'That's what he was there for.'

'But the situation has worsened in the last few hours,' Marlowe continued. 'Now that the press have got hold of the full story—'

'Yes, how *did* that happen?' the Home Secretary wondered.

'I couldn't say. But I can assure you, there were no leaks from my office,' Marlowe lied. 'Anyway, that's beside the point. The press *have* got hold of it, and whilst it was a big story before they learned about Major Maitland, it's a *huge* one now. Which means – inevitably – that we're all suddenly under considerably more scrutiny.'

'Yes, I know that,' the Home Secretary said. 'I'm expecting questions in the House about it.'

'And given the changed circumstances, I can't help wondering if perhaps Mr Slater-Burnes isn't now just a little out of his depth,' Marlowe continued.

'Out of his depth?' the Home Secretary repeated. 'What do you mean by that?'

'Merely that, while I'm quite willing to believe that he's an expert in all the theoretical aspects of police-work, he does show a tendency – which I'm sure the press will pick up on and blow out of all proportion – to be a little lost when he finds himself in more practical situations.'

'Be more specific, if you don't mind, Chief Constable,' the Home Secretary said, with a sudden hardness in his voice.

'Of course,' Marlowe said smoothly. 'Major Maitland's main aim, as you know, is to have his wife's case re-opened. It's always been my view that we should stand firm against any demands backed up with firearms—'

'Hear, hear!' the Home Secretary said.

'. . . but it's not a view that Mr Slater-Burnes seems to share. He's all for giving in to the Major's demands. I've gone along with him so far – albeit reluctantly – because he *is* a senior Home Office official, and because he *does* have the backing of Chief Inspector Woodend, who—'

'Woodend?' the Home Secretary interrupted. 'Isn't he the man who left Scotland Yard under a bit of a cloud, a few years ago?'

It was all going so beautifully that Marlowe had to restrain himself from chuckling.

'I think you're being rather generous in the way you phrase that, Home Secretary,' he said. 'The truth is that Woodend was practically *booted* out of the Yard.'

'Then he certainly doesn't seem to be the right man to be handling this situation.'

'Oh, I agree with you entirely on that, Home Secretary. But the problem is, you see, that as long as we continue to pursue the approach Mr Slater-Burnes seems so eager to follow, we really have no choice *but* to use Woodend.'

'Why?'

'Because he's the only officer Major Maitland seems willing to speak to.'

'I see.'

'My main concern is the safety of the hostages,' Marlowe said, 'as I'm sure yours is, too.'

'Quite.'

'But men in our positions are forced to look beyond that – to take a wider view.'

'A wider view?'

'If this whole unfortunate incident ends in a bloodbath – and given the way things are being conducted at the moment, it very well might – there will be public outrage. Heads will roll. And not just heads at the lower levels. Not just heads at the *county* level.'

'Go on,' the Home Secretary said cautiously.

'I'm not really concerned about my own position – I just want to do the right thing,' Marlowe said, 'but since Mr Slater-Burnes seems to have no interest in protecting you from all this, I feel the responsibility falls on me.'

'I find myself in something of a dilemma,' the Home Secretary said worriedly. 'On the one hand, I quite take your point about the difficult position I seem to be being thrust into. On the other, I don't want to seen to be undermining one of my own officials.'

'Quite,' Marlowe agreed. 'I would never, for a moment, suggest you do such a thing. But . . .'

'Yes?'

'But I *do* think there's a case for arguing that, given his attitude to this particular crisis, it might be wiser to keep Mr Slater-Burnes out of the loop for a while.'

'Do you have an alternative strategy to the one Mr Slater-Burnes is advocating?' the Home Secretary asked.

'As a matter of fact, I do,' Marlowe replied.

'Then you'd better let me hear it.'

Marlowe quickly outlined the plan which had been evolving in his head for most of the day.

'Tricky,' the Home Secretary said when he'd finished.

'I prefer to think of it as *imaginative*,' Marlowe said.

'Oh, it's that, all right,' the Home Secretary agreed. 'It's *very* imaginative. What I'm not sure about is whether or not it's entirely legal.'

'It could certainly be argued that it's not *illegal*,' Marlowe countered. 'And even if it were, by the time any ruling's made, the crisis will be over – and you will have emerged from a very sticky situation totally unscathed.'

'I'll consult my advisors on the whole matter,' the Home Secretary said cautiously.

'You do that, sir,' Marlowe replied. 'But I wouldn't take too long about it – because there's no telling when things might blow up here.'

When he put down the phone, the Chief Constable was feeling well pleased with himself. Slater-Burnes had tried to

94

shift the responsibility for any failure on to him, he thought, and what he'd just done was to shift it squarely back again. That, in itself, was a cause for self-congratulation.

But there was more. If his scheme worked out as he thought it would, then the Home Secretary – one of the most influential men in the whole government – would be in his debt. And if he chose to run for parliament himself – which was very much on the cards – the man would have no choice but to give him his backing.

Marlowe ambled over to his drinks cabinet, and helped himself to a generous – celebratory – shot of his twelve-year-old malt. He had hated offering such a fine whisky to an uncouth lout like Charlie Woodend – a real case of putting pearls before swine – but it had been necessary at the time, and so he had clenched his teeth and done it.

Now – and as a direct result of the sacrifice of that excellent whisky – Woodend probably fondly imagined that he had his Chief Constable's full backing. The truth, of course, was quite the opposite. The truth was that the unmanageable Chief Inspector in the scruffy tweed jacket was being used as no more than a decoy in the game which was being played out. And if that decoy happened to get shot – as many decoys did – well, that was just one of the risks he ran.

Marlowe took a sip of his whisky, and chuckled to himself. The Chief Inspector would be furious when he realized just how badly he'd been duped, he thought.

Fifteen

Constable Beresford had often looked at this table in the Drum and Monkey with longing, but had never allowed himself to dream that he would actually ever sit at it. This was the table at which the giants of his world – Woodend, Rutter and Paniatowski – solved their cases. And now here he was, his elbows resting on the table as if they actually belonged there.

'Sergeant Paniatowski thinks that if Judith Maitland *didn't* kill Burroughs, then the murderer has to be someone with a motive that has nothing to do with Judith at all,' Woodend said.

Beresford, unsure of whether or not he was expected to comment at this stage, nodded his head in what he hoped was a wise and knowing way.

'In other words,' Woodend continued, 'not only does Judith have no connection with Burroughs' death, but she doesn't even know the killer.' He paused and took a sip of his pint. *'That's* what Sergeant Paniatowski thinks. An' she may well be right. But I don't want to take the chance that she isn't.'

Was now the time to speak? Beresford wondered. And if it was, what was he expected to say?

He decided it would be wiser to settle for a second nod.

'Do you spend much of your free time in art galleries, Beresford?' Woodend asked.

Art galleries? What was this all about?

'Not a lot, sir,' Beresford said.

'Not a lot?' Woodend echoed.

'None at all, if the truth be told,' Beresford admitted.

'Then you're missin' out,' Woodend told him. 'You can learn a lot about life from art.'

'If you say so, sir,' Beresford replied, dubiously.

'Take one of them pictures of the Madonna an' Child, which painters were so fond of in the Middle Ages,' Woodend said. 'Your eye is drawn straight away to the Baby Jesus, which is, of course, what the artist intended to happen. But if you leave it at that, you're only gettin' part of the experience.'

'I wouldn't really know about that, sir,' Beresford said, feeling as if he were sinking in deep, dark water.

'Well, listen, then you will,' Woodend said. 'If, when you're lookin' at one of them paintings, you focus all your attention on the baby, you miss out Mary an' Joseph, the shepherds an' the wise men. An' they're important to the story – because the way Jesus acted, an' the way society *reacted* to him, were functions of the times in which he was livin'.'

'I'm afraid I'm not really much of a church-goer myself, sir,' Beresford admitted.

Woodend sighed heavily, and began to wonder if he'd picked the right man for the job.

'I'm not much of a church-goer either, lad, but that's not

the point,' he said. 'It doesn't have to be a paintin' of the Nativity we're talkin' about. That's just an example. It could be *any* paintin' at all – from the *Mona Lisa* to that peculiar thing Élite Catering's got hangin' in its lobby. The point I'm tryin' to make is that if you focus on one particular detail, you run a risk of missin' the big picture.'

'And that's what it would be like if we focused only on Burroughs?' Beresford asked, uncertainly.

'Exactly!' Woodend agreed. 'So while Sergeant Paniatowski's concentratin' on the centre of the picture, we should take a careful trip around the edges of the frame.'

'And that would be Judith Maitland?'

'Now you're startin' to understand where I'm goin' with all this, lad,' Woodend said, greatly encouraged. 'You see, lookin' at it that way, we can believe that Judith Maitland didn't kill Clive Burroughs – or even want him killed – an' yet, at the same time, not completely rule out the idea that his death might in some way be *connected* to her.'

'You mean, this ex-boyfriend of hers – the one that Major Maitland told you about – might have appeared on the scene again and killed Burroughs out of jealousy?' Beresford asked.

'Not necessarily him – but that's the *kind* of thing I mean,' Woodend said. 'Of course, the chances are that Burroughs' death *doesn't* have anything to do with Judith – but until we've investigated all the possibilities, we'll never know.'

'I think I'm catchin' on, sir,' Beresford said.

'Maybe,' Woodend agreed. 'But there's one major aspect of workin' in the CID that you *do* seem to have missed.'

'What's that, sir?' Beresford asked, worriedly.

Woodend grinned at him. 'When you see your boss's glass is empty, you immediately order him another pint,' he said.

Monika Paniatowski didn't know at exactly what time she'd fallen asleep with her head on the desk, but when – with bleary eyes – she looked at her watch, she saw that it was a quarter past one in the morning.

She reached for a cigarette, lit it up, and studied the two stacks of documents which lay intimidatingly on the desk in front of her. To the left were the bank statements from Burroughs' builders' merchant's business. To the right the statements from his personal account. They all went back a full ten years – no one could accuse Chief Inspector Baxter of not being thorough. And just before she'd decided to close her eyes for a second – some considerable time earlier – she'd found things in both piles to quicken her interest.

The cheques written on the business account were mainly to meet bills submitted by wholesale suppliers, though there were also some to cover utility payments and property taxes. There had been no trouble for most of the period which they related to, but during the last year or so of Clive Burroughs' life, the bank had refused to cash several cheques on the grounds that the account contained insufficient funds.

Which would suggest, Paniatowski thought, that Hal Greene had been right when he'd said that the business was in serious trouble.

Had Judith Maitland really been the woman whom Burroughs expected to pull him out of the hole he found himself in? the sergeant wondered.

And if she had, just what kind of hold did Burroughs have over her?

Paniatowski switched her thoughts to the other pile of statements – the personal ones. As with the business statements, they mostly followed a set, regular pattern, but here, too, there was an anomaly. And in this case, the anomaly had not occurred towards the end of Burroughs' life, but a full seven years earlier.

For a whole month in the late 1950s, the statements revealed, Burroughs had been writing a weekly cheque to Piccadilly Holdings Ltd. What the cheques were to cover was explained in a bill stapled to one of them. Mr and Mrs Burroughs, it appeared, had been staying at the Westside Hotel in Manchester, which was part of the Piccadilly Holdings chain.

Now why would they have done that? Paniatowski wondered.

It surely couldn't have been a holiday. Manchester had its charms, it was true, but they weren't enough to occupy the Burroughses for a whole month! Bloody hell, even *London* would start to lose its appeal after a couple of weeks!

Perhaps he'd used the hotel for business purposes, then.

But in that case, why hadn't it been paid for out of the business account, rather than the personal one?

Besides, most deals could be done perfectly satisfactorily over the phone. And even if this one couldn't be – even if whoever he was dealing with had insisted on face-to-face meetings – Burroughs surely wouldn't have gone to the expense of living there on a full-time basis, when his own home was less than a couple of hours' drive away?

Paniatowski groaned. A new idea had just come into her mind, and had made what looked like a promising lead quite melt away.

It said 'Mr and Mrs Burroughs' on the hotel bill, she thought, but it hadn't been Mr and Mrs Burroughs at all. The 'Mrs Burroughs' had been just one of Clive's long list of conquests. The hotel had been nothing more than the base they'd used for their affair.

She lit a new cigarette from the stub of her old one, and wondered where this new and unwelcome insight left her.

Nowhere. Nowhere at all.

This whole thing has been a waste of time, she thought. I might as well have gone back to Whitebridge and slept in my own bed.

Bob Rutter would have made more sense out of the statements than she ever could. Bob loved this kind of work – thrived on sitting at a desk and reading people's lives through what they spent and where they had gone.

She wished he was sitting beside her at that moment – patiently explaining, as only he could, what she had missed in the statements, and the questions she should be asking about what *wasn't* there.

She wished that she'd never fallen in love with Bob Rutter. Or that he'd never fallen in love with her. Or that he'd fallen *in* love with her and *out* of love with his wife.

But most of all, she wished that Maria had never been murdered: because while everything else that had happened could have been reversed – or at least overcome – that had changed things for ever.

Bob would never stop grieving and feeling guilty. Neither would she – his one-time lover. And Charlie Woodend – who had almost learned to forgive them both *before* Maria's death – had taken two steps back, and was now almost a hostile stranger.

'Nobody loves poor little Monika,' she said softly. 'Nobody at all.'

'I always think that when you start talking to yourself, it's time to call it a day,' said a voice from the doorway.

Paniatowski looked up, and saw the bulky form of Chief Inspector Baxter standing there.

'I . . . I thought you would have gone home long before now, sir,' she said weakly.

Baxter smiled warmly. 'It's not only you young uns who can put in the hours when the occasion calls for it,' he said. 'Even us old farts can make the effort once in a while.'

He wasn't really an old fart at all, Paniatowski thought, looking at him closely for perhaps the first time.

He was older than her, certainly, but he was several years younger than Woodend, and she had never considered Cloggin-it Charlie to be actually *old*.

'What would you say to the idea of a drink, Sergeant Paniatowski?' Baxter asked.

'I'd love it,' Monika admitted. 'But I would have thought the canteen would be closed by now.'

'And you would have thought right,' Baxter agreed. 'It pulled down its shutters over two hours ago. But while power may have its responsibilities, it also has it perks.'

'Perks?'

Baxter patted his jacket pocket. 'I just happen to have a key to the canteen in here. So if you want a good strong coffee, I'll make it for you myself.'

'I'm not sure I—'

'And if you fancy something stronger, there'll be no problem with that, either.'

'A coffee would be nice,' Paniatowski said. 'Provided it's got a vodka chaser.'

'Just what I was thinking myself,' Chief Inspector Baxter said.

The Siege: Day Two

Sixteen

It had not been an easy night for the loved ones of those unfortunate men and women who were hostages in the Cotton Credit Bank. They, too, felt that they were the victims of the gunman: that even though they were not being physically restrained in the bank themselves, their very *futures* – the lives they and their partners had planned out – were being held hostage.

Their relatives and friends had rallied round them, insisting that they should not spend the night alone. They meant well, these kindly concerned folk, but in some ways their presence only made matters worse. For while they maintained an air of confidence and optimism while speaking to the 'victims' themselves, their tones quickly changed to urgent and desperate whispers when they were talking about the situation with each other.

Many of the 'victims' did not wish to go to bed, but their friends and relatives insisted they must –

'You need the rest. You'll feel better for it.'

And since they somehow could not summon the strength to resist, they meekly did as they'd been bidden.

Once upstairs, they spent the night tossing and turning in beds which had been built for two – but might never accommodate more than one again. And all through that dreadful night – whether fitfully asleep or miserably awake – they listened out for the ring of the telephone bell – or the knock on the door – which could confirm their worst fears.

Dawn finally came – a crisp, clear December dawn – but rather than bringing with it any hopes of a new beginning, it merely served to emphasize the fact that the siege was now entering its second day.

And though the 'victims' tried their best not to let any negative thoughts into their heads, it seemed to all of them that the longer this went on, the more the chances something would go terribly wrong.

Major Maitland's team had worked in shifts throughout the night – two hours on watch, four hours off, and then two hours on again – and since he knew that if trouble came it was most likely to come at first light, Maitland had reserved the dawn shift for himself.

He looked down at his hostages, huddled together on the floor of the vault, sharing their fear as they shared their body heat. Some were asleep, some were merely pretending to be asleep, and some were so paralysed by their fear that they were neither asleep nor awake.

They didn't deserve to suffer like this, the Major told himself. They were all ordinary decent people, and at this time of the morning they had a right to be at home with their loved ones.

And what about you! screamed a voice from somewhere deep inside his brain – deep inside his soul.

Don't you deserve to be at home with your loved one?

He looked down at his hostages again, and forced himself to redefine their situation.

He was on a mission, far into enemy territory, he told himself, and so different rules applied. Put simply, anyone who was not with him was against him. It was a battle between the Maitlands and the rest of the world – and these hostages were definitely not part of the Maitlands.

He wondered, suddenly, if he'd lost his mind – and decided that he probably had.

No matter! If he had gone mad, it was because he had been forced into his madness. If he had gone mad, he had no choice but to use that madness to achieve his stated objective.

There was no turning back now.

Monika Paniatowski stirred uncomfortably in a bed which did not feel in the least familiar to her, then opened her eyes to gaze at a ceiling she was sure she had never seen before.

She wondered, briefly, if she were dreaming. But her dreams never involved anything as mundane as bedroom ceilings. Her dreams contained labyrinths and pits. They were peopled by goblins with grotesque bodies but familiar

104

faces; with sharpened spikes which threatened to penetrate her, and bombs which exploded to drench her with bitter memories. And when she awoke from these dreams, she was not merely bemused – as she was now – she was sweating and trembling.

She became aware of a slight pressure against her side, and turning, saw that she was lying next to a great barrel of a man's chest which was covered in curly greying hair.

Now she knew where she was. *Now* she understood that in her weakness – her vulnerability – she had done something she would probably regret.

Joan Woodend was still sleeping when her husband carefully eased himself out of bed. The Chief Inspector tiptoed across the room, and padded downstairs to the kitchen of the hand-loom weaver's cottage where they had lived ever since the powers that be in Scotland Yard had decided they had had quite enough of Cloggin'-it Charlie and sent him into exile, back to his native Lancashire.

It was sometimes a battle to beat his wife down to the kitchen, Woodend thought, as he filled the kettle. Joan was one of those women who still believed that since it was the husband who brought home the bacon, it should be the wife who cooked it. But despite her protests, he still tried – when-ever possible – to outmanoeuvre her, to present her with the *fait accompli* of a cup of tea in bed.

'I like to spoil you, love,' he'd say.

But they both knew it wasn't that at all – were both well aware that he was doing it because, after her heart attack while on holiday in Spain, the doctor had insisted Joan should get as much rest as she possibly could.

Woodend looked out of the window on to the moors, the wild, beautiful moors on which he had walked as a child. It was a view he had never tired of – as relaxing as a pint of best bitter, as soothing as a Capstan Full Strength – but on that particular morning it did nothing at all for him.

The hostages in the Cotton Credit Bank were his responsi-bility – and his alone – he told himself. If any of them died, it was because he had not done his job properly.

'*You can't go takin' the weight of the whole world on your*

105

shoulders, our Charlie,' his mother had told him often enough, when he was growing up.

'*I know that, Mam,*' the young Charlie had replied.

And he *still* knew that – knew it better, in fact, than he had when he was a kid. But it still didn't stop him trying.

Judith Maitland lay in her narrow iron bed, watching the first rays of the morning sun spread across the high ceiling.

Though there was no need – from a strictly medical point of view – to continue confining her in the prison infirmary, the authorities had decided that if a Suicide Watch was to be maintained, then the infirmary was the easiest place to keep it.

The prison psychiatrist had been to see her the previous day.

'Do you now regret attempting to take your own life?' he'd asked her.

'Yes,' she'd said.

'Are you sure? Are you saying it because you mean it, or because you think that's what I want to hear?'

'I'm saying it because I mean it.'

She hadn't been lying. She should never have *tried* to kill herself – she should have *succeeded*!

Her failure had resulted in the worst of all possible outcomes. She was still alive, and her poor, darling husband – spurred into action by the obvious desperation her attempt had signalled – had embarked on a mad, dangerous course which he hoped would save her.

She thought of the hostages – terrified almost beyond endurance, and starting their second day of captivity.

She thought of her husband, who might, at that very moment, be caught in the cross-hairs of a sniper's rifle.

She could not allow this horrific situation to continue for much longer, she decided – not when she had the solution to it in her own hands.

She would request a meeting with the Governor. They would refuse her at first, telling her the Governor was too busy. But she would persist – claiming that she had something very important to say – and in the end they would have to agree.

She would not tell him *everything* when she had finally

been ushered into his presence. She would willingly endure a thousand painful deaths rather than do that. But she was now prepared to confess that she had murdered Clive Burroughs.

Seventeen

The origins of the Dunethorpe Industrial Estate stretched back into the time when fine Yorkshire wool had made the whole of England rich, and many of the older buildings on it still bore signs of their previous use as wool mills. There were also other, newer establishments, however – hastily erected prefabricated buildings which would have shocked and horrified the proud stonemasons who built the mills – and Burroughs' Builders' Merchant was one of these.

Monika Paniatowski parked her MGA between a small lorry and a builder's van, and lit up a cigarette. She had come to the estate with two purposes in mind. One was to talk to the nightwatchman from the building opposite Burroughs', a man whose evidence had been crucial in Judith Maitland's trial. The other was to learn what she could from the people who had actually worked with the victim.

She checked her watch. She was not due to meet the nightwatchman for nearly an hour. She would make a start with Burroughs' former employees.

The moment Paniatowski stepped through the door of Burroughs' Builders' Merchant, she found her passage blocked by a man in a three-quarter-length khaki coat.

'Can't you read, love – or are you just stupid?' he asked rudely. 'The sign outside says we're a *builders'* merchant. That means it's *builders* we deal with, you see. We don't sell to members of the general public.'

'I'll bear that in mind if I ever *do* want to buy any of the second-rate tat you've got on offer,' Paniatowski said.

'Second-rate tat?' the man repeated.

'At best,' Paniatowski told him. She produced her warrant card. 'Is the manager around?'

'I'm the manager,' the man said, in a tone of voice that fell neatly between his previous hostility and a new concern. 'My name's Mr Sanders. Is anything wrong?'

Paniatowski gave him a quick once-over. Middle thirties, black slicked-down hair, quite handsome in a shifty sort of way, but not her type.

No, she thought, not my type at all. Based on the best available evidence, my type now appears to be pipe-smoking middle-aged chief inspectors with hairy chests, whom I seem to be willing to sleep with at the drop of a hat.

'*Mr* Sanders,' she said, as if pondering the words for hidden implications. 'Do you know, I don't think I've ever come across anybody with "Mr" as a first name before.'

'I've no idea what you're talking about,' the manager said. 'My first name's Alfred.'

'Well, *Fred*, let's go and have a cosy little chat in your office, shall we?' Paniatowski suggested.

It was not so much an office as a storage place for goods which didn't quite belong anywhere else, but Sanders produced two rickety chairs, and they both sat down in a canyon between boxes of ceramic tiles and stacks of copper piping.

'Before we go any further, I should tell you that I'm not here to investigate any of your little fiddles,' Paniatowski said.

'Pardon?' Sanders said.

'Your little fiddles,' Paniatowski repeated patiently. 'The merchandise you sell over the counter, but somehow forget to put through the books.'

'I'm not sure I—'

'The bricks you pick up cheap, because there's no invoice to go with them, and sell-on cheap for exactly the same reason.'

'I can assure you, Sergeant, that nothing of that kind goes on here,' Sanders protested.

'Of course it does,' Paniatowski said dismissively. 'And given half an hour, I could tell you *exactly* which fiddles you're running. But I don't like doing that kind of work unless I'm in a really bad temper. And I don't *get* into a bad temper when people answer the questions I put to them quickly and honestly. Am I getting through to you here?'

108

Sanders nodded. 'Yes, I think you are.'

'Good,' Paniatowski said pleasantly. 'Then let's make a start, shall we? How long have you been working here?'

'Twelve years.'

'And how long have you been the manager?'

'Only since Mr Burroughs was murdered. I was the assistant manager until then.'

'There *are* some people who'll kill for a promotion,' Paniatowski said. 'You're not one of them, are you?'

'Now, look here—' Sanders blustered.

'Only joking,' Paniatowski said sweetly. 'So you know the business well, do you?'

'Well enough.'

'And you must have known Clive Burroughs well enough, too, mustn't you, now?'

'He was my boss,' Sanders said. 'You never know that much about your boss, do you?'

'Oh, I'm not so sure about that,' Paniatowski said airily. 'I seem to know a fair amount about mine. You were aware, weren't you, that Clive Burroughs was a bugger for the ladies?'

'I knew he had girlfriends, if that's what you mean.'

'*Single* men have girlfriends,' Paniatowski said. '*Married* men have mistresses.'

'I knew he had *mistresses*, then,' Sanders said sullenly.

'And you didn't see the need to inform his wife of the fact?'

'No. It wasn't my place to.'

'Quite right,' Paniatowski agreed.

'What?'

'I said you're quite right – it wasn't your place to.'

'Well, in that case, maybe we don't really need to talk about—'

'Did you know about his last mistress – the one who allegedly picked up a hammer and bashed his brains in?'

'No, but I knew about . . . about . . .'

'About what?'

'Nothing.'

'About the fact that he was sleeping with the landlady of the Philosophers' Arms?'

'Well, yes.'

'And did you know all about the mistress whom he took to Manchester with him?'

'What?'

'Don't mess me about,' Paniatowski said impatiently.

'I'm not. I promise. But Mr Burroughs took a lot of his girls into town for the night. They liked it. Bright lights, big city. That sort of thing.'

'I'm not talking a single night,' Paniatowski said. 'I'm talking about *a month*.'

Sanders looked blank.

'Oh, come on, Freddie, boy!' Paniatowski said. 'Round about seven years ago, he spent a whole month in Manchester with one of his mistresses. You *must* remember it.'

'I remember him being away for a month. It was the first time he left me in charge of the business. But I didn't know he was in Manchester, and I didn't know he was with a woman.'

'Didn't you? Well, it's not really important,' Monika Paniatowski said dismissively.

'Look, I really am trying to help you, but—'

'I said it wasn't important. I was merely testing the range and extent of your knowledge.'

'Pardon?'

'You're not very bright, are you, Freddie? I wanted to establish just how much you *did* know, so I could decide which line of questioning it would be profitable to follow. I merely used the question of his mistresses as a tin-opener – so I could see what was in this particular can of worms.'

'You've lost me,' Sanders confessed.

'Of course I have. I never expected anything else. So let me put it in even simpler terms – ones even you can understand. I'm not interested in his mistresses, Freddie, old son. The only person who actually concerns me is the one who battered him to death.'

'But that *was* one of his mistresses, wasn't it?' Sanders asked.

'That remains to be seen,' Paniatowski said. 'Tell me about Clive Burroughs' enemies.'

'He didn't have any.'

'Pull the other leg, why don't you? It's got bells on,' Monika Paniatowski said sceptically.

'It's true what I'm telling you. Mr Burroughs was a salesman, through and through.'

'So?'

'Salesmen get along with everybody. It's an instinct they develop. They can't help themselves.'

'Doesn't seem to have rubbed off on you,' Paniatowski said. 'You're sure about this, are you? He didn't have *any* enemies? Not even the husbands of his mistresses?'

'They never found out. Mr Burroughs was very clever about keeping his affairs quiet.'

Which was pretty much what Hal Greene had said, Paniatowski thought. And Greene was living proof of it. *He* didn't know about his wife's affair with Clive Burroughs until she told him herself.

'Nobody can avoid unpleasantness altogether,' she said. 'Clive Burroughs must have had disagreements with *somebody*.'

'Customers got annoyed occasionally, when they didn't get exactly what they ordered, but Mr Burroughs would take them out for a pint, and it would all be forgotten.'

'And you don't recall anything a bit more serious, in the weeks before he died?'

'No, I can't say that I do.'

'What about worries? Did he have any?'

'None.'

Monika laughed. 'Come on, Alfredo, this is your old mate, Sergeant Paniatowski, you're talking to here. Don't try to piss me about or I'll find a way to make you regret it.'

'The business was in trouble,' Sanders admitted. 'We were finding it difficult to pay our bills. But Mr Burroughs said all our worries would soon be over – that there was a big injec tion of cash coming into the company. He sounded very confid ent about it, and I believed him.'

'And was his confidence justified? *Was there* a sudden injection of cash into the business?'

'Well, no,' Alfred Sanders conceded. 'But there might have been, mightn't there?'

'Might there?'

'Yes, of course. Who's to say what would have happened if Mr Burroughs hadn't died when he did.'

111

'Let me see if I've got this straight,' Paniatowski said. 'The business was ailing?'

'Yes.'

'And Burroughs was killed before he could do anything about it?'

'That's right.'

'So why does the sign over the door still say *Burroughs'* Builders' Merchant? Why isn't somebody else's name there instead?'

'Because *Mrs* Burroughs owns the business now.'

'And where did *she* find the money from to keep the company afloat?'

'Where do you think?'

'I don't know. That's why I'm asking.'

'It came from the insurance company, of course! Mr Burroughs had a whacking great policy on his life – and it paid double if he happened to meet a violent death.'

As Paniatowski walked back to the car park, she couldn't help noticing that she had developed a bounce in her step.

Well, why not? she asked herself.

Life didn't always have to be serious. Or earnest. Or tragic. You were allowed to enjoy yourself once in a while.

And she *had* enjoyed the interview with Sanders. He was an unpleasant, self-important man who had lorded it over her when she entered the builders' merchant's, and it had been a real pleasure to make him jump through all the hoops.

But the interview had been rewarding in other ways, she thought. Up until the moment she'd spoken to Sanders, the investigation had been focused on – almost *obsessed* with – a single possible motive for Clive Burroughs' murder. He had been killed, so the thinking had gone, because someone – either Judith Maitland or a person or persons yet unknown – had hated him enough to want to see him dead.

Now, another possibility had presented itself. Alive, Clive Burroughs was in imminent danger of losing his business, and possibly his home. Dead, his widow would have enough money to save both of them. And any scruples she might have had about killing for money would surely have been mitigated by the fact that, though murder was always wrong, it was *less* wrong when the victim was a right proper bastard like Burroughs.

Yes, Paniatowski thought, she could well imagine Mrs Burroughs using that as a justification for reducing her husband's brain to a pulp.

Eighteen

The White Swan Restaurant – better known, by everyone who used it, as the Dirty Duck – was just off Whitebridge High Street, a location which would normally guarantee it a steady trade, especially during the Christmas period. But it wouldn't be doing much business on that particular day, Woodend thought, as he knocked on the side door of the restaurant – not with the High Street itself completely blocked off, and parking temporarily prohibited on all the streets that fed into it.

Woodend knew the man who answered the door, and thus also knew that though he looked as if he were in his late forties at most, he was, in fact, pushing sixty. So if Giles Thompson was anything to go by, the Chief Inspector decided, the restaurant business must be far less stressful than police-work.

The two men shook hands. 'It was good of you to spare me the time, Giles,' Woodend said.

'If I can do or say anything to help Judith, then I'm more than willing to,' Thompson replied. 'I'd crawl on my hands and knees over broken glass for that sweet girl.'

The restaurant owner led Woodend up to the office, and offered him a chair. 'Judith had her wedding reception here at the Swan, you know,' he said. 'She could have catered it herself, or chosen somewhere much posher. But as far as she was concerned, it *had* to be here. She never forgets her old friends, doesn't Judith.'

'If she had the reception here, you must have met her husband,' Woodend said.

'I did. But only briefly.'

'Still, you must have formed some kind of impression of him. How did he strike you?'

113

'As a thoroughly decent sort of chap. And I can't tell you how relieved I was at the time, because I'd always felt that Judith deserved more than life had thrown at her. And now this.' He pointed in the direction of the Cotton Credit Bank. 'Whoever would have thought it?'

'Whoever would have thought Judith would murder her lover?' Woodend asked provocatively.

Thompson's eyes flashed with sudden anger. 'He *wasn't* her lover, and she didn't *murder* him.'

'Do you know somethin' about the case that the bobbies investigatin' it didn't?' Woodend wondered.

'I know *Judith*,' Thompson said.

'Then tell me about her,' Woodend suggested.

'Not if you're going to twist everything I say round, just so it will fit into your preconceived theories,' Thompson said, his anger still evident.

'I said what I just did to see how you'd react,' Woodend told him. 'And maybe I shouldn't have.'

'Damn right, you shouldn't have,' Thompson growled.

'The truth is, I agree with you about Judith,' Woodend continued. 'I don't think Burroughs was her lover, an' I don't think she killed him. But believing it is one thing, an' provin' it is quite another. To get proof, I'm goin' to need your help – so why don't you tell me what you can about her?'

'All right,' Thompson agreed, though there was still an edge of caution to his voice. 'She was fifteen when she first came to work for me. There'd been talk of her staying on at school – maybe even of going to university – but when her dad died, her mother said that just wasn't an option any more.'

'*How* did her dad die?' Woodend wondered.

'If you're looking for something mysterious about his death, then you're out of luck,' Thompson told him. 'The poor bugger had cancer. He was riddled with it, from what I heard. Anyway, her mother said Judy needed a job in order to be able to help out with the household expenses – and needed it quick. So that's how I met her.'

'What kind of work did she do?'

'The menial sort at first – washing-up, floor cleaning, and the like – as befits somebody starting at the bottom of the ladder, with absolutely no experience of catering. But she

114

worked so hard at the jobs I'd given her that it wasn't long before I'd promoted her to vegetable preparation. The next thing was, she asked if she could wait on the tables, and she was soon one of the best waiters I'd ever had. Which was just as well, really, because she'd never have managed to live on just a skivvy's wages after her mother left.'

'Her mother left? Where did she go?'

'To Australia. To start a new life.'

'And Judith didn't want to go with her?'

'She wasn't *invited* to go with her,' Giles Thompson said bitterly. 'Her mother had remarried by then, and her new husband didn't get on with his stepdaughter. So when they talked about a new life, what they really meant was a life without Judith.'

'How did she manage?'

'Very well, as you would have expected, if you'd known her like I did. She got her own little flat – no mansion, but it suited her well enough – and set about mastering the few aspects of the business she'd yet to learn. She was content enough. No, more than content, she was *happy*. Everything was going along swimmingly – and then she met *him*!'

'Him?'

'Sebastian-bloody-Courtney-Jones. He was the regional manager of one of the big wine firms. You know the sort of man I'm talking about – sports car, blazer, regimental tie. He really had a high opinion of himself. The only problem was, Judy shared it. She went out with him for two years. She thought he was going to marry her.'

'But that didn't happen.'

'No, of course it bloody didn't! When push came to shove – when she demanded to know where they were going with their relationship – he told her that he couldn't wed her, because he had a wife and three kids already. Then, straight away, he put in for a transfer and got moved down south. The bastard!'

'She took it badly?'

'She was totally devastated. It had never occurred to her that he might be stringing her along, you see – because that's the last thing she'd ever think of doing to anybody else herself. Anyway, her work went completely to pot. She turned up late, and even when she was here, I couldn't rely on her. And she looked terrible. So in the end, I called her into the office and said she needed to get herself some professional counselling.'

'That took some guts on your part,' Woodend said.

'Well, I certainly hadn't been looking forward to it,' Thompson admitted. 'Some people hit the roof when you tell them they should see a shrink. But Judith accepted it all quite calmly. She said she thought I was right. In fact, she told me, she'd already looked into the possibility herself, and had found a place that would take her in for a course of residential treatment. Her one worry was that she wouldn't have a job to come back to.'

'An' what did you say to that?'

'I said I was delighted she was being so sensible about it all. I told her there'd always be a job for her here, however long it took her to get herself straight. One year, two years – it made no difference to me.'

'That was generous of you.'

'She was worth it. But as it turned out, she didn't need that much time at all. She was back within a few months.'

'An' how was she when she returned?'

'I'd be lying if I said she was a completely new woman. You could tell she'd been to hell and back. But at least I could see some evidence of the *old* woman – the woman Judy had been – just below the surface.'

'Did you give her her job back, as you'd promised you would?'

'The offer was still there, certainly, but she said that wasn't what she wanted any more. She told me she'd been doing a lot of thinking while she was away, and she'd decided she wanted to make something of her life. Her exact words, if I remember correctly, were, "I want to create something that I can call my own." Then she asked me if I'd help her fulfil her dream.'

'She wanted money, did she?'

Thompson shook his head. 'You really don't know Judy at all, do you? All she asked was that I'd serve as guarantor for the loan she'd negotiated with the bank, and I said I'd be more than willing to.'

'You were still takin' a bit of a chance, weren't you?'

'Not really. I knew that she'd make a success of *whatever* she'd set her mind to.'

'Still, most men would have thought twice before makin' themselves responsible for somebody else's debts – especially in a risky enterprise like caterin'. You must surely have had just a *few* misgivings.'

'None at all. And what if her business *had* flopped? I'm a single man, with no heirs to consider. I've made a fair amount of money out of this restaurant in my time, and could well have stood the loss.'

'I see,' Woodend said, thoughtfully.

'Anyway, I made the right judgement, didn't I?' Thompson continued. 'Judith's business turned out to be a roaring success. She could probably buy me and sell me now.' Thompson gulped. 'Did you hear that?' he asked. 'I talked as if she were still around. But I can't help it. It's almost impossible to imagine a vital girl like Judy in prison.'

'Did you see her often in the last couple of years?'

'Not as often as I used to do. She was very busy. She catered all over Lancashire. We met perhaps three or four times, and then only briefly.'

'No heart-to-hearts?'

'Not really.'

'So if she had been havin' an affair with this man Burroughs, you wouldn't have known about it?'

'I told you, there's absolutely no possibility that she—'

'Yes or no, Giles!'

'If she'd been looking for a bit on the side,' Thompson said reluctantly, 'she'd have most likely gone back to her old love, Sebastian Courtney-Jones, don't you think?'

'But the affair had been over for years, hadn't it? There was probably no possibility of going back.'

'That's what you or I might think, but it certainly wasn't a view that Courtney-Jones seemed to share.'

'What do you mean by that?'

'A couple of months before she was arrested, Courtney-Jones turned up here. Said that he wanted to speak to Judy. You see what that means, don't you? The bastard had shown so little interest in her since he jilted her that he didn't even know she didn't work for me any more.'

'So you told him to sod off, did you?'

'Yes, but he wouldn't go. He said that it had taken him a

while to realize it, but he'd finally come to understand that Judy was the only woman he'd ever loved. He told me he'd divorced his wife as soon as the kids had grown up, and now he wanted to start again where he'd left off – only this time he *would* marry her.'

'An' you told him he was too late?'

'And I told him he was too late,' Thompson agreed. 'She was married herself now, I said, and she wouldn't want any more to do with him. But still he wouldn't go. He pleaded – and I mean *pleaded* – for her address. He said he just wanted to talk to her – to ask for her forgiveness.'

'An' you gave him the address, did you?'

'Not at first. I asked him to wait, and I phoned Judy. I told her that he was here, and that if I didn't tell him where she lived, he'd find out from somebody else soon enough. She said not to worry. She could handle him, no problem at all. So I gave him the address.'

'An' do you know if he actually went an' saw her?'

'Oh, he went and saw her, all right. She rang me up straight after he'd been, and told me all about it.'

'How did the meeting go? Did he ask for her forgiveness?'

'He did not! That was just a line he'd fed to me. He told her that he really *did* want to marry her – but if that wasn't on the cards, he'd settle for an extramarital affair. Judy sent him packing, as I'd known she would. But I will say one thing for him – I think he was being sincere when he told me she was the only woman he'd ever really loved.'

'An' what makes you think that?' Woodend wondered.

'Judy said that when he left her house, he was in tears. If I hadn't heard it from her, I'd never have believed that a man like him could actually break down and cry.'

'Did he strike you as the kind of man who'd do whatever it took to get what he wanted?' Woodend asked.

'Definitely,' Thompson said. 'He'd absolutely no consideration for anybody but himself.'

'And he wanted Judith?'

'I don't think I've ever seen a man want anything more.'

Nineteen

The business trading on the opposite side of the road from Burroughs' Builders' Merchant had a large billboard in front of it which proudly announced it as:

Paradise Garden Features

It was a large site, surrounded by a high wire-netting fence, and within it lay all those articles which the billboard further promised would enable Paradise's customers to give their 'little palace' the garden it 'truly deserves'.

Peering through the wire-meshing, Paniatowski could see most of what the place had to offer. There were fountains and fibreglass paddling pools; children's slides and climbing frames; sheds, gazeboes and conservatories. In the middle of it all stood a wooden building indistinguishable from most of the sheds, save that it had a sign on it which identified it as the office and salesroom.

Paniatowski heard a car approaching, and turned to look at it. It was an ancient Austin A40, but even from a distance it was possible to see that it had been lovingly maintained.

The car came to a halt by the gate, and a man, wearing a blue serge security guard's uniform, climbed out of it. He was in his middle-to-late fifties, Paniatowski guessed. His grey hair was extremely short – almost to the point of being shaved – and he sported a pencil-thin moustache.

Paniatowski took a step towards him. 'Mr Goodrich?' she asked.

'That's right,' the man replied.

'You needn't have bothered to wear your uniform,' Paniatowski told him. 'Not when you're off-duty.'

Goodrich gave her a hard stare. 'This being in the nature of a semi-official interview, I deemed it appropriate,' he said. 'You are Detective Sergeant Paniatowski, I take it.'

'Yes, I am.'

'And can I also take it that you have some sort of official identification on your person to prove that?'

Monika produced her warrant card. 'Will this do?' she asked, flicking it closed again.

'I'd like to have a much closer look at that, if you don't mind,' Goodrich told her.

Paniatowski handed him the card, and he studied it for perhaps half a minute before handing it back.

'Yes, that seems to be in order,' he conceded. 'So how may I help you, Sergeant Paniatowski?'

'I'd like to retrace your movements on the night of the murder,' Paniatowski told him.

'Is that strictly necessary, Sergeant? It's all down in black and white, in the statement I gave to the local constabulary at the time.'

'True, but I'd like to *physically* retrace your steps, rather than just follow them on paper,' Paniatowski said.

Goodrich considered the idea for a moment. 'Well, I don't see there can be any harm in that,' he said finally. 'If you'd care to follow me.'

He led Paniatowski through the main gate.

'Look at this fence,' he said, pointing in disgust at the chain-link. 'Any villain worth his salt could cut his way through it in a few seconds, providing he had a decent pair of wire-clippers.'

'True,' Paniatowski agreed.

'Electrification! That's the answer!' Goodrich told her, with sudden, unexpected enthusiasm. 'I said as much to the boss of this place myself. Put a few thousand volts through that fence, I advised him, and you'd soon deter any would-be thief.'

'And what did he say to that?'

'What do you think he said? He said the namby-pamby bureaucrats down at the town hall wouldn't stand for it. According to them, it goes against health and safety regulations. Well, *I* say that any robber who gets himself burned to a frazzle only has himself to blame.'

'I'm sure you're easily as much a deterrent as any electric fence ever could be,' Paniatowski said ingratiatingly.

'You're right about that,' Goodrich agreed. 'Since me and my dog have been on patrol, nobody's pinched a thing.'

The detective sergeant and the security man negotiated their way through a clump of grinning garden gnomes and came to a halt next to some large ornamental flowerpots.

'This is just where I was standing when I heard the first vehicle,' Goodrich said.

'That would be Clive Burroughs' car?'

'Correct. He parked it over there, then went through the side gate to his office.'

'You're sure that's where he went?'

'Definitely. The proof is that once he was inside the building, he turned the light on.'

'Did Burroughs often return to his premises at that time of night?'

'No, he didn't. In fact, it was the first and only time I remember him doing it.'

'So what happened next?'

'I carried on with my rounds. But I hadn't even reached the far end of the perimeter fence when I heard another vehicle. I thought it was strange there'd be two cars here at that time of night, so I turned around to have a look. It was that Mrs Maitland, in her van.'

'You're sure it was *her* van?'

'I most certainly am.'

'Describe it to me.'

'It was a white Vauxhall six hundredweight, and it had a sign on the side which said Élite Caterers.'

Paniatowski peered through the fence at the building across the road. 'It was dark at the time, wasn't it?' she asked.

'It was just *going* dark.'

'But yet you still managed to read the sign on the side of the van?'

'There's a street lamp just there on the corner,' Goodrich said, pointing it out for her. 'When it's on, it lights up the whole area as bright as day. And – before you ask – I have excellent vision.' He reached into his pocket. 'I always carry my optician's report with me, in case my competence is called into question. You may examine it, if that is your wish.'

'That won't be necessary,' Paniatowski assured him, 'So

121

Mrs Maitland pulled up outside the builders' merchant's, did she?'

'Yes, she most certainly did.'

'And how long was she there?'

'Fifteen minutes.'

'She said in her statement that she was there a much shorter time – only a minute or two.'

'So I've heard. But she was lying, wasn't she?'

'You're sure it was a *full* fifteen minutes?'

'Positive.'

'Did you time her?'

'I didn't need to,' Goodrich said.

'Why not?'

'Because it was right after she arrived that I took my break.'

'And where, exactly, did you take it?'

'Just follow me, and I'll show you,' Goodrich offered.

He led Paniatowski through a maze of gazeboes and summer houses to an unassuming garden shed which was all but hidden from sight.

'My office,' Goodrich said, without a hint of irony in his voice.

He swung the door open and invited Paniatowski to step inside. There was a battered armchair in one corner of the shed, and a small table at the other. On the table were a kettle, a large mug, a sugar bowl, a bottle of sterilized milk, a spirit stove, and a transistor radio.

'All the comforts of home,' Goodrich said. 'This is where the dog and I take our break every two hours. I give the dog a couple of biscuits, boil up the kettle, make myself a brew, drink it, and then we're out on patrol again. It takes us fifteen minutes. Not a minute more – and not a minute less. And even if I *had* taken more, all that would prove was that *Mrs Maitland* stayed even longer than she claimed, now wouldn't it?'

'That's true,' Paniatowski said gloomily. 'Let's assume the fifteen minutes are up. What do we do next?'

'We head back to the main gate, to make sure nobody's been tampering with the lock while we've been away.'

'Then let's do that now.'

Goodrich led the sergeant back through the maze of garden

buildings again. When they reached the gate, he mimed checking the lock, even though the gate itself was wide open.

'The van was still there at this point?' Paniatowski asked.

'The van was still there,' Goodrich confirmed. 'And it was just after I'd finished examining the lock that Mrs Maitland appeared.'

'She came out of the office?'

'She did indeed. She was running as if she had the Devil himself on her tail. She got straight into her van, and drove away.'

'You're sure it was her?'

'Yes.'

'It couldn't have been some other woman of roughly the same height and build?'

Like Mrs Burroughs, for example? Paniatowski thought to herself.

'It was Mrs Maitland,' Goodrich said. 'I picked her out of the police line-up without a moment's hesitation.'

'What was she wearing?'

'A black-and-white check business suit, a pale blouse, and a pair of flat-heeled shoes.'

'You're very observant,' Paniatowski said.

'Yes, it's something I pride myself on,' Goodrich agreed.

'Most men might have remembered the suit, but they wouldn't have noticed the shoes at all.'

'Maybe they wouldn't. But I was surprised she was moving so fast, so I checked to see what she had on her feet.'

'What about her overall?' Paniatowski asked.

'Overall?'

'The Duncthorpe Police think that when she killed Burroughs she was wearing her catering overall. That's why there were no traces of blood on her other clothes.'

'I wouldn't know about that,' Goodrich said.

'But she definitely wasn't wearing the overall?'

'She was not!'

'Nor carrying it in her arms?'

'Nor carrying it in her arms. Her arms were swinging. They do when you're running.'

Besides, Paniatowski thought, if she had been holding the overall, then some of the blood on it would have been almost bound to rub off on to her smart business suit.

123

'Did you tell the Dunethorpe Police that Mrs Maitland had nothing in her hands?' she asked.

'I did.'

'And what did they say to that?'

'They said I must have been mistaken. But I *wasn't*! I'll swear on a stack of Bibles that I wasn't!'

Twenty

Someone had finally decided to switch off the bloody twinkling fairy lights in the shop windows, but other than that, the drama being played out on Whitebridge High Street had become as much a frozen tableau as the nativity scene which was annually put on display outside the Catholic Church.

What *had* changed from the previous evening, Woodend decided, was the atmosphere. Then, there had been a tense expectation emanating from the armed officers crouched behind their cars, and the sharpshooters on the roofs. Now – as the siege entered its second day – there was only a feeling of listlessness.

'It was a bit like this durin' the war, wasn't it?' Woodend asked the man walking beside him.

'I'm sorry?' Stanley Keene said.

'You didn't want to fight, did you? Far from it! But you got so all-pumped-up for action that if the fightin' didn't start when it was supposed to, you began to feel mildly depressed.'

'I wouldn't know anything about that,' Keene said. 'I wanted to join up, but the Army turned me down flat.'

'On medical grounds?'

'That's what they said. But we all know the real reason they turned me down, don't we? They didn't want a camp old queen in their man's army. So, since they wouldn't let me fight for my country, I spent *my* war as a barman at the Windmill Theatre in London. It wasn't much of a contribution to the war effort, but at least it gave me a chance to help make life a little pleasanter for the men who *were* risking their lives.'

'Don't do yourself down so much, Mr Keene,' Woodend

said. 'You did at least *try* to join up, when a lot of other fellers were doin' their level best to get out of it. An' livin' in London, with all them German bombers comin' over every night, can't have been any picnic.'

'No, it wasn't,' Stanley Keene agreed, with a shudder. 'Some nights I thought the bombing would just *never* stop. I still jump whenever I hear a loud explosion.' He giggled, nervously. 'I certainly hope we're not going to hear any explosions today.'

They had almost drawn level with the bank door, and Woodend came to a halt. 'You wait here,' he told Stanley Keene.

'But I thought you said I'd be going in with you,' Keene protested.

'No, I didn't,' Woodend contradicted him. 'I said once *I* was inside, I'd decide whether or not it was a good idea.'

The Chief Inspector stepped inside the bank, and closed the door firmly behind him. 'Shop!' he called loudly.

The door behind the counter slowly opened, and Maitland emerged, his submachine gun held at shoulder level, sweeping the room as he moved.

'What have you got for me so far?' the Major demanded, when he'd satisfied himself that the camera hadn't lied, and Woodend had come alone.

The Chief Inspector looked down at the cuffs of his trousers. 'I don't see any cycle clips,' he said, seemingly mystified.

'Cycle clips?' Maitland repeated.

'Aye,' Woodend agreed. 'I thought I *must* be wearin' a set. I certainly couldn't think of any other reason why you might mistake me for a grocer's delivery boy.'

'Look here—' Maitland began.

'No, *you* look here,' Woodend interrupted. 'You can't just order up a pound of justice an' expect me to deliver it the next mornin'. I'm doin' the best I can for you, but I can't perform miracles.'

Maitland nodded, accepting that Woodend had a point. 'But you do believe that my wife is innocent, don't you?' he asked.

'I believe there's a strong possibility that she might be,' Woodend said carefully.

'I want more than that,' Maitland snapped.

125

'Well, you can't bloody have it,' Woodend told him.

Maitland seemed to experience a sudden mood change, and laughed. 'Isn't it your job to reassure me?' he asked.

'No,' Woodend countered. 'It's my job to get you to trust me – an' I can only do that by bein' completely honest with you.'

'Suppose I gave you an incentive to work harder?'

'Like what?'

'Like killing one of my hostages.'

Woodend felt a cold shiver run through his entire body.

'I told you yesterday that if you harmed a single hostage, I'd have nothin' more to do with any of this,' he said.

'So you did,' Major Maitland agreed. 'But I've been thinking about that, and I've come to the conclusion that I don't believe you.'

'Is that right?'

'Certainly it is. I think that as long as there's even *one* hostage alive, you'll do your damnedest to get me what I want. Your conscience wouldn't let you do otherwise.'

'Maybe you're right about me,' Woodend agreed. 'But what I think, or what I might do, wouldn't matter any more – because as far as the people outside are concerned, you'd have put yourself beyond the pale.'

'The people outside,' Maitland mused. 'What a pleasant – if rather vague – euphemism. And *who* exactly are "the people outside"? The police? The Army? The politicians?'

Woodend sighed. 'All of the above. I've spoken to them. They all think like civilians – even the ones wearin' uniforms – an' they'd be so outraged at the death of even one hostage that they'd storm the place however many more lives it cost them.'

'Ah, I wondered when you'd start trying to create a bond between us,' Maitland said. 'And now you have.'

'Have I?'

'Certainly you have. You're trying to suggest – in a scarcely subtle way – that it's you and me against the world.'

'Don't flatter yourself,' Woodend said harshly. 'I don't approve of what you've done, an' if, without hurtin' any of your poor bloody hostages, one of the marksmen could take you out now, I wouldn't have a second's hesitation in tellin'

him to do it. So I'm not on *your* side at all, Major Maitland –
but I *am* on your wife's.' He paused to light a cigarette. 'I've
got somebody outside who'd like to talk to you,' he continued.

'And who might that be?' Maitland wondered. 'A priest?'

'No,' Woodend said. 'Your wife's partner.'

'Stanley's here?'

'That's right.'

'And he's actually prepared to come into the bank, and face
a man pointing a weapon at him?'

'He is.'

Maitland laughed. 'I didn't think he was so brave.'

'Then you seem to have underrated him,' Woodend said.
'Will you see him or not?'

'I'll see him,' Maitland said.

Woodend walked over to the door, and signalled that Stanley
Keene should be allowed to pass through the cordon.

Keene was wearing his conservative suit again. Perhaps he
wore it to give himself confidence, Woodend thought. But he
didn't *look* very confident. In fact, he seemed as if he were
about to mess his pants.

'Come closer, Stanley,' Maitland said, and Woodend realized that the soldier was actually enjoying the caterer's discomfort.

'How are you, Thomas?' Keene asked, in a trembling voice.

'Have you given even a moment's consideration to the position I'm in?' Maitland asked.

'Well, yes, I—'

'I'm in a bank, totally surrounded by armed men who'll
shoot me the first chance they get. I haven't had more than
two hours' continuous sleep in the last twenty-four hours. So
how do you *think* I am, Stanley?'

'I . . . I . . .' Keene said helplessly.

'I'm on top of the world,' Maitland said. 'Never felt better
in my entire life. I tell you, Stanley, this is all like a holiday
to me.'

'I know it must be hard,' Keene said.

'Hard!' Maitland repeated. 'What does a *so-called* man like
you know about hard?'

This had all gone far enough, Woodend decided. 'I think
you'd better leave now, Mr Keene,' he said.

But instead of taking his chance when it was offered to him, Keene stood his ground.

'I don't think you're being fair to Judith, Thomas,' he said. 'Honestly, I don't.'

'Fair to her? What are you talking about? Who do you think I'm doing all this for, if not for *her*?'

'Loving someone isn't about doing what *you* want for them,' Stanley Keene said.

'Then what is it about?'

'It's about doing what they want for *themselves*. And Judith wouldn't want this.'

For the first time since his initial encounter with Maitland, Woodend sensed that the Major was starting to feel slightly unsure of himself. Stanley Keene might not have served in the war, but he certainly deserved a medal for this, the Chief Inspector thought.

'What do you know about what Judith would want?' Maitland asked sneeringly.

'I'm her partner,' Keene replied.

'Her *business* partner. You shared an interest in making money. Nothing more than that.'

'*Much* more than that,' Keene said quietly.

'I've shared a bed with her, which is more than you've ever done – or ever could do. I know how she thinks, and how she feels. She *loves* me.'

'She loves me, too,' Keene said.

'Oh, I'm sure she does! I'm absolutely convinced of it! Who *wouldn't* love you, Stanley?'

'She doesn't love me in the same way as she loves you,' Keene said, ignoring the jibe. 'I would never try to claim that. But it *is* still love. And I love her. I'd never make her suffer in the way you're making her suffer now.'

'If you love her, why don't you prove it?' Maitland hectored. 'Why don't *you* confess to the murder?'

'If I thought I could convince the police it really was me who did it, then I would,' Stanley Keene said. 'If I had the choice of which of us should spend the next twenty-five years in gaol, I'd choose me.'

Mistake! Woodend thought. Keene should never even have raised the *possibility* that Judith would serve her full sentence. But it was too late to do anything about it now.

The implication of Keene's words had made Maitland rock slightly on his heels.

'But Judith's not *going to* spend the next twenty-five years in gaol,' he said, almost desperately. 'The police are soon going to find Clive Burroughs' real murderer, aren't they?'

'Yes, yes, of course they are,' Stanley Keene said, unconvincingly.

'Liar!' Maitland said, spitting out the words. 'You don't really believe they will, do you, Stanley?'

Stanley Keene flapped his hands helplessly in the air. 'What do you want me to say, Thomas?' he asked.

'I want you to say that everything's going to be fine, you bloody simpering idiot!'

'I'm . . . I'm sure Mr Woodend is trying his very best to do what you want him to, but—.'

'Get out!' Maitland screamed. 'Get the hell out of here. I'm sick of the sight of you, you mincing little queer.'

'Thomas—'

'Call me *Major Maitland*, you nasty little poof!'

'Major Maitland, please, if you'll just listen—'

The submachine gun had been pointing at Woodend, but now Maitland swung it round and aimed it directly at Keene.

'You've got five seconds to get out,' he said. 'If you're still here after that, I'll spatter your pathetic little body all over the walls.'

For perhaps three seconds, Keene did not move, then panic engulfed him and he turned and fled out into the street.

'He doesn't even *run* like a real man,' Major Maitland said in disgust.

'There's more than one way to be a man,' Woodend told him. 'An', in my book, Mr Keene's up there with the best of them.'

Stanley Keene was leaning heavily against one of the police cars. Without its support, Woodend guessed, he would probably have fallen over.

'I made a complete mess of the whole thing, didn't I?' Keene asked plaintively.

'It turned out to be a mess, all right,' Woodend agreed, 'but hardly any of it was your fault.'

What *had* gone wrong, he'd already decided, was that Maitland – who was prepared to lay down his own life for his wife – simply couldn't bear the thought that there was someone else out there who loved her, and was also prepared to make sacrifices for her.

'He didn't mean it,' Keene said.

'Mean what?'

'All those names he called me. He must have seemed like a vicious bully, but that's not really Thomas at all. He's a very decent man, you know. It's just that he's under a lot of pressure.'

'That's very forgivin' of you,' Woodend said.

'And when he threatened to shoot me – to spatter my pathetic little body all over the walls – he didn't mean that, either. I *knew* he didn't mean it. I was almost sure I'd have been perfectly safe to stay there. But I still ran away. I just couldn't help myself.'

'There's very few people who *wouldn't* have run, under those circumstances,' Woodend said.

Tears were forming in Keene's pale eyes. 'Do you really think so, Chief Inspector?' he asked.

'I'm sure of it,' Woodend said.

Stanley Keene took a deep breath. 'If you want me to go back into the bank, I will,' he said. 'It won't be easy for me, but I'm almost certain that I can force myself to do it.'

'There'd be no point in your goin' back in,' Woodend said. 'He won't talk to you again. I'll consider myself lucky if he'll even talk to *me*.'

'If only I'd been able to handle it differently,' Keene agonized.

'You did your level best, Mr Keene, an' that's all any of us can do,' Woodend said.

'So what happens now?' Keene asked. 'Now that I've failed so miserably.'

Woodend looked around him – at the sharpshooters on the roofs, at the barricades at the end of the street.

'What happens now?' he said. 'To tell you the truth, Mr Keene, I've absolutely no bloody idea!'

Twenty-One

Back in her temporary office in the rabbit warren which was Dunethorpe Central Police Station, Monika Paniatowski gazed down despondently at the stack of documents Chief Inspector Baxter had so assiduously collected on the Burroughs case.

There was a nagging feeling in some far corner of her mind that she'd missed something. That at some point the previous evening – either just before she'd fallen asleep, or shortly after she'd woken up – she'd come across a document which, if she'd been feeling sharper, she would instantly have homed in on.

The problem was that she had no idea which document in the large pile it could be, or even which aspect of the late Clive Burroughs' life it related to. Yet it was there – she was almost *certain* it was there.

She heard a gentle tapping on the open door, and when she looked up she saw that Chief Inspector Baxter was standing there.

'Woke up this mornin', and found my baby gone,' he sang in a voice that sounded passably like Mick Jagger's.

He was making a joke of it, Paniatowski thought. But just below the surface, there was clearly a rebuking edge to his tone. And joke or not, she didn't like being referred to as his 'baby'.

'Yes, I did slip out rather quietly,' she admitted, sounding – even to herself – ridiculously prim. 'I didn't want to disturb you.'

Not *quite* true. What she hadn't wanted to do was to *talk* to him – not until she'd got all her feelings about the previous night properly sorted out.

'Never mind, we'll make up for it by going somewhere nice for lunch,' Baxter said.

'I'm not sure I'll have time for lunch, sir.'

Baxter's smile turned to a frown. '*Sir?* You didn't call me "sir" last night, Monika.'

131

'That was then, this is now,' Paniatowski said, smiling to blunt the apparent sharpness of her words.

'I'm not sure I know what you mean,' Baxter said – though it was perfectly clear from his expression that he did.

'*Then*, we were two lonely people, seeking a bit of comfort in each other's arms,' Paniatowski clarified. 'And maybe we will be again. But *now*, we're two working bobbies, both snowed under with our current assignments, as working bobbies always are.'

'Is that really how you see us?' Baxter asked wonderingly. 'As working bobbies?'

'As nothing more than two lonely people.'

'You don't seem to have ever seriously considered Mrs Burroughs as a suspect,' Paniatowski said.

'What?!'

'You investigated the case amazingly thoroughly, you've collected mountains of background material, but you don't seem to have ever seriously considered Mrs Burroughs as a suspect.'

'Ah, I see. That's a way of telling me not to bring our personal life into the office,' Baxter said.

'When I'm working on a case, I don't *have* any personal life,' Paniatowski countered.

Or even when I'm *not* working on a case, she added silently.

'So what happened last night, if it wasn't a personal life?' Baxter wondered.

'I really would much prefer to talk about the investigation, sir,' Paniatowski said, insistently.

Baxter nodded. 'All right. If that's the way that you want to play it, Monika.' He paused and took a deep breath. 'In answer to your question, no, I didn't really consider her a suspect, *Sergeant Paniatowski*.'

'Why not? She had plenty of reasons to despise her husband, and stood to gain a great deal of money from his death.'

'All that's true enough. But I already had my *prime* suspect – locked up in the cells.'

'So what happened to your prime suspect's overall? According to your theory, she was wearing it when she killed Burroughs.'

'That's true.'

'Yet you never found it.'

132

'She must have destroyed the overall before we picked her up in the lay-by. Given the time element, she'd certainly had ample opportunity to do so.'

'That would imply she took it with her when she left the crime scene.'

'Of course.'

'The nightwatchman said she didn't.'

'You're putting words into the witness's mouth. What the nightwatchman actually said was that he didn't *see* her carrying it. That certainly doesn't mean that she wasn't.'

'So he was observant enough to notice that she was wearing flat-heeled shoes, but yet somehow completely missed the fact that she was carrying a bloodied overall in her arms?' Paniatowski asked sceptically.

'It's possible.'

'But not likely.'

Baxter ran his fingers through his wiry, greying hairs. 'You should know yourself that if you ask six different witnesses to describe an incident, you'll get six vastly different versions of what actually happened,' he said.

'You disappoint me, sir,' Paniatowski said. 'I thought you were my kind of bobby. But you're not, are you?'

'Aren't I?'

'No. I'll admit that you did a superb job of collecting up all the available evidence, but does that really count for much when you've already made up your mind about the case? You weren't really conducting an investigation at all, were you? You were just going through the motions.'

Baxter shook his head again, almost despairingly. 'You may have all the drive and energy of youth – you may have a very quick brain – but you've still got an awful lot to learn about detective work.'

'Maybe I have. But you could claim that about anybody. Even an old dog should try to learn a *few* new tricks occasionally,' Paniatowski said cuttingly.

Baxter looked hurt. 'In life, as distinct from popular fiction, the obvious suspect is almost always the right one,' he told her.

Charlie Woodend would never have said anything like that, Paniatowski thought.

Cloggin'-it Charlie approached every new case with a totally open mind. For him, evidence was a broad light which helped to illuminate the whole picture, not a narrow beam which focused on one aspect of it.

Why hadn't she seen that when they'd been having their argument the previous day? she wondered.

Then she realized that it wasn't so much that she *hadn't* seen it as that she'd chosen to ignore it – chosen to cast Woodend in the role of dinosaur, because a dinosaur's opinion of you didn't really matter.

She saw now that having just almost lectured Baxter on his inability to keep the personal and professional sides of his life distinct, she'd been falling into exactly the same trap with Woodend. And what was even worse, she'd let her personal feelings *warp* her professional judgements.

'If you don't mind, sir, I have to make a phone call in connection with my investigation,' she said.

'And you'd rather I wasn't here when you did it?'

'Exactly.'

'Right then,' Baxter said, turning to face the corridor. 'I'll see you around, Sergeant.'

'About lunch?' Paniatowski said.

'Yes?' Baxter asked over his shoulder.

'I really don't have time today, but if I'm still here tomorrow, it's certainly something we could think about.'

Woodend made use of the phone when he had to, but he didn't care for it. He liked to study the face of the person he was talking to, and a disembodied voice emerging from a piece of moulded plastic was no substitute for that at all. Thus, whilst he was pleased that Monika Paniatowski had phoned in her report – because he had been just a *little* bit concerned about her mental balance – he couldn't help wishing that she was sitting opposite him instead.

'You might just be on to somethin' there,' he said, after Paniatowski had told him about Judith Maitland's uniform. 'Good work.'

'Yes, it was, wasn't it?' Paniatowski's voice crackled at him from the other end of the line.

Cocky young bugger, Woodend thought. Still, it was nice that she felt she *could* be cocky again.

134

'What's your view on this month that Burroughs spent in Manchester?' he asked.

'It was a long time ago,' Paniatowski said. 'Besides, I think I know what he was doing there – and it has nothing to do with the case.'

Woodend lit up a cigarette, but said nothing.

'It hasn't, has it, sir?' Paniatowski asked, with a note of uncertainty creeping into her voice.

'Hasn't what?'

'Hasn't anything to do with the case?'

'Probably not,' Woodend conceded. 'But if you want to learn somethin' new about a feller, you shouldn't study the ordinary things he'd done – you should look at the *extraordinary* ones.'

'So are you saying that I should go down to Manchester to chase this lead up?'

'If you were given all the resources you needed to do the job properly, then you most certainly should,' Woodend replied. 'But we both know that's never goin' to happen – that you're always goin' to have to juggle with what you've actually got. An' since you already seem to have enough balls in the air to keep you busy, there's no point in goin' lookin' for any more.'

'So what do you think I *should* do?'

It was nice that she was asking his advice again, Woodend thought. 'If I was you, I think I'd pay another visit on the grievin' widow,' he said.

'And what should I do when I see her? Ask her straight out if she picked up a hammer and battered her husband's brains in?'

Woodend chuckled. 'Aye, why *not* do just that?' he said. 'She's bound to break down an' confess immediately.'

'You think so?'

'Of course. You should have seen enough of Perry Mason on the telly to know that's what *always* happens.'

Paniatowski laughed. 'But on the off-chance that it doesn't, maybe I should try a slightly different approach,' she suggested.

'Perhaps that *would* be wise,' Woodend concurred. 'You might be best to build on the pally relationship you already seem to have established with her. You could try givin' her the impression that you think the whole investigation's a waste of time, for example. That should relax her, an' with her guard down, she just might say somethin' very interestin'.'

'It's a thought,' Paniatowski agreed. 'Well, if there's nothing more, sir, I think I'll—'

'Hang on just a minute,' Woodend said.

'Yes?'

'Was there any particular reason why you didn't check in with me before you left for Dunethorpe this mornin'?'

There was a significant pause on the other end of the line, then Paniatowski said, 'As a matter of fact, sir, the reason I didn't come to see you was because I wasn't actually *in* Whitebridge at all this morning.'

'No?'

'No. I spent the night here in Dunethorpe.'

She was suddenly sounding unnaturally casual, Woodend thought – and wondered why that should be.

'Booked yourself into a hotel, did you?' he asked. 'Well, given the way the minds of our bean-counters work, I hope you settled for a modest bed-and-breakfast, rather than drownin' yourself in three-star luxury.'

The pause was even longer this time.

'I didn't actually check into a hotel at all,' Paniatowski admitted. 'DCI Baxter gave me a mountain of material to look at, and I spent the night at the station, working my way through it.'

Now that just didn't ring true, Woodend told himself.

'So you had no sleep at all?' he asked.

'I . . . er . . . managed to grab a couple of hours at my desk.'

'Well, don't overdo it, Monika,' Woodend advised. 'I need my bagman to keep her mind razor-sharp. You're no bloody good to me when you're completely knackered.'

'I won't work straight through the night again,' Paniatowski promised. 'In fact, I was planning to come back to Whitebridge early enough to make sure I get a good night's sleep in my own bed.'

'Very wise.'

'So shall I see you in the Drum and Monkey, as usual? Say at about nine o'clock?'

'Grand,' Woodend said. 'It'll give you a chance to meet the new member of the team.'

'New member of the team? *What* new member of the team?' Paniatowski asked sharply.

Oh dear, oh dear, Woodend thought, the children can get jealous of one another, can't they?

'He's only with us temporarily,' he said aloud.

'Who is?'

'Constable Colin Beresford. You probably remember him from the Pamela Rainsford case, don't you?'

'I thought he was *Uniformed Branch*,' Paniatowski replied, saying the words not as if they were a description of his position in the police hierarchy but more as a slur on Beresford's general character.

'Aye, he is normally one of the pointed helmet brigade,' Woodend agreed. 'But dress him up in a decent suit, an' you could almost pass him off as a normal person.'

'I see,' Paniatowski said, sounding far from convinced.

'You were new to the CID yourself once,' Woodend reminded her. 'I hope you remember that, an' try not to give the lad too much of a hard time.'

'I'll be like a mother to him,' Paniatowski promised.

'I don't want you goin' that far,' Woodend cautioned.

'And as long as he can just avoid stepping on my feet with his big thick boots, he probably won't be too much of a liability to the investigation,' Paniatowski concluded.

'Very gracious of you to look at it that way,' Woodend said dryly. 'Nine o'clock tonight, then?'

'Nine o'clock,' Paniatowski agreed.

Twenty-Two

Constable Colin Beresford, dressed in the suit his mum had helped him to choose, was already relishing his first interview for the CID.

True, the person he was questioning didn't exactly *look* like a master criminal. Nor was there much of a chance she actually *was* one, since only very rarely were master criminals middle-aged women with frizzy orange perms and a slight weight problem.

The setting, too, lacked something of the seedy glamour of a police interview room. The bright lighting which surrounded him came not from an interrogator's lamp, but from the neon strip lighting mounted over the kitchen range in the Dirty Duck restaurant.

Still, he told himself, everybody had to start somewhere, and he was starting here.

'Am I right in thinking that of all the staff who were working at the Dirty Duck when Judith Maitland was here, you're the only one remaining, Mrs Newton?' the constable asked.

'Yes,' the woman agreed. 'But you mustn't refer to this place as the Dirty Duck when Mr Thompson's around,' she cautioned.

'Why?'

'He hits the roof. And that's not a pretty sight, I can assure you, because he's got a terrible temper when he's roused. So, all in all, it'd be safer to make sure you call it the White Swan.'

'I'll bear that in mind,' Beresford said. 'So, what *can* you tell me about Judith?'

Mrs Newton shrugged. 'I don't know what to say, really. She was a nice enough girl.'

'What exactly do you mean by that?' asked Beresford, searching for nuances he could get his teeth into, as any good interrogator should.

'Well, I suppose I mean that she was a good worker, who never tried to get out of doing her fair share. An' that she was always very pleasant to everybody in the kitchen.'

'I see,' Beresford said.

'She didn't seem as if she had a mean bone in her body,' Mrs Newton ploughed on, in an attempt to find something useful to say. 'Which is why you could have literally knocked me over with a feather when I heard she'd been arrested for murder.'

'Interesting,' Beresford said seriously.

But it wasn't, really, he was forced to admit to himself.

Cases weren't solved by the officers who were conducting

them learning that someone was 'a nice girl' or 'always pleasant to everybody'. There was plainly more to this CID work than first met the eye. He wondered how Inspector Rutter or Sergeant Paniatowski would have handled this particular interrogation.

'Did you know the man who Judith was going out with while she was working here?' he pressed on. 'The one who jilted her?'

'I saw him a few times, when he came to pick her up. I can't say I ever really took to him.'

This wasn't going *at all* well, Beresford thought. 'Did he seem to have a violent nature?' he asked.

'Violent nature. Well, he didn't smash up the kitchen while he was here, if that's what you mean.'

'No, I—'

'An' Judith never came into work battered and bruised, as a couple of the girls who've worked here have. So I suppose I'd have to say no, he really didn't strike me as violent.'

Hopeless, Beresford told himself. Absolutely hopeless.

'Mind you, there are other ways you can hurt a girl than knockin' her about,' Mrs Newton said. 'She was in a terrible state after he left her.'

'Was she?'

'I should say so. Cryin'! Pullin' her hair! The whole thing was makin' her quite ill. She even threw up a couple of times. An' you can't have that kind of thing goin' on in a kitchen, now can you? Health inspectors tend to take a very dim view of vomit in a food-preparation area.'

'I suppose they must,' Beresford agreed. 'Judith went away from Whitebridge for a while, didn't she?'

'Yes.'

'Do you know why that was?'

Though there was nobody else in the kitchen, Mrs Newton still checked over her shoulder to make sure they were not being overheard, and only when satisfied they were truly alone did she mouth the words, 'Nervous breakdown!'

'But she got over it, didn't she? She was completely cured when she came back?'

Mrs Newton shrugged again. 'Couldn't really say. It'd take a doctor to know for sure.' She paused for a moment. 'I suppose she must have been cured,' she conceded, 'or they would never have let her out of the loony bin at all, now would they?'

'I wasn't asking you for a medical opinion,' Beresford said. 'What I meant was, looking at her as just one person seeing another, you must have noticed some differences in her. Am I right?'

'Not really.'

'She can't have been *exactly* the same when she came back as she was when she went away,' Beresford said, almost desperately.

'Probably not, but I can't say that I picked up on it myself. I didn't see much of her, to tell you the truth.'

'But surely, once you started working together again—'

'Are you *sure* you're a detective?' Mrs Newton interrupted.

'Well, yes,' Beresford said, wishing he really did sound like one.

'Then let me give you a tip. You should get your facts right before you start asking other people questions.'

'Pardon?'

'Judith *didn't* come back to work at the Dirty Du— ... at the White Swan ... at all.'

'No?'

'No! She just popped in a couple of times to have a talk with Mr Thompson. And you know what they were talking *about*, don't you?'

'Well, yes,' Beresford lied.

'So you don't need me to—'

'But I'd much rather you told me all about it in your own words.'

Mrs Newton glanced round the kitchen again, just as she had done before she'd told Beresford about Judith Maitland's nervous breakdown.

'She was starting up her own business, an' she needed money for that,' the woman said, in a hushed, conspiratorial voice. 'They do say – an' I don't know whether or not there's any truth in it – they do say that Mr Thompson gave her *five thousand pounds* out of his own pocket.'

Constable Beresford whistled, softly. 'That's a lot of money for anybody to part with.'

'It would be for the likes of you or me, but not for Mr

Thompson,' Mrs Newton said. 'This place is a real gold mine, you know.'

'Well, it certainly always looks busy enough when I walk past it,' Beresford admitted.

'Busy? I'll say it's busy. We can do sixty or seventy covers – easy – on a good night.'

'Is that a lot?'

'It certainly is. Most restaurants would be over the moon if they had that kind of business. And then there's the market days. You can't move in this restaurant on market days for all the people who want feedin'. Besides,' Mrs Newton continued, dropping her voice even lower, 'there's other considerations to be taken into account, aren't there?'

'Are there?'

'There are indeed. Considerations which go well beyond bits of paper with the Queen's face on them.'

'What ... er ... kind of considerations?' Beresford wondered.

'Mr Thompson – an' this I *do* know for a fact, because I've seen it with my own eyes – Mr Thompson has been in love with Judith from the first day she started workin' here.'

'You don't say.'

'I *do* say. An' when the heart's already surrendered, the head has no say in what happens to the brass, does it?'

Twenty-Three

'You're back again, are you?' Mrs Burroughs asked, in a pleasant but slightly puzzled way, when she opened her front door to find Monika Paniatowski standing on her doorstep.

'Yes,' Paniatowski replied, with an air of mock-resignation. 'I am indeed back again.'

'Well, all I can say is that, however much you might criticize her, your mum must be a saint,' Mrs Burroughs told her.

'Sorry?' Paniatowski said.

'To spend so much of her free time babysitting your kids,' Mrs Burroughs explained.

'Oh that!' Paniatowski said, making a mental note that the next time she told Mrs Burroughs a lie, she'd remember which lie she'd told. 'Yes, she really is very good about looking after them.'

Mrs Burroughs glanced up and down the street, as Paniatowski had noticed people often do when they're unsure about what to say next.

'So what can I do for you this time, Sergeant Paniatowski?' the widow asked, after a few seconds had passed.

'It's Monika,' Paniatowski reminded her. 'And if you don't mind, Helen, I'd like to ask you a few more questions. Just to finally wrap things up.'

'I think I *do* mind,' Mrs Burroughs replied. 'To tell you the truth, I don't really see the need of it.'

'And to be honest, neither do I,' Paniatowski replied. 'But the boss wants it done, and whatever I think about him personally, he *is* still the boss. Besides, I could use the overtime. So would you mind if I came in?'

Mrs Burroughs looked dubious. 'Well . . .' she began.

'Forget it,' Paniatowski said. She glanced at her watch. 'The pubs are open, aren't they? Well, then, I'll just go and sit in the nearest boozer for an hour or so, then tell Octopus-Man that I've spent the time talking to you. He'll never know the difference.'

'There's no point in drinking alone, when you can do it in company,' Mrs Burroughs said, softening. 'Come in. I've got—'

'A bottle of white wine nicely chilling in the refrigerator?' Paniatowski guessed.

And both women laughed.

The little girl, Emma, was not in evidence in the living room.

'She's upstairs, taking her nap,' Mrs Burroughs explained. 'Thank God kids seem to need so much sleep.'

Emma's older brother, Timothy, was playing with his train set in the corner of the room, and refused to leave even when his mother offered him the customary bribe.

'You'll have to be very quiet, then,' Helen Burroughs said, giving in. 'As quiet as a mouse.'

'Mouses aren't quiet,' Timothy countered. 'They squeak. And you can hear them running behind the wall.'

His mother sighed. '*Quieter* than a mouse then. Otherwise, you go upstairs whether you want to or not.'

'I'll be quiet,' Timothy promised. 'I don't *want* to listen, anyway. Grown-ups' talk is boring.'

His mother raised an exasperated eyebrow, and Paniatowski – as was obviously expected of her – nodded sympathetically.

Mrs Burroughs filled two wine glasses right up to the brim. 'Cheers!' she said.

'Cheers!' Paniatowski echoed. 'What made you decide to keep on the business after your husband's . . .' She glanced at Timothy, still sitting in the corner, '. . . after your husband went away for a while?'

Mrs Burroughs shrugged. 'My father always used to tell me that having money's no use unless that money is working for you. And he was spot on about that. The builders' merchant's is a good business as long as it's in the right hands – and Al Sanders' hands *are* right.'

'Al Sanders?' Paniatowski repeated, conjuring up a mental picture of the creepy Sanders easily enough, but managing to sound as if she'd never heard the name before.

'He's the manager of the firm now. Very competent. And not a bad-looking chap, either.'

Paniatowski giggled girlishly. 'To hear you talk, you'd think there was something going on between the two of you,' she said. 'Is there?'

Mrs Burroughs giggled, too. 'You mind your own business,' she said, wagging her finger at Paniatowski.

'Have you never thought of moving away from this area, Helen?' Paniatowski asked.

'Why should I have?'

'Well, to get right away from all the bad memories you must associate with the place.'

'I suppose I could do that,' Mrs Burroughs admitted. 'But I still like Dunethorpe, and, on the whole, I'd rather stay and block out all those bad old memories with good new ones.'

'Good new ones like Al Sanders?' Paniatowski asked.

Helen Burroughs giggled again. 'That'd be telling!'

The phone in the hallway rang.

'Damn!' Mrs Burroughs said.

She swayed slightly as she stood up. She was not yet drunk,

143

strictly speaking, but she was certainly working her way steadily towards it.

Mrs Burroughs had left the door open, and Paniatowski had no difficulty at all in hearing her side of the telephone conversation.

'They've done what?' Mrs Burroughs demanded. 'But that's ridiculous. Can't they . . .? No, I bet they bloody won't.'

She slammed the phone down and stamped furiously back into the living room.

'Is something the matter?' Paniatowski asked, solicitously.

'You could say that. One of the bloody suppliers has just turned up at the yard with a lorry load of bathroom suites.'

'And is there something wrong with them?'

'Nothing at all. Al thinks they're just what we wanted. The problem is that some of the paperwork's not gone through yet, and the driver says I'll have to sign for them personally. He *also* says he's in a big hurry. Well, that's too bad, isn't it! He'll just have to wait – because I can't get there in less than an hour, what with having to get the kids ready and everything.'

'How long would it take you *without* the children?' Paniatowski asked casually.

'Not long at all. Ten minutes to get there, five minutes to sign the papers and another ten minutes to get back. But that's still nearly half an hour I'd be out of the house, and I can't possibly leave the kids on their own for all that time.'

'*Don't do it, Monika!*' a voice in Paniatowski's skull urged her. '*Don't even think of doing it!*'

'I could easily look after them for half an hour, if you'd like,' she heard herself say.

'You're sure?' Mrs Burroughs asked.

'No trouble at all. I'll check on Emma every five minutes or so, and if Timothy gets bored, I'll play a game with him.'

'Well, that would make things a lot easier,' Mrs Burroughs conceded, already heading back into the hallway. 'Help yourself to another glass of wine when you need one.'

I have been very stupid, Paniatowski thought, as she heard the front door slam. Very, very stupid.

She could imagine herself standing in the witness box, if she was ever called to give evidence against Mrs Burroughs.

144

'*You told my client that you had two children of your own,*' she could hear the defence counsel saying. '*Is that correct, Sergeant Paniatowski?*'

'*I don't—*'

'*Is that what you told her?*'

'*Yes.*'

'*And that you always left them in the care of your mother when you were at work?*'

'*Yes.*'

'*But none of that was true, was it?*'

'*No. My mother's dead. She had a hard life, which sent her to an early grave.*'

'*And your children?*'

'*I don't have any. I'm barren. I can* never *have any – however desperately I might want to.*'

'*I see. So having established that you're a liar, let's move on. Is it a part of your function — it is written into your job description, shall we say – that you should offer to baby-sit for any woman you are in the process of interrogating?*'

'*No.*'

'*Then why did you do it on this occasion?*'

'*To be helpful? To show at least one member of the public the human face of policing?*'

'*I suggest you had quite another motive, Sergeant Paniatowski. I suggest you did it, purely and simply, to further both your investigation into Mrs Burroughs and your own career.*'

She'd already gone that far, and there was no backing out of it. But she didn't need to go any further – she didn't *have* to make matters any worse.

'*And once you were alone with the child – the poor, inno-cent little boy – what did you do then?*' she heard the imag-inary barrister ask her in her head.

'*I . . .*'

'*You interrogated him, didn't you? His mother trusted you to look after him, and you repaid that trust by treating him no better than you'd have treated a common criminal!*'

The way out of *that* possible dilemma was simple enough, Paniatowski decided.

If Timothy made any move to speak to her, she would say

she didn't want to talk because she had a headache. He might not like that, of course, but it was never too early to learn that part of growing up was accepting that you had to put up with *a lot* of things you didn't like.

The boy abandoned his toys, and crawled over to where she was sitting.

'Do you know my daddy?' he asked, looking up at her.

'Headache!' Paniatowski's internal warning system screamed. *'For God's sake, say you've got a headache.'*

'No, I don't know him,' she said. 'But he sounds like a very nice man. Why don't you tell me all about him?'

'Mummy says that he's gone to London for a while – but I know that he hasn't.'

Oh Christ, I'm going to be the first person he chooses to confide in! Paniatowski thought. I'm going to be the first one to be told that he thinks his father is dead!

But she couldn't back out now, even if she wanted to – because if the boy *had* decided to face his fears, who could guess what damage it might do to him if she refused to face them with him?

'Where do *you* think your daddy is?' she asked gently.

'He's in New Zealand,' the boy said firmly.

'New Zealand?'

'That's right. Do you know where New Zealand is?'

'No, I don't.'

'It's right on the other side of the world.'

'Is it? And where else is on the other side of the world?' Paniatowski wondered.

The boy considered for a moment. 'Whitebridge,' he said.

'Why do you think he's in New Zealand?'

'Because that's what he told the lady,' the boy said, slightly scornful of her ignorance.

'Which lady?'

'The lady that me and my daddy – the lady that Daddy and *I* – used to go out with.'

'And where did you go with this lady?'

'All kinds of places. We went to the zoo, and saw lots of different animals – monkeys and tigers and bears. And we went out on a boat in the river. The lady liked it.'

'How do you know?'

'Because she was always laughing.'

'And your daddy told her he was going to New Zealand, did he?'

'He told her we were *all* going to New Zealand – me and Emma and Mummy.' Timothy looked suddenly troubled. 'She didn't laugh much after that.'

Twenty-Four

Woodend had been an enthusiast of best bitter for all of his adult life, and saw no good reason to start surprising his liver now it had reached middle age. As a result of his single-minded dedication, he knew almost nothing about wine – and even less about wine companies. Thus, as he drove towards the Kensington Wine Company's regional headquarters in Bolton, he had no real idea what to expect, though he rather imagined it would be somewhat like a brewery warehouse, full of oak barrels and stacked crates of bottles.

What he actually *found* was so different to his imaginings that it quite surprised him. Kensington's office was housed in a medium-sized building in the better part of town. It clearly had no warehousing facilities of any kind, and was entered through a black plate-glass door with a very impressive coat of arms etched on it.

Sebastian Courtney-Jones, in contrast to his place of work, presented no surprises at all. He was pretty much what Woodend would have expected from Giles Thompson's description of him – mid-forties, smooth, and obviously very impressed with himself.

'I really don't know how I can help you, Chief Inspector,' he said genially, when he had invited Woodend to sit down in an office which smelled of expensive polished wood and old leather. 'It must be some years now since I've even *talked* to Judith.'

'That's not quite true, now, is it?' Woodend asked. 'Accordin' to what I've been told, you saw her no more than a few months ago, when you first moved back to the area.'

'Ah, so you've heard about that, have you?' Courtney-Jones asked, slightly uncomfortably.

'Possibly you don't fully appreciate the nature of a police inquiry,' Woodend said gravely. 'It's a serious matter, and if you mislead it, you could well be charged with obstruction of justice.'

'Over one little white lie?'

'There's no such thing as a *white* lie in the eyes of the law,' Woodend told him. 'There's lies, an' there's the truth – an' what you've just told me falls squarely into the former category, doesn't it?'

'Well, yes, I suppose that, strictly speaking, it does,' Courtney-Jones admitted. His hand hovered over the intercom on his desk. 'Would you care for a drink, Chief Inspector? We've just received a shipment of a red wine from the Côte de Blaye which I'm sure you'll find rather palatable.'

'Do you know, I'd quite forgotten why I was so glad to leave London behind me,' Woodend said.

'And why were you?'

'Because it was chock-full of fellers like you.'

'I beg your pardon?'

'Self-important prats,' Woodend amplified. 'Smarmy, complacent dickheads.'

'I must say that I rather object to you using that kind of—' Courtney-Jones began.

'Tell me about the last time you spoke to Judith Maitland,' Woodend interrupted. 'An' I mean, the *last* time.'

'I did go to see her once – just for old times' sake,' Courtney-Jones said sulkily.

'You went to see her with the explicit purpose of findin' out if you could pick up again where you left off, seven years ago,' Woodend corrected him.

'You *are* well informed,' Courtney-Jones said.

'Yes,' Woodend replied. 'I am, aren't I?'

'I suppose I'd better come clean,' Courtney-Jones said.

'That might be a good idea,' Woodend agreed.

'I found myself back in my old hunting ground, both foot-loose and fancy-free. I went to see Judith because it seemed the ideal opportunity to renew an old acquaintanceship – especially when the old acquaintance in question was so *very* good in bed.'

'You didn't tell her you loved her? You didn't say that you now realized she was the only woman in the world for you?'

'Who told you that? Was it Judith herself?'

'It doesn't really matter who it was. Just answer the question.'

'I may well have said something of that nature. Men will talk all kinds of rubbish when there's a good chance of them getting back into a girl's knickers, won't they?'

'*Some* men, maybe,' Woodend agreed. 'Some two-legged creatures that *pass themselves off* as men. But what I really want to know is why you decided to break up with her in the first place.'

'She suddenly had the urge to start taking things far too seriously. I simply couldn't allow that. I had my family to consider.'

'Pity you didn't consider them before,' Woodend said dryly. 'What made her want to become more serious, do you think?'

'I've absolutely no idea,' Courtney-Jones said.

But he blinked as he spoke, and Woodend knew he was lying.

'Were you aware, at the time you last saw her, that she supposedly had a lover in Dunethorpe?' the Chief Inspector asked.

'No, I didn't even know the man existed, until I read about him in the papers,' Courtney-Jones said – and the eyes blinked again.

'Do you know what I think?' Woodend asked.

'No,' Courtney-Jones said, squaring his shoulders and thrusting his chin out, 'I have absolutely no idea at all. And, to tell you the truth, Chief Inspector, I'm not really interested.'

'I'll tell you anyway,' Woodend said. 'I think you were speakin' no more than the truth when you said you'd finally realized you loved her. I think you'd have married her if she'd been willin' and – apart from the occasional fling – you'd have stayed true to her.'

'That's the most ridiculous thing I've ever heard in my life,' Courtney-Jones blustered.

But though he was trying to hold back the tears, he was fighting a losing battle.

'It must have come as a real shock to you to find out that

you had a heart after all,' Woodend pressed on relentlessly. 'It doesn't square with how you see yourself, does it? To a man like you, normal human feelings must have seemed almost like a weakness.'

A single tear rolled down Courtney-Jones' cheek, and fell on to his desk blotter.

'We could have been so happy together,' he said. 'I just *know* we could have been.'

Constable Beresford's dealings with banks had never previously extended beyond talking to the clerk behind the grille, so he had no idea of what to expect from the manager's office of the Wakefield and District Bank, into which he was now being ushered.

His first impressions were of opulence and seriousness – a large, expensive-looking wooden desk; heavy flock paper covering the walls; a sombre portrait of the bank's founder, which somehow managed to convey the impression that although he was long-dead, he was still watching you.

The manager himself had a shiny bald head and a large grey moustache. He was probably in his mid-fifties, and it was almost impossible to imagine that he had ever been any younger.

'So what can I do for you, Constable Beresford?' he asked.

'That's *Detective* Constable Beresford, sir,' Beresford replied, telling himself that Woodend would probably never find out he'd stretched the truth a little – and *perhaps* wouldn't mind, even if he did.

The manager smiled benignly. 'Of course,' he corrected himself. '*Detective* Constable Beresford.'

Beresford cleared his throat. 'As you may know, we've re-opened the Judith Maitland case,' he said.

'*We?*' the manager said, in the tones so often employed by a teasing uncle. 'Am I to take it, then, *Detective* Constable Beresford, that you played a major part in this decision?'

Beresford felt himself starting to flush. 'It . . . it was mainly my boss's decision,' he admitted.

The manager chuckled. 'Yes, I rather imagined it might have been.'

So now, instead of being treated like a kid in a uniform, he was being treated like a kid in a suit, Beresford thought – and wondered if the manager had somehow learned he still lived with his mum.

'I am right in assuming that Mrs Maitland was a customer of yours, aren't I, sir?' he pressed on.

The manager wagged his finger playfully. 'You shouldn't say "customer", *Detective* Constable Beresford. This is a bank, not an ironmonger's shop, and we much prefer the term "client".'

'Then she was a *client* of yours?'

'Now that sounds better, doesn't it? Yes, she was a *client* of ours.'

Beresford imagined the manager going home after his day's work and having his wife in stitches as he described the way he had made the young constable jump through the hoops.

Well, that wasn't going to happen, he decided, as he felt his earlier humiliation being driven out of him by a growing anger. It wouldn't happen because he'd give the manager such a grilling that the bastard wouldn't even want to *think* about what had gone on once he got home.

He started softly, still playing the role of the stumbling, unsure constable – which was not really quite a role at all.

'What were your impressions of Mrs Maitland, sir?' he asked diffidently.

'My impressions? I suppose I'd have to say I thought her a rather personable young woman.'

'Personable?' Beresford said. 'That's one of those "dressed-up" words, like client, isn't it?'

'I beg your pardon?'

'It sounds better – more respectable – to say "client" rather than "customer", and it sounds better to say "personable" than "a real cracker". But really, they both just mean the same.'

A slight tick had suddenly developed in the bank manager's left eye.

I was right, Beresford thought triumphantly. He fancied her rotten. It was probably her he was picturing when he was lying on top of his missus – thrusting half-heartedly as part of their weekly ritual. But he can never admit it – even to himself – because bank managers are pillars of the community. They're not *supposed* to be dirty old men.

151

The manager seemed to have got his tick under control. 'Mrs Maitland certainly had a pleasing aspect to her, yes,' he admitted. 'But that wasn't what I meant at all.'

'No?'

'No. When I called her "personable", I was referring to her character – to her businesslike attitude and her obvious energy. *Now* do you understand what I'm talking about?'

Beresford grinned, but made no reply.

'Have I inadvertently said something to amuse you?' the bank manager wondered.

'Not really. I was just thinking that, if I'd been a bit older, I might have had the hots for her myself.'

'The *hots* for her?' the manager repeated, horrified.

'And if I'd been your age – and in your position – I might well have been persuaded to take the same risk you did.'

'Risk?' the bank manager asked, still flushed from the discovery that this boy in his Sunday suit had somehow managed to learn of his secret yearnings. 'What risk?'

'The risk of lending a great deal of money to a young woman with absolutely no experience of running a business on her own,' Beresford explained, with growing self-confidence. 'Now that's a case of your heart leading your head, if I ever heard of one.'

'Are you daring to suggest . . .?' the bank manager began.

'Still, you didn't completely lose your self-control, did you?' Beresford continued cheerfully. 'Once she'd charmed you into agreeing to lend her the money – once her spell had worn off a little – you did at least have the good sense to insist that she got a guarantor for the loan.'

'You're quite wrong in almost all your assumptions,' the manager said heatedly. 'Mrs Maitland never cast a spell on me, and I most certainly never lent her any . . .'

He dried up, realizing he had said too much.

'What was that, sir?' Beresford asked.

Now they were back in the familiar territory of money matters, the bank manager seemed more in control of himself again. He folded his arms decisively. 'Any dealings which this bank has with any of its clients are an entirely confidential matter,' he said.

'Perhaps I'm being unfair to you,' Beresford pondered.

'Maybe there was never a question of a loan from the bank at all. Maybe it was more a case of the bank merely agreeing to manage the money that Mr Thompson had put into Mrs Maitland's account. Have I got it right this time?'

The manager unfolded his arms, and pressed a button on his desk.

'This interview is over,' he said coldly. 'And the next time your Chief Inspector wants me to answer any questions, I suggest he sends someone else to ask them.'

By the time Mrs Burroughs returned from the builders' merchant's, Timothy had already become bored with talking to Paniatowski about his father, and had drifted back to his train set in the corner of the room.

'Were they any trouble?' the mother asked the policewoman.

'None at all,' Paniatowski replied. 'Timothy's been playing quietly, and there hasn't been a peep out of Emma.'

'That's typical, isn't it?' Mrs Burroughs said, sitting down and immediately reaching for the wine bottle. 'People look after your kids for half-an-hour or so, and go away with the impression that they're little angels. What they don't realize is that when we're alone – just me and them – they can be right proper sods. You probably find the same with your own kids, don't you, Monika?'

'Absolutely,' Paniatowski agreed. 'Did you get the delivery sorted out all right?'

'No problem at all,' Mrs Burroughs said, taking a generous gulp of her wine. 'It's an easy business to run if you're just a little bit careful. Profitable, too, if you watch the till. But Clive never did.'

'Are you saying that other people were stealing from him?' Paniatowski asked.

'No, Clive was too cunning to ever allow anybody else to get one over on him.'

'Then . . .?'

'The problem wasn't the employees – it was him. He couldn't keep his *own* hands out of the till.'

Paniatowski nodded understandingly. 'He liked to live well.'

'He liked to have plenty of money in his pocket to lavish on his whores! God knows how much he got through in the last few years, what with posh dinners and expensive presents.'

'And hotel bills,' Paniatowski suggested.

'Oh yes, them as well,' Mrs Burroughs agreed, starting to slur her words slightly now. 'A quick screw in the back of the car wasn't good enough for him and his women. They had to do it in fancy hotels, with silk sheets and private bathrooms. It makes me sick to my stomach just to think about it.'

'And it wasn't always just the one night in those expensive hotels, was it?' Paniatowski asked.

'What do you mean?'

'Well, I've seen the bills,' Paniatowski explained. 'They're all in the evidence file.'

'Oh yes?' Mrs Burroughs said, and now there was a hint of caution in her tone.

'And if I remember correctly, there was a time, a few years ago it must have been, when he paid for a hotel room in Manchester for a whole month,' Paniatowski continued.

The air in the room had been pleasantly warm, but now its temperature seemed to drop by several degrees.

'Get out!' Mrs Burroughs said.

'What?'

'Get out! I want you out of my house!'

'Look, if I've said something to offend you, I'm sorry,' Paniatowski told her. 'Believe me, I certainly never meant it.'

Mrs Burroughs rose shakily to her feet – and her shakiness was only partly a result of the wine, Paniatowski thought – and pointed to the door.

'Out!' she said firmly.

'I'll go, if that's what you want. But would you mind if I just finished my wine, first?'

'Yes, I bloody well would mind!'

It was her house. There was nothing for it but to simply comply with her wishes.

Paniatowski stood up. 'Perhaps I'll come back later, when you're not quite so upset,' she suggested.

'You will not,' Mrs Burroughs told her. 'I never want to see you again,' she continued, a little calmer now. 'And if you try to talk to me – even if it's only over the phone – I'll imme-

154

diately put a complaint through to your superior. I'll tell him you came to my house and got drunk.'

'But I—'

'Disgustingly drunk. I might even tell him what you called him. Octopus-Man, wasn't it?'

Paniatowski feigned concern. 'Please don't do that,' she said.

'I won't – unless I have to,' Mrs Burroughs said. 'If you can keep your nose out of my business, then I'm perfectly willing to keep mine out of yours. If you don't – well, you know now what will happen.'

As threats went, it was quite forceful, Paniatowski thought, and wondered *exactly* what had turned Mrs Burroughs from an amiable lush into a towering harridan in less than a heartbeat.

Twenty-Five

The landlord of the Drum and Monkey looked across at the corner table in the public bar which, over the years, had become almost an unofficial annex of Whitebridge Police Headquarters.

It was good to see the old team back in action again, he thought. But he couldn't help feeling a slight twinge of resentment that the seat which used to be filled by DI Rutter was now occupied by someone else a young feller wearing what was obviously his best suit. He seemed a pleasant enough lad, the landlord had to admit. Bright enough, too. But try as he might, he couldn't imagine the lad ever quite being able to fill Bob Rutter's shoes.

Woodend took a swig of best bitter, and lit up a cigarette.

'I think it'd be a good idea to run through our list of possible suspects,' he said. 'An' the one I'd like to start with is Sebastian Courtney-Jones – the answer to every young maiden's prayer.'

'Really?' Monika Paniatowski asked doubtfully.

'Really,' Woodend confirmed. 'I know I shouldn't say this – what with justice bein' even-handed an' all that – but I'd

155

be tickled to death if that bastard *did* turn out to be our murderer.'

'But why should he have killed Clive Burroughs?'

'Because he was still in love with Judith, and he saw Burroughs as his main rival for her affections. She refused to come back to him, remember, and he might just have thought that with Burroughs out of the way, she'd be more amenable to changin' her mind.'

'But Burroughs *wasn't* his rival,' Paniatowski pointed out. '*He* was having an affair with the landlady of the Philosophers' Arms.'

'Is there any law which says a man can't be conductin' two affairs at the same time?' Woodend asked.

'From everything we've learned about both Judith *and* Burroughs, I don't think they'd ever have considered having an affair,' Paniatowski said.

'I admit it doesn't seem *very* likely,' Woodend conceded, 'but there's nowt as queer as folk, an' you can never really tell who's goin' to decide to hop into bed with who, can you?'

Oh shit, I shouldn't have said that! Woodend told himself.

Not to Monika.

Not quite so bluntly.

And especially not in the presence of Constable Beresford, who knew nothing about her affair with Bob Rutter.

He risked a quick glance at Paniatowski's face, to see how she'd taken his gaffe.

His sergeant *did* seem to have suddenly fallen into a pensive mood, he decided – but he got the distinct impression that whatever she was thinking about, it wasn't Bob Rutter.

'An' if Judith wasn't havin' an affair with Burroughs, exactly what hold did he have over her?' the Chief Inspector pressed on. 'Because there's no doubt that he did have a hold of *some* kind.'

'I'd like to throw another name into the hat, if I may,' Constable Beresford said, speaking very quickly, as if he'd only just summoned up the courage to speak at all.

'Go on, then,' Woodend said encouragingly.

'Giles Thompson.'

'Giles Thompson!' Woodend repeated. 'But he's a grand lad, is Giles. I've known the feller for donkey's years!'

156

'Does . . . does that mean he couldn't possibly be a murderer, sir?' Beresford asked.

'Well, no, of course it doesn't,' Woodend admitted. 'In my time, I've come across any number of murderers who seemed to be grand lads on the face of it. In fact, I've come across a good few who really *were* grand, an' were just pushed past the point of endurance. So why do you think Giles Thompson might be our killer, Beresford?'

'For the same reason you think Courtney-Jones might have done it,' Beresford replied. 'Love!'

'Are you sayin' Judith might have had an affair with Giles Thompson an' all?'

'No, sir. I'd think it was more a case of *paternal* love. Judith started working for Thompson just after her father died. She was very young at the time, and I think Thompson sort of took her under his wing. And once her mother had abandoned her and moved to Australia, I think he might have started to see himself as the only family she'd got.'

'That's possible,' Woodend said, though he seemed a long way from being convinced.

'In fact, he felt *so* responsible for her that when she needed the money to establish Élite Catering, he was the one who provided it,' Beresford continued.

'Now hold on a minute,' Woodend said. 'That's not what Giles told *me* at all. According to him, all he did was guarantee the bank loan.'

'I'm sure he did say that,' Beresford replied. 'But I think he was lying.'

'An' what are you basin' this assumption on?'

'On what they told me at the Wakefield and District Bank.'

'You went to the *bank*?'

'Yes, sir.'

'Who did you speak to?'

'The manager.'

'You've got some nerve,' Woodend said, with a hint of admiration in his voice. 'Even *I'd* think twice before I started strong-armin' a bank manager. An' did the bank manager confirm that Giles Thompson had actually given Judith Maitland the money?'

Beresford considered giving his new boss a verbatim account of the meeting, then rapidly decided against it.

'He wouldn't confirm that Thompson provided the money, sir,' he said. 'But he wouldn't exactly deny it, either.'

'So, according to your theory, Giles killed Burroughs out of his love for Judith?'

'It's certainly a possibility, sir. He'd already stood by and done nothing while one man wrecked her life. He may well have decided he wasn't going to let anything like that ever happen again.'

'I still don't see it,' Woodend confessed.

'And he has a temper,' Beresford pointed out. 'All his staff confirm that you've only got to call his restaurant the Dirty Duck, instead of the White Swan, and he'll go ballistic.'

'You're both missing one vital point,' said Paniatowski, who seemed to have emerged from her reverie.

'An' what's that?' Woodend wondered.

'Would either Thompson or Courtney-Jones have let the woman they loved go to prison for a crime they'd committed themselves?'

'Would you care to field that one, Beresford?' Woodend asked.

He'd expected the constable to look flustered, as all new recruits did the first time their pet theory was shot down in flames, but Beresford seemed to take it in his stride.

'I think both Thompson and Courtney-Jones might *well* have let her take the blame,' the constable said seriously. 'You see, it seems to me there's a very big difference between doing something *for* the woman you love and suffering *instead* of her.'

'Such wise words from one so young,' Paniatowski said.

'Monika!' Woodend said sharply.

'Sorry, that came out wrong,' Paniatowski said, and she really did sound apologetic. 'As a matter of fact, what Constable Beresford's just said makes a lot of sense. But I still think your general theory's wrong. I still think the prime suspect is to be found in Dunethorpe.'

'Mrs Burroughs?'

'Or Alfred Sanders. Or both of them. Mrs Sanders had both emotional and financial reasons for wanting to get rid of her husband.'

'An' Sanders?'

'He may be in love with her – he almost certainly *is* sleeping with her. Besides, with Mrs Burroughs controlling the company, he's the manager. Whereas, if Burroughs had lived, the company might well have gone broke and he'd have had no job at all.'

'So did they deliberately set out to frame Judith Maitland for the murder? Or was that just an accident?'

'It really doesn't matter, does it? Accidental or deliberate, the end result's the same.'

The landlord leaned out across the bar counter. 'Phone call for you, Sergeant Paniatowski,' he shouted across the noisy pub, in his 'last orders' voice.

'Now I wonder who that could be?' Woodend said.

'I have absolutely no idea,' Paniatowski told him.

Paniatowski took the phone as far away from the bar as the cable would allow her to, and then wrapped herself around it.

'Monika?' said a voice at the other end of the line.

'How did you find me?' Paniatowski asked.

DCI Baxter chuckled. 'I'm a detective, remember. I'm trained to track people down.' He paused. 'Is anything wrong?'

Was there?

Paniatowski wasn't sure.

'Why are you calling?' she asked.

'I just thought it'd be wise to confirm our lunch date for tomorrow.'

'We don't *have* a definite lunch date,' Paniatowski retorted. 'I said we'd do it if I could make the time.'

The pause was longer this time, then Baxter said, 'Listen, Monika, I'm a blunt, no-nonsense Yorkshireman. If you'd rather not see me again, you've only got to say the word.'

'I don't . . . I haven't . . .' Paniatowski found herself spluttering. She took a deep breath. 'I think – I'm almost sure – I want to see you, but it's all so complicated,' she continued.

'Is that right?' Baxter asked.

'Yes. You may not believe it, but it is. I was very involved with another man until quite recently . . .'

'But that's over, is it?'

'Yes.'

'And there's no chance of you getting back together?'

'None at all.'

'Then what's the problem?'

'And . . . and then there's the investigation. I'm up to my neck in it right now, and I just can't think of anything else.'

'Then let's say no more about it, for the moment,' Baxter suggested. 'But if you *are* in Dunethorpe tomorrow, we'll try to grab a bite of lunch together. And whether we do it as lovers, friends, colleagues – or even casual acquaintances – is entirely up to you. Fair enough?'

'Fair enough,' Paniatowski agreed.

Woodend had been watching his sergeant, and noticing how tense she seemed to be as she spoke into the phone.

Now he turned to Beresford and said, 'Why do I get the distinct feelin' that when you started tellin' me about Giles Thompson, your nervousness was only partly due to the fact that you were the new boy at the table, makin' his voice heard for the first time?'

'I don't know, sir,' Beresford said, deadpan.

'But there *was* another reason for it, wasn't there?'

'Yes, sir.'

'An' would you like to tell me about it?'

'I'd really rather not.'

Woodend shook his head. 'It doesn't work like that, lad. If you're goin' to be part of the team – even for a short time – you're goin' to have to learn to tell me what's on your mind.'

'I spoke out when I did in order to save Sergeant Paniatowski from further embarrassment, sir,' Beresford said.

'Now I wasn't expectin' that!' Woodend admitted. 'Would you mind spellin' out for me exactly what you meant?'

Beresford swallowed hard. 'You were talking about love affairs in general terms, sir, but I thought that there was a real danger that Sergeant Paniatowski might take it personally.'

'An' why should she have done that?'

'Don't you know, sir?'

'That's not the question, lad. I'm more interested in what *you* think *you* know.'

Beresford gulped again. 'For over a year, Sergeant Paniatowski was having an affair with Inspector Rutter,' he said.

160

'An' who *else* in Whitebridge HQ knows this – or, should I say, *thinks* they know this?'

'I can't speak for anybody above the level of sergeant.'

'Then don't. Who knows among the rank an' file?'

'Everybody,' Beresford said.

But of course they did, Woodend thought. He'd been foolish to ever imagine otherwise.

The servants in big houses the length and breadth of the country knew everything their masters were getting up to; the common soldiers, whether in barracks or out on the battlefield, were more aware of their officers' doings than the officers themselves ever dreamed they might be – and there were no secrets that could be hidden from the police canteen.

'Have you always had this instinct for protectin' other people like you just tried to protect Sergeant Paniatowski, Constable?' he asked.

'No, sir, it's something that's developed quite recently.'

'An' why do you think that might be?'

'I'd rather not say,' Beresford told him. 'And this time, I *mean* it.'

'Fair enough,' Woodend agreed.

Paniatowski returned to the table, and the moment she'd sat down she knocked back the rest of her vodka.

'Was that call anythin' to do with the case, Monika?' Woodend asked.

'No,' Paniatowski replied.

Woodend waited for her to tell him more, and when it became plain she wasn't about to, he said, 'So exactly where are we, in terms of the investigation, do you think?'

'We've got a fair number of leads to follow up on, but none of them are strong enough to indicate that it's the one we're really looking for,' Monika Paniatowski said.

'Which means?'

'That we have no choice but to keep plugging away at them until we get a breakthrough.'

'Aye,' Woodend agreed. 'An' while we're doin' that, we just have to pray that Major Maitland can keep control of his end of things, an' that the Chief Constable doesn't suddenly decide to go an' do somethin' bloody daft.'

Beresford looked down at his watch. 'If there's nothing else, sir, I think I'd better go,' he said.

'Go?' Woodend repeated. 'But there's three-quarters of an hour's drinkin' time left yet.'

'I know that,' Beresford agreed. 'But, you see, sir, my mother will be waiting.'

Woodend wondered if he was joking – and decided that he wasn't. 'Well, you'd better get yourself off, then,' he said.

Beresford stood up. 'Good night, sir. Good night, Sarge.'

As soon as the constable had gone, Woodend ordered more drinks.

'So what do you make of our new lad?' he asked Paniatowski.

'When you told me over the phone that he was on the case, I was annoyed,' Monika admitted. 'I didn't like the idea of bringing in somebody green – somebody who had no idea of how we work.'

So it's 'us' again, is it? Woodend thought. The way *we* work.

'Go on,' he said.

'I can't say I'm impressed by the fact that he's still so tied to his mother's apron strings that he has to dash off home well before closing time,' Paniatowski continued. 'But, despite that, I think I rather like him.'

'An' so you should,' Woodend said.

'Why?'

Because he stood up for you when your boss put his big size-ten foot right in it, Woodend thought.

'Doesn't matter,' he said aloud. 'Do you have any more thoughts on the case, or can we devote the rest of our evenin' to bitchin' about our beloved Chief Constable?'

'I've had more thoughts,' Paniatowski said. 'I've been worrying over what you said about learning more about people from extraordinary things they do than you ever can from the ordinary ones.'

'Yes?'

'That month which Burroughs spent in Manchester, seven years ago, doesn't fit into any pattern of behaviour he's displayed either before or since.'

'So?'

'So even though we're working against the clock, I think I'd like to take the time to go down to Manchester, and find out exactly what he was doing there.'

'An' what about your investigation in Dunethorpe?'

'As soon as I've finished in Manchester, I'll drive straight there and carry on where I left off.'

'So when do you think you'll actually be back in DCI Baxter's territory?' Woodend asked.

'Not too late,' Paniatowski replied, with a casualness which spoke volumes. 'I'll probably arrive in Dunethorpe shortly after lunch.'

The Siege: Day Three

Twenty-Six

Constable Colin Beresford awoke – just as he'd trained himself to – the moment he heard his mother moving around.

'Don't you try to do anything for yourself, Mum,' he called loudly. 'I'll be down to help you in just a minute.'

Up until a year earlier, he had always thought of Alzheimer's – on the rare occasions he had thought about it all – as an old people's disease. So it had been truly devastating to be told by the grave-looking doctor that his own mother had become a sufferer.

'But she's only sixty-one!' he'd protested.

The doctor had nodded, understandingly. 'I know. And it's rare for it to occur in anyone of your mother's age. But I'm afraid there's no doubt that that's what it is. It seems as if some people are just unlucky that way.'

Unlucky?

The word bounced around in Beresford's brain. Unlucky . . . unlucky . . . unlucky . . .

It wasn't unlucky at all! It was bloody tragic!

'What exactly will it do to her?' he asked – trying to be grown-up, trying to be brave.

'She'll become forgetful,' the doctor explained. 'The names of people and things she's familiar with will slip her mind. She won't remember certain events from the past. She may have trouble adding up her shopping bill.'

'And is that it?' Beresford asked, somewhat relieved. 'Is that as bad as it gets?'

The doctor shook his head. 'I'm afraid not. As the disease progresses, she may neglect to do simple everyday things.'

'Like what?'

'Comb her hair or brush her teeth, for example. Beyond that, she may take to wandering away from home with no fixed purpose. And she will almost certainly become unreasonably aggressive.'

167

'Is there nothing you can do about it?' Beresford had asked, anguished. *'No medicine? No injections?'*

'Nothing at all, I'm afraid. The disease will simply run its course.'

'Is it . . . is it my fault?' Beresford had asked.

The doctor frowned. 'How could it possibly be your fault?'

'My mum . . . my mum had me late in life. She was nearly forty when I was born.'

'I suspect that has nothing to do with her present condition,' the doctor told him. 'Many women have babies in middle age, but very few of them are struck with Alzheimer's, as your mother has been.'

Beresford should have left it at that – but he couldn't.

'Are you saying you could definitely rule it out as a reason, then?' he persisted.

The doctor hesitated – as if considering whether or not to tell a kindly lie – then said, 'Quite frankly, Mr Beresford, we know so little about the disease that we can't rule anything out.'

So that had been it. Beresford had gone straight round to the estate agent's office and told him he was no longer interested in taking the flat he had already put a deposit down on.

He had lost the deposit, but he didn't mind that.

He had lost his freedom – and he tried not to mind that, either.

Beresford dressed quickly, and went downstairs. His mother was standing in the kitchen. She was holding the kettle in her hand, but seemed uncertain about what to do with it.

'You're wearing your best suit,' she said, when she saw him. 'Why aren't you wearing your . . . your . . .'

'My uniform, Mum,' Beresford said patiently. 'Why aren't I wearing my *uniform*.' He paused, giving time for the word to sink into his mother's increasingly confused mind, then continued, 'Do you remember what I told you the day before yesterday, Mum?'

'The day before yesterday?' Mrs Beresford repeated.

'I said I'll be working with the CID for a while, didn't I? That's why I'll be wearing my suit instead of my . . . Instead of my *what*?'

168

'Instead of your . . . your uniform,' his mother said.

Beresford smiled. 'Good girl! I'll fix you your breakfast, then I'll have to go out. But don't worry, Mrs Watkins from across the road will pop in to see if you're all right in about half an hour.'

His mother looked at him blankly. 'Who's Mrs Watkins?' she asked.

Time had no real meaning in the vault of the Cotton Credit Bank, Major Maitland thought. Down here there were no shades of light and dark – no early mornings or late evenings.

And it was not only time which had gone awry. The whole world beyond the vault had ceased to be real to him. He could hardly conceive of buses and postboxes, of trees and flowers. He even found it difficult to picture Woodend – up there somewhere on the surface – conducting an investigation which just might clear his wife of murder charges.

He had experienced feelings like this before – on missions in the Middle East and in the Malayan jungle. Then, as now, the universe had contracted until it contained only the small area which was his immediate responsibility.

He looked down at his hostages. He had seen to it that they always had plenty of water. He had fed them with combat rations which, while being virtually tasteless, had been nutritious enough. When they had wished to go the toilet, he had granted them as much privacy as was possible in the circumstances. He had not physically abused them, nor – apart from the implied menace of the weapons he was carrying – even threatened to do so. He could justly claim that – according to the standards set by the rules of warfare – he had treated his prisoners well.

But all that would count for nothing once his world had expanded again, and he was on the outside once more. Nor, he admitted frankly, should it. He had done wrong – even by his own lights – and if he was picked off by a sniper's bullet, he would have no complaints.

He only hoped that it had not all been for nothing. That all the suffering he had put these people through – and the pain that was yet to come – would at least result in his darling wife gaining her freedom.

A new feeling began to creep through his body, making his nerve-endings tingle.

He recognized it for the warning it was.

It had always been like this, he reminded himself.

After days in the jungle – when nothing much had happened or even seemed likely to happen – he had known, instinctively, when violent confrontation was not far away.

Entering a probable enemy safe house in Aden, he had sensed the enemy lurking long before the first shot had been fired.

So that was it, then. This was the day that the siege would finally be ended – one way or another.

It was now twenty-four hours since Judith Maitland had first requested an interview with the Governor – and what a long, frustrating and agonizing twenty-four hours it had been.

She had expected the warden to say he was too busy to see her at first, but what she had not anticipated was how that same warden would react to her repeated requests.

'You're becoming hysterical again, Maitland,' Miss Donaldson had told her, when she'd made her second request an hour later.

Again? Judith thought. What does she mean – again!

'I've never been hysterical,' she said.

Miss Donaldson looked sceptical. 'And I suppose you think you never tried to kill yourself, either. Well, just look down at your wrists.'

'I'm fully aware I tried to kill myself, and I know what mental state I was in when I made the attempt,' Judith countered. 'I wasn't hysterical then, and I'm not hysterical now. And I demand to see the Governor!'

'Any more of this, and I'll call the nurse and have you sedated,' Miss Donaldson threatened.

Judith had waited a full two hours before she tried again. 'What I have to tell the Governor will end the siege in the bank in Whitebridge,' she said.

'Talk about delusions of grandeur!' Miss Donaldson scoffed.

'It's true! The man who's holding the hostages is my husband.'

'So criminality runs in the family. I can't say I'm surprised.'

*   *   *

It was not until late in the afternoon that Judith hit on the right approach.

'I know I've been difficult today, and I'd just like to thank you for the sympathetic way you've dealt with me,' she told the warder.

'Sympathetic?' Miss Donaldson repeated, mystified.

'I've been thinking about how to show my appreciation, and I've decided that the best way would be to make a donation to your favourite charity,' Judith continued. 'A hundred pounds seems just about right. You do have a favourite charity, don't you, Miss Donaldson?'

'Never really thought about it,' the warder confessed.

'Well, do think about it,' Judith urged her. 'And the next time my partner comes to see me, he'll bring the money in a plain envelope, so you can make the donation yourself.'

'All right,' the warder agreed. 'And about that other matter, Maitland? Your request to see the Governor?'

'Yes?'

'I'll see what I can do.'

Even with the bribe, she hadn't been granted an appointment that day, but she had been promised one for early the next morning. And now the morning had come!

So it will soon be over, Judith thought. I'll confess, and that will be the end of it.

Unless it was already too late! Unless Thomas had already gone off the rails, and hurt – perhaps even killed – one of the hostages.

They wouldn't tell her about it, even if he had. They'd listen to her confession – listen to her giving up all hope of ever getting a retrial – and say nothing to indicate that she was making a pointless sacrifice.

So perhaps she shouldn't do it at all!

Perhaps she should just keep quiet.

But she knew she couldn't do that – knew that even if there was the slightest chance of getting Thomas and his hostages out alive, she must grasp that chance wholeheartedly.

Twenty-Seven

Molly Ryder, who worked as a management trainee at Élite Catering, was a 23-year-old brunette who was nicely rounded – without being overblown – and had the most sparkling green eyes that Constable Colin Beresford had ever seen.

She was the sort of girl that any well-intentioned young man would want to take to meet Mother, Beresford told himself.

But how could he introduce *his* mother to anyone? How could he possibly start a relationship with a girl while knowing that, because of his mother's condition, they would have to do most of their courting at home – and that, as her condition gradually worsened, home would become an increasingly difficult and unpleasant place to be?

'I thought you were here because you wanted to ask me some questions,' Molly Ryder said.

'What?' Beresford asked, startled.

Molly laughed. 'You were miles away, weren't you?'

'Yes,' Beresford admitted. 'I was.'

'Then why don't we go right back to the start,' Molly suggested. 'Here I am in the kitchen, my only company the two dozen chickens that Mr Keene has told me to cook for the Rotary Club's monthly lunch. Right?'

'Right.'

'Then in walks a handsome young policeman – only I don't know he's a policeman at first, because he's wearing his Sunday suit. "Can I ask you some questions?" this handsome policeman asks, and I reply with a breathless, "Yes." I'm naturally disappointed when he reveals these questions are not on the lines of, "Do you come here often?" or "How about a dance?" Still, I agree. I abandon my chickens without a moment's regret, and we come into the office. But once we're here, I don't get the third degree, as I'm expecting – and almost looking forward to. Instead, the handsome young policeman – who should, by

172

rights, have been *very* interested in me – falls into some kind of trance.'

'Sorry,' Beresford said.

'So you should be,' Molly Ryder told him – and laughed again, to show she wasn't really offended.

'I wanted to ask you about Mrs Maitland,' Beresford said, trying his best to inject gravity into his tone.

'Yes, I thought that might be what this was all about,' Molly Ryder said, suddenly growing more serious. 'We all went into shock when we learned she'd been arrested. To tell you the truth, I think most of us are *still* a little bit in shock, even after all these months.'

'You got on well with her, then?'

'Yes, I did.'

'Try an' find out what Judith Maitland was really like, lad,' Woodend had advised Beresford. *'See if you can build up an accurate picture of her. That won't prove her innocence – if, indeed, she is innocent – but it might just give us somethin' to build on.'*

'How would you rate Mrs Maitland as a boss?' Beresford asked.

'Rate her?'

'Yes. You must know the sort of thing I'm after. How does she compare to the other people you've worked for?'

'I couldn't really say. I came here straight from catering college, so I haven't got anyone else *to* compare her and Mr Keene with. But I will say this – if all my future bosses measure up to them, then I'll have no complaints.'

'Did you notice any change in her state of mind in the weeks leading up to Mr Burroughs' murder?' Beresford asked.

'I did, as a matter of fact,' Molly Ryder said. 'Up until those last few weeks, she'd always been a very positive person. You know what I mean – lively, energetic, unflappable, even-tempered.'

'I get the picture.'

'But she suddenly became the opposite of all those things. She was moody, and irritable. She didn't really seem to care whether the job got done or not – and that was just not like her. At first, I put it down to nothing more than women's problems. We can all get a bit difficult at a certain time of the month. But it all went on a little too long for that.'

'And she was like this – you know, difficult – right up until the time she was arrested?'

'No, actually, she wasn't. She seemed much happier during the last few days. Maybe it was her brush with death that did it. You know how it is – you think all your problems are enormous, then you go through something like that, and it puts everything in perspective. Anyway, she—'

'Hang on a minute!' Beresford interrupted. 'What was that you just said about a brush with death?'

'You mean you don't know about it?'

'Obviously not.'

'She had a crash in her van.'

'The one she was arrested in?'

Molly Ryder laughed again. 'You'd not have needed to ask that question if you'd seen the van.'

'Messed up, was it?'

'It was a complete write-off. Anybody looking at it, without knowing the circumstances, would have thought the driver must have been killed. But Mrs Maitland came out of it with hardly a scratch. She was lucky that day. She's not been very lucky since, has she?'

'How did the crash happen?' Beresford wondered. 'Was she in a head-on collision or something?'

Molly Ryder shook her head. 'No, nothing like that. There weren't any other vehicles involved.'

'So what *did* happen?'

'Her brakes failed. I still don't see how it could have come about, because if there's one thing Mr Keene and Mrs Maitland always insisted on, it was that all vans went through regular safety checks.'

Chief Constable Henry Marlowe stood at the corner of the High Street, flanked by Slater-Burnes and Colonel Danvers. Overnight, two military armoured cars had been moved into position to replace the police vehicles which had previously been parked near the bank, but other than that very little about the scene had changed since the first morning of the siege.

'The longer this situation continues, the less the chances of

174

bringing it to a safe conclusion,' Colonel Danvers said ominously.

'Surely, that can't be right, can it?' Slater-Burnes asked.

'Why can't it?' Danvers wondered.

'Well, it seems to me that the longer it lasts, the more exhausted the hostage-takers become, and thus, the easier it is for a well-rested squad of men to catch them with their guard down.'

'Exhaustion can make men careless,' Danvers agreed, 'but it can also make them more nervous and more irrational. Once they're in that state, even a slight noise outside could make them think they're under attack, whether they are or not. What's even worse is that some word or action from one of the hostages – however innocuous – could drive them into an irrational rage. And if either of those things does happen, they may well start killing their captives.'

'But what can we do about it?' Slater-Burnes asked. 'As long as they've got the hostages wired up to explosives, we're helpless.'

'I'm not sure I still believe they *are* wired up,' Danvers said.

'You're not? What's changed your mind?'

'I've been going through Maitland's service record. He's tough. There's absolutely no doubt about that. But he's not one of the more . . . er. . .'

'More *what*?'

'Shall we just say that he doesn't strike me as one of the more "irresponsible" of our combat officers.'

'And what conclusions do you draw from that?'

'That I don't believe he's ever put civilians any more at risk than he needed to. That he just doesn't seem to me like the kind of man who would turn non-combatants into human bombs.'

'I want to be sure that I understand this properly,' Slater-Burnes said. 'You think he had no intention, at the beginning of the siege, of harming any of his hostages?'

'Correct.'

'But you believe that as time goes by – as he grows more tired and more irrational – his attitude to them may change, and he may positively *want* to hurt them. Have I got that right?'

'Essentially, yes, you have.'

'In that case, I think that we should storm the building as soon as we possibly can,' Slater-Burnes said. He turned his attention to Marlowe. 'What do you think, Chief Constable?'

'Me?' Marlowe asked, as if surprised to be finally consulted. 'Listening to the two of you discussing the situation, *I* think you both seem to have forgotten that you are here merely as advisors, and that I am still the man in charge.'

'Neither of us was trying to suggest—' Danvers began.

'And unlike you, I still have confidence in the men working under me,' Marlowe continued. 'Chief Inspector Woodend is a fine officer – a credit to his rank – and as long as he is of the opinion that the best way to proceed is as we have been doing so far, I am prepared to back him to the hilt.'

'I'm . . . er . . . surprised you place *so much* confidence in Mr Woodend,' Slater-Burnes said.

'Are you? And why might that be?'

'Well, to be perfectly honest with you—'

'Oh, by all means, *do* be perfectly honest with me,' Marlowe told the man from the Home Office. 'Honesty, as we all know, is a pearl beyond price.'

'Very well, since you now seem finally able to cope with an *honest* response, it is this,' Slater-Burnes said angrily. 'At the start of the crisis, I got the distinct impression that you had little idea what to do yourself, and no faith in Chief Inspector Woodend at all.'

Ah, but at the start of the crisis, I didn't see any way to turn things to my advantage, Marlowe thought. I was so busy trying to protect my own back, in case anything went wrong, that I didn't see how I could emerge with credit if everything went *right*. But I do now. And better yet, if things still *do* go wrong, the two people who'll find themselves up to their necks in shit are the Home Secretary and Charlie-bloody-Woodend.

'You're mistaken about my attitude to Chief Inspector Woodend, Mr Slater-Burnes,' he rebuked. 'I always have – and always will – support my men. I'm well known for it.'

Woodend and Beresford sat in the police canteen, mugs of steaming tea sitting in front of them, and cigarettes burning away in the ashtray. The woman behind the counter, who had been half-watching them since they first came in, thought the Chief Inspector looked deeply troubled – and she was right.

'Let me see if I've got this absolutely straight,' Woodend said, taking a sip of the tannin-drenched solution he'd just been served. 'You think there was an attempt to kill Judith Maitland just a few days before she was arrested for killing Clive Burroughs, do you?'

'I think there *may have* been an attempt,' Beresford said cautiously. 'The results of the tests carried out at the police garage are inconclusive. It's certainly *possible* that the braking system of the van was tampered with, but no one I talked to was prepared to rule out a mechanical failure, either.'

'But the vans *were* checked regularly?'

'Yes. That's what Molly Ryder told me, and when I asked Mr Keene, he confirmed it. In fact, the actual van that Mrs Maitland crashed had been in for a full service only a few days earlier.'

'So, given that the matter was never fully resolved, why wasn't there a follow-up investigation?'

Beresford shrugged. 'There probably would have been if Mrs Maitland hadn't then been arrested for murder, but once the supposed victim was out of the way – and likely to *stay* out of the way for a very long time – the investigation seemed to lose momentum. Besides . . .'

'What?'

'There's nothing about this in writing, you understand, sir, but I got the distinct impression that the experts had decided that if the brakes *had* been tampered with, they'd probably been tampered with by Mrs Maitland herself.'

'In other words, she tries to commit suicide, an' when that fails she thinks she might as well commit a murder instead?' Woodend asked sceptically.

'That's about the long and short of it,' Beresford admitted. 'There seems to be a general assumption at the police garage that there's no telling which way a disturbed mind will jump next.'

'So the glorified mechanics who call themselves forensic experts think they can do the psychologist's job as well, do they?' Woodend said. 'What's next? Will we be havin' the shrinks changin' wheels, and the CID washin' the windows?'

He paused to light a fresh cigarette from the smouldering butt of his old one. 'What do you think yourself, lad?'

'I wouldn't care to speculate, sir.'

'Then you're in the wrong job, son. Speculation is our stock in trade.'

'I *do* have an idea,' Beresford admitted. 'But it seems very far-fetched.'

'Let's hear it, anyway.'

'I think it's possible that Mr Burroughs tried to kill Mrs Maitland, and she just sort of . . . well . . . retaliated.'

'Or someone who had her best interests at heart – someone who'd worked out for himself what Burroughs had probably done – decided to retaliate *for* her?'

'That's possible, too,' Beresford agreed, relieved that Woodend had not dismissed his idea out of hand.

'How easy would it have been for Burroughs to tinker with the van, if he'd wanted to?' Woodend asked.

'As far as I can tell, there'd have been no problem at all. There are several vans in the fleet, and they were left on an unsupervised car park next to the catering company offices. On the morning of the crash, Mrs Maitland drove her own car to work, then transferred to the van. The accident – if that's what it was – happened a couple of minutes after she set off.'

'In other words, Burroughs could have doctored the van overnight, without anybody seeing him?'

'Yes.'

'But why the bloody hell would he?' Woodend asked, exasperatedly. 'What possible motive could he have had?'

'I don't know.'

'The problem is – an' always has been – that we don't understand anythin' like enough about the Maitland–Burroughs relationship,' Woodend said exasperatedly. 'Accordin' to his wife, they were lovers, but according to Judith, they weren't. The landlord of the Philosophers' Arms told Sergeant Paniatowski that a woman who he thought was Judith was about to bail Burroughs out of the hole he'd dug himself into. But we've no bloody idea why she should ever want to do that. We need answers, an' we're not getting' them – because Judith *won't* tell us, and Burroughs *can't*.'

'It's difficult,' Beresford said.

Woodend gave him the sort of look which had sent a shiver running through the veins of many an aspiring young detective before him.

'Nay, lad, you've got it wrong,' the Chief Inspector said. 'Walkin' a tightrope across Niagara Falls is *difficult*. The task we're facing is bloody near *impossible!*'

Twenty-Eight

The Westside Hotel made great play in its advertisements of being convenient for both Manchester's Victoria Railway Station and the city's main shopping streets. But it was also, Paniatowski noted, discreetly located on a side street, which meant that guests who were entering or leaving it would be unlikely to accidentally run into anyone they knew. It was, in other words, the ideal sort of hotel in which to have a lovers' tryst, and if she and Bob had ever brought their affair to Manchester, it was just such a hotel they would have been looking for.

Paniatowski had been prepared to pull all kinds of psychological levers in an effort to jolt the reception clerk's memory, but none of them proved to be necessary. The moment she showed him the picture, he nodded his head knowingly.

'Yes, I know him,' the clerk said 'He came here for years.'

'You're sure it was him?' Paniatowski asked – concerned that anything could be quite as easy as that. 'Couldn't you be confusing him with someone who just looked vaguely like him?'

'Absolutely not. I make a point of remembering all our regular customers, because if you know their names when they first come through the door, there's a better chance of a tip when they leave. But in Mr Burroughs' case, there's also the fact that he got himself murdered and had his face splashed all over the papers. I can even recall reading the article about it in the *Evening News*, and thinking to myself: Well, you've had the last ten bob tip you'll ever get out of him, Steve.'

'Did he come alone?'

The clerk grinned. 'You're testing me, aren't you?'

'Maybe,' Paniatowski conceded.

'He always brought his wife with him.'

'Really?'

'Really! The only thing was, it was a different wife every time,' the clerk said, in a tone which was half-disapproving, but also half-envious. 'I've lost count of the number of "Mrs Burroughses" who've tried out for themselves the strength of our bedsprings.'

'How long did they normally stay here – Mr Burroughs and all the Mrs Burroughses?'

'Only the one night. Mr Burroughs didn't need more than that. He knew what he wanted from them – and he knew where they kept it.'

'He once paid a bill for a whole month's accommodation,' Paniatowski pointed out.

'Yes, he did,' the clerk agreed. 'But that was different.'

'*How* was it different?'

'Well, for a start, the one he brought with him that time wasn't like his other women. She was no more than a girl, really. Very young, and very frightened-looking. A bit like how you'd imagine an injured fawn to be.'

'Very poetic,' Paniatowski said dryly. 'With your way with words, you're wasted in the hotel business. But you said the fact that she was only a girl was just a start. What else was different about her?'

'He normally booked a double room to entertain his lady-friends in, but this particular time he booked two single rooms with a connecting door. Of course, that wasn't really much of a surprise to me. I could see when they walked in that he hadn't brought her here for his usual purposes.'

'Why was that? Because she was so young? Or because she looked so frightened.'

'Neither,' the clerk said. 'It was because she was so *pregnant.*'

'What?'

'Didn't I say? She was nearly full-term. She went straight from here to the maternity hospital.'

*   *   *

Woodend and Paniatowski arrived at the prison within minutes of each other, and were shown into the visitors' room together. Judith Maitland did not seem particularly pleased to see the addition of a new face, but there was a steely resolve in her eyes and she was clearly not to be deterred from her purpose by Monika Paniatowski's presence.

'You're here because the Governor's told you about our interview, aren't you?' she asked.

'I'm not sure I know what you're talkin' about, Mrs Maitland,' Woodend admitted.

'You're not?'

'No.'

Judith Maitland sighed wearily. 'I asked for a meeting with the Governor yesterday morning,' she explained. 'I said it was urgent, but this place being what it is, I didn't get to see him until just over an hour ago. Once I was in his office, I told him everything.'

'About what?' Woodend asked.

'About the murder. I confessed that I had done what I was convicted of – that I had killed Clive Burroughs.'

'An' did you also explain *why* you killed him?'

'Yes.'

'Then explain it to me.'

'Why should I?'

'Because I'm askin' you to. An' because you really need to have me on your side.'

Judith Maitland nodded. 'All right. I killed Clive because he was my lover and—'

'You always said he wasn't.'

'I always said I didn't *kill* him. But that wasn't true, either.'

'Are you sayin' that Mrs Burroughs was right? That you actually carried on this affair of yours with his son Timothy present?'

'Not always. Sometimes Clive came alone.'

'But *some* of the time you did?'

'Yes.'

'In places like the *zoo*?'

'Not *in* the zoo, no. When we left the zoo, we'd drive somewhere else. With all the excitement, Timothy would be tired by then, and he'd fall asleep. That's when we'd do it.'

'In the car? Within touchin' distance of the boy?'

'Once Timothy was asleep, nothing would disturb him for a good hour. If he was in the front passenger seat, we'd do it in the back. If he was on the back seats, we'd have to manage somehow in the front. Occasionally, if we were in the countryside, we'd get out of the car and go behind some bushes. But we were always close enough to hear him if he woke up.'

'While you were *doing it*?'

'That's right.'

'I'm surprised that a woman from your background would use that phrase,' Woodend said.

'What phrase?'

'Doing it!'

'What would you expect me to say?' Judith asked scornfully. 'That we were having sexual intercourse?'

'No,' Woodend told her. 'What I'd expect you to say was that you were makin' love.'

'There was no love involved. I *love* my husband.'

'And yet you betrayed him?'

'I couldn't help myself.'

'Why did you kill your lover? Sorry, why did you kill the man you were *doin' it* with?'

'He said he didn't want to see me any more. I became hysterical. I don't remember reaching for the hammer, but I must have done, because the next thing I knew, it was in my hand and Clive was lying dead on the floor.'

'What happened to your overall?' Woodend asked.

'What overall?'

'The one you always carried in the back of your van.'

'Oh that. It was covered with blood.'

'So you were wearin' it when you went into the builders' merchant's, despite what you've said previously?'

'Yes.'

'An' despite the fact you were about to meet the man you were havin' an affair with?'

'Yes.'

'Funny that. Even if it was purely sexual, I'd have thought you'd have taken some care over your appearance.'

'Burroughs liked me in my overall. He found it sexy.'

'Well, there's no accounting for taste. So, because the overall was covered with blood, you got rid of it?'

'Yes.'

'How?'

'I threw it out of the van window on the way to the lay-by where the police found me.'

'The nightwatchman, who was one of the chief prosecution witnesses, said you weren't carryin' anythin' when you left the buildin'.'

'He was mistaken.'

'So you just threw it out of the van?'

'Yes. That's what I just said. Weren't you listening?'

'Then why was it never recovered?'

'I can't answer that. I can only tell you what happened. And now I have told you, I want to speak to my husband.'

'Why?' Woodend asked.

'Isn't it obvious? He's holding all those poor people hostage because he believes I'm innocent. Once I tell him myself that he's got it all wrong, he'll let them go. So can you please take me to see him?'

'Later, maybe,' Woodend said. 'But first, you're goin' to have to answer a few questions.'

'For God's sake, time is running out,' Judith Maitland said. 'And the sooner I can see him, the sooner I can put an end to this whole terrible business.'

'If he believes you,' Woodend pointed out.

'Of course he'll believe me! Why wouldn't he?'

'Because you haven't convinced *me* – an' I don't know you half as well as he does. So let's start again, Mrs Maitland. An' this time, we'll do it properly. This time, you'll tell me the whole truth. Will you agree to that?'

Judith Maitland's shoulders visibly slumped. 'What choice do I have?' she asked.

'None at all,' Woodend said. 'Let's begin with an easy question, shall we? When did you first meet Clive Burroughs?'

'I've told you that a dozen times! I met him at a reception that I catered in Dunethorpe last year.'

'Wrong!' Woodend said. 'I don't know exactly *where* you met, but I do know when. An' it wasn't last year at all. It was *seven* years ago.'

Judith Maitland already had a prison pallor, but now she turned even whiter. 'You . . . you . . .' she began.

'I know all about the baby, yes,' Woodend said. 'It's just the details I need you to fill in for me.'

Twenty-Nine

'I hadn't had much experience with men when I met Sebastian Courtney-Jones,' Judith Maitland said. 'He was tall and handsome, kind and attentive, and I suppose he simply swept me off my feet. I knew he was married, of course, but he said that he hardly even spoke to his wife any more, and that as soon as it was possible, he'd divorce her and we could be married.'

'An' then you got pregnant,' Woodend said.

'That's right. I was delighted at first. I thought it would do no more than speed our marriage up.'

'But when you told Courtney-Jones about it, he was somewhat less than thrilled?'

'He was furious. He said he didn't know how it could have happened. He said I must have tricked him into getting me pregnant. Unless, of course, the baby wasn't really his at all. I couldn't believe he was saying all these things. He didn't sound like my Sebastian at all.'

'I imagine that he said he'd be willin' to pay to get rid of it,' Woodend guessed.

'Yes, he did. He assured me it wouldn't be dangerous or unpleasant. Nothing like a back-street abortion, no hot bath and bottle of gin or a knitting needle. The man he'd send me to would be a proper doctor, though, of course, he wasn't allowed to practise any more.'

'You turned him down?'

'I had to. I knew I couldn't keep the baby myself – I'd never have coped – but I couldn't bring myself to have him aborted, either. I told Sebastian what I felt, and he said that if that was my attitude, then I was on my own. He wouldn't answer my calls after that, and a couple of weeks later he got his company to transfer him down south. I didn't know what to do.'

And then the man rings her. He has such a pleasant, reassuring voice on the phone.

'You don't know me,' he says, 'but I've heard about your difficulties, and I think I might have a solution.'

'Who told you?' she asks.

'That doesn't really matter, now does it?' the man answers, so softly, so kindly. 'Would you like to hear what my solution is?'

Yes, she desperately wants to hear – wants to be told that there is at least some possibility of a light at the end of the tunnel.

'There are many wonderful couples who desperately want to have children of their own, but can't,' the man says. 'Your baby would be like a gift from heaven for them.'

'Why don't they go to an adoption society?' Judith asks suspiciously.

'You've no idea how long their waiting lists are. And these couples don't want to wait. They want to give the best years of their lives to some lucky child, not leave it until they're too old to play a really important part in that child's growing up. And think of the advantages for you.'

'What advantages?'

'If you give your child to an adoption society, you'll have no idea who he's gone to. If you work through me, I'll allow you to meet the prospective parents, and if you don't like them, I'll find you another couple that you will like. Besides, these couples so desperately want to have children that they'll be happy to pay all your expenses from now until the child is born.'

'What's in it for you?' Judith asks.

'I collect a small fee – just to cover my administrative costs – but that's no concern of yours, because the new parents will pay it.'

'I agreed to go ahead with it,' Judith Maitland said. 'It seemed the best thing all round.'

'Did you meet the couple who were going to take your baby?' Woodend asked.

'Only the man.'

185

'My wife would love to have met you,' Clive Burroughs says, 'but she's simply not feeling strong enough at the moment. She's so very worried this will all fall through, and she's so set her heart on having a baby.'

And at the time, Judith believes it, because Burroughs seems so kind and so understanding. Later on, she will form a different opinion entirely. She will see how Burroughs likes to control every situation he finds himself in. She will understand that the Burroughses are not so much adopting a baby together as Clive is presenting the baby to his wife as a gift. To keep her quiet. To earn himself credit, so that when his next affair comes to light, she will forgive him again.

But Judith sees none of this now. When Burroughs suggests that she speak to his wife over the phone, she agrees, and Mrs Burroughs sounds like a very nice woman.

Monika Paniatowski's mind was back in Dunethorpe Police Headquarters, looking at the pile of documents which made up Clive Burroughs' personal papers. She'd known at the time that she was missing something important, and now she'd worked out what it was.

'Was the little girl also adopted?' she asked.

'No,' Judith Maitland replied. 'They'd always been told they couldn't have children, but then Mrs Burroughs got pregnant and had Emma. Apparently, it often happens that way.'

Tax forms, driving licences, passports, Paniatowski thought. Fishing permits, insurance policies, club membership cards. Burroughs' whole life had been documented on that desk. There'd been a birth certificate for Emma in that pile, too – but there hadn't been one for Timothy.

'Was it always planned that Burroughs would spend the entire last month of your pregnancy with you?' Woodend asked.

'Not as far as I know,' Judith Maitland said.

No one had even suggested it at first. But as the moment of giving birth draws closer and closer, Judith begins to have doubts about the course she has chosen – begins to think that she will keep the baby after all.

She does the decent thing, and tells the man who first contacted her. And he tells Clive. And Clive comes to see her.

'I know what the problem is,' he says. 'You're so worried

about having this baby on your own that you're really not thinking straight.'

She had not thought that was the problem, but he says it with so much conviction that she begins to believe it well might be.

'You poor girl,' Burroughs says. 'Well, I won't let it happen like that. You won't be alone. When it comes close to your time, I'll always be around. In fact, I'll book us a couple of rooms in a nice hotel I know, so that if you need me – at whatever time of day or night – you only have to call.'

She believes that he is doing it for her, *out of kindness. Later on, of course, she will realize that he did it for himself – because he knows that as long as he is close to her, he can nip in the bud any idea of her keeping the baby.*

'So the baby was born, and Burroughs took him away,' Woodend said. 'An' then, last year, you unexpectedly met Burroughs again, at an event which you were caterin'.'

'I'd never even considered the possibility, but the moment I saw him, I recognized him,' Judith Maitland said. 'And I realized that if he was there, my baby couldn't be far away.'

'You asked him if you could see your son?'

'Yes. I only wanted the briefest peek at him, yet I would have understood if Burroughs had said no. But he didn't. He said his wife must never find out, because she wouldn't agree to it, but if I was willing to keep her in the dark, he was quite prepared not only to let me see my child but to actually go out on excursions with him.'

'That's why you changed your mind about selling up your share of the business and moving around with your husband?'

'Yes. I'd only just found Timothy again. I simply couldn't bear the thought of going away from him.'

'Clive Burroughs' offer must have seemed like a dream come true,' Woodend said.

'It did.'

'But it was really the start of a nightmare?'

'Yes.'

'Burroughs' business was already in trouble, an' when he met you again – an' realized you were a successful caterer – he saw a way out of all his difficulties. But he played it craftily.

187

He let you see your son for almost a year before he put the squeeze on, didn't he?'

'And even then, he didn't come out and simply demand it,' Judith Maitland said bitterly. 'That wasn't his way.'

'So what *did* he do?'

'He said that if his business went bankrupt, he'd move his family to New Zealand. But I knew exactly what he meant – exactly what he was asking for.'

'So what did you do?'

'I talked it over with my partner, Stanley.'

'Why?'

'Because I needed to draw a substantial amount of capital out of the business, and there was no way I could do it without his consent.'

'And did he give that consent?'

'Not at first. But it wasn't the money he was worried about.'

'No?'

'Not at all. He said that even without checking the books, he knew the business was going so well that we could easily afford it.'

'Then what *did* he object to?'

'To giving in to blackmail. He said there'd be no end to it. Burroughs might claim he'd be happy with just the one payment, but he wouldn't be. He'd be back next year for another one. And the year after that, and the year after that. Stanley said I'd never be free of him.'

'An' Stanley was right,' Woodend said.

'I know he was. I even knew it at the time. But I was so desperate that I would have done anything. So I pleaded with Stanley. We had the first real argument we've ever had as partners, and it was a bloody one. But still he wouldn't budge.'

'But he *did* budge in the end, didn't he?'

'Yes.'

'So what made him change his mind?'

'I had a car accident. I wasn't really harmed at all, but it *could* have been very serious.'

'I know. I've heard about it.'

'It shook Stanley up almost as much as it shook me up. Maybe even more. He said if I had died, my last thought would probably have been about him – and how he had refused

188

to help me. He was in tears, even as he was telling me. Then he said that our friendship was worth more to him than all the money in the world. He still thought I was making a mistake, but if paying the blackmail was what I wanted, then he didn't feel he could stop me.'

'Did you actually get as far as paying Burroughs?'

'No. The reason I went to see him on the night he died was to tell him that we'd been getting the money together, and he could have it the next day.'

'Why did you keep quiet about Timothy being your child after you were arrested?' Woodend asked. 'You must surely have realized that if you'd told the judge that Burroughs was using your own son to blackmail you, you'd never have been given the sentence you were.'

'I'm not a fool! Of course I realized that.'

'Then why didn't you say anything?'

'Because it's bad enough that, when Timothy gets a bit older, he'll learn that his father was murdered. Imagine how much worse for him it would be if he was also told that the person serving time for that murder was his natural mother!'

Thirty

'Do you know what's goin' through my head right now, Monika?' Woodend asked, as he and Paniatowski walked across the car park towards Whitebridge Police Headquarters.

'I couldn't even begin to guess, sir,' Paniatowski replied.

'I'm thinkin' that if I come out of this bloody mess in one piece – an' it'd be a foolish man who'd be prepared to put any money on that – I just might have a bit too much to drink tonight.'

'Good idea.'

'In fact, I think I might just have *a lot* too much to drink. I could even achieve that state which students of philosophy call "utter leglessness", if I really put my mind to it.'

A man was coming out of the main door. He had his head down, and was holding his attaché case tightly under his arm.

'Good evenin', Mr Slater-Burnes,' Woodend said.

The man from the Ministry stopped, and looked up. His face was black with rage.

'The chap's a viper!' he said hotly.

'You'll be talkin' about our esteemed Chief Constable, will you, sir?' Woodend asked.

'He blindsided me,' Slater-Burnes complained. 'Went completely behind my back. Can you *believe* that?'

'Very easily,' Woodend said. He turned towards Monika. 'How about you, Sergeant? Can *you* believe it?'

'It's not really my place to comment on the actions of my superiors, sir,' Monika Paniatowski said, deadpan.

'I had no idea what he was doing until the very last minute,' Slater-Burnes continued angrily. 'Not a clue. And by the time I did get a glimpse of the way his devious, twisted mind was working, it was too late to do anything. Now he looks like the shining hero of the hour, and I look like nothing more than some kind of bumbling nincompoop.'

'You have my sympathies, sir,' Woodend said.

'Thank you, Chief Inspector. But bearing in mind that I'll be on the train for London in an hour, while you have to stay here and continue to work with the bloody bastard, I think you need my sympathies much more than I need yours,' Slater-Burnes replied.

The Chief Constable was sitting at his desk. Behind him, on the wall, were framed photographs of him shaking hands with important people, and certificates he had collected by attending courses at institutions located conveniently close to good golf courses.

The look on his face suggested that he thought the world was a very benevolent place to live in if your name happened to be Henry Marlowe – and that he had been waiting patiently to explain, to his least-favourite chief inspector, just why that should be.

'Ah, Mr Woodend, I'm glad you're here,' he said expansively, 'because I've got a little job I want you to do for me.'

'Have you, sir?' Woodend asked. 'An' what might that be?'

'Nothing much. Nothing that should stretch even *your* capabilities. I'd simply like you to go down to the Cotton Credit Bank on the High Street, and bring the siege to an end.'

'I'm sure we'd *all* like that, sir,' Woodend said. 'But I'm not entirely sure how I should go about it.'

'Of course you're not,' Marlowe said. 'But, you see, I am.' He picked up an impressive piece of paper which had been lying conveniently to hand on his desk, and held it out for the Chief Inspector to examine. 'All you have to do is show this to Major Maitland.'

'It's a Royal Pardon,' Woodend said, scanning it. 'I've never seen one before.'

'Few people have. It's not the kind of document you can get your hands on by merely collecting cigarette coupons.'

'An' it's for Judith Maitland.'

'It is, indeed, for Judith Maitland,' the Chief Constable agreed. 'The Home Secretary took a lot of persuading, but I did finally talk him into using his influence to get it issued.'

'Aren't you worried about the precedent it might set, sir?' Woodend wondered.

'Precedent? I don't know what you mean?' Marlowe said.

Of course he did, Woodend thought. He knew perfectly well. But he was playing out the game to its full extent – stretching his moment of triumph as far as he possibly could.

'It just might send out the message that if you have a relative in gaol, all you need to do to get him pardoned is take a few hostages,' Woodend said, playing a game of his own.

'That certainly would be the case if Mrs Maitland were to be allowed to get away with it scot free,' the Chief Constable said.

'But she won't be?'

'No, she most certainly won't.'

'Then what *will* happen to her?'

'The moment the hostages are freed, she'll be re-arrested. This time she won't be charged with *killing* Clive Burroughs, but only with causing him grievous bodily harm. Of course, she can't be given as long a sentence for GBH as she was for murder, but most of the public seem to think her current sentence was too harsh anyway. And so do the newspapers.'

'Ah, yes, the newspapers,' Woodend said.

The papers were Marlowe's Bible, he'd long ago realized, and if one of the popular ones suggested that it would be a good thing if all chief constables painted their backsides bright yellow, Henry Marlowe's hand would reach straight for the paint brush.

'So Judith Maitland ends up serving a stiff – but not excessive – sentence, and everybody's happy,' the Chief Constable concluded.

'Very clever,' Woodend said.

'I think so, too,' Marlowe said complacently.

'But I'm afraid that I can see just two little flaws to the plan,' Woodend added.

'And what might they be?'

'Well, the first is that you'll be trying her for the same crime twice. An' you can't do that under the rule of double jeopardy.'

'Haven't you been listening?' Marlowe demanded, irritably. 'It's the same *crime*, but a different *charge*.'

'Even so, it's splittin' hairs a bit, isn't it?' Woodend said dubiously. 'I'm almost sure that Judith Maitland's lawyers will find some grounds on which to object.'

'Well, of course her lawyers will find grounds on which to object, you bloody idiot. They'll be submitting motions to the Court of Appeal as soon as they learn what we're doing. And they won't stop there. They'll take it as high as the House of Lords, if they have to. And they might even win in the end.'

'Then I don't see—'

'But that will take *years*. We'll have all moved on by then – or, at least, *I* will. And do you think the general public will still care by that point? Of course not! They'll have completely forgotten about it.'

'But they'll still remember you as the man who found a way to end the siege of the Cotton Credit Bank,' Woodend said.

'Well, exactly!' Marlowe replied, pleased that the Chief Inspector had finally got the point.

'It's certainly very ingenious,' Woodend admitted. 'I don't think I would ever have come up with anythin' like that myself, even if I'd thought about it for a thousand years.'

'Quite,' Marlowe agreed. 'And that, Chief Inspector, is why I'm sitting in this chair, and you are not.'

'Yes, that must be the explanation,' Woodend agreed.

The taste of triumph in Henry Marlowe's mouth was

acquiring a slightly sour edge to it. For a moment, he wondered why that might be. And then he thought he knew.

It was not at all like Woodend to give in so easily and – for him – so gracefully, he told himself. The obnoxious Chief Inspector had to at least *believe* he had one more card left to play.

'Let's have it!' the Chief Constable said.

'Have what, sir?'

'You said that there were two flaws to what is – as you've admitted yourself – my *very* clever plan.'

'Yes, sir,' Woodend agreed. 'Now you come to mention it, I think I *did* say that.'

'Well, we've dismissed the first of your objections easily enough, haven't we? We've agreed that whatever ultimately happens to Mrs Maitland, I'll come out of the whole affair smelling of roses.'

'Have we, sir?'

'Haven't we, Chief Inspector?'

'Not really. If you do decide to charge Mrs Maitland with GBH, then I think you'll come out of it smellin' of somethin' else entirely.'

'I'm losing my patience with you, Chief Inspector,' Marlowe said. 'Why don't you just come right out with what's on your mind?'

'All right,' Woodend agreed. 'If you're goin' to charge anybody with GBH, then I think it should be the person who swung the hammer which stove in Clive Burroughs' skull.'

'And?'

'An' that, sir, *wasn't* Mrs Maitland.'

Thirty-One

It had been dark for more than an hour when Woodend and Colonel Danvers passed through the police barricade and entered the High Street. It had not been a particularly warm day, and with the setting of the sun it had grown bitterly cold.

From somewhere in the distance, Woodend could hear the

strains of the Salvation Army Band, playing their traditional carols. He'd almost forgotten that Christmas was so close, and he found himself wondering if, when the Queen made her Christmas Day Speech, he'd still be alive to watch.

'Maitland's been in there for over fifty hours now,' Colonel Danvers said, as they approached the nearer of the armoured cars. 'I know from experience that the strain must have been almost intolerable. God alone knows what state he's in, or what he's likely to do.'

'Well, you certainly do know how to motivate a man who's about to set off on a dangerous mission,' Woodend said dryly.

'You don't have to go, you know,' the Colonel told him. 'You could let me go, instead. I'm a soldier, like him. He'll listen to me.'

'No, he won't,' Woodend told him. 'It has to be me.'

'Then at least put on a flak-jacket before you enter the bank.'

Woodend shook his head. 'That'd be sendin' out all the wrong signals. He'll think I'm only wearin' it because there's an assault group followin' right behind me. If this is goin' to work, it has to be because he's sure that he trusts me.'

Danvers shrugged. 'Well, it's your funeral,' he said.

'You really *are* good at this motivational stuff, aren't you?' Woodend countered.

For the fourth time since the siege had begun, Woodend opened the heavy glass door and stepped inside the bank. He looked up at the camera Maitland had installed over the counter, waved his hand, and waited.

He did not have to wait long. The door behind the counter opened, and Major Maitland appeared.

'I didn't send for you,' he said angrily. 'You're only supposed to come when I send for you!'

He wasn't happy when things didn't go strictly according to his plan, Woodend thought. He liked to be in total control at all times. That was how the military mind operated.

But if this situation was going to work itself out without any loss of life, the Major was going to have to learn – and learn very quickly – to be a lot more flexible.

'Well, what's your explanation?' Maitland demanded.

'If I was the kind of feller who only came when he was sent for, I'd also be the kind of feller who wouldn't be of much bloody use to you,' Woodend replied.

'I gave you orders!'

'You told me what you wanted – which is not quite the same thing. An' I've done what you asked.'

'Has . . . has Judith been released?' Maitland asked – and there was a slight tremble detectable in his voice.

'No, she hasn't,' Woodend said. 'Not yet. But a Royal Pardon's been issued, an'—'

'I don't want *that*!' Maitland said, in a voice which was almost a scream. 'I don't want her *let off* for something people still think she did – I want it proved that she *didn't* do it at all.'

It's a pity Henry Marlowe isn't here on the firing line to listen to this, Woodend thought – a pity he isn't able to witness for himself how the brilliant scheme, which he'd thought would make his name, would never have worked.

But then, it had never been on the cards that the Chief Constable *would* be there, had it? The words 'Marlowe' and 'firing line' had never belonged in the same sentence.

'I know you wouldn't be happy with just a pardon,' he said to Maitland. 'An' you don't have to be. I know who the real murderer is, an' when you've let the hostages free, I'll arrest him.'

'Why not do it the other way round?' Maitland demanded. 'Why not arrest the killer first?'

'Because that will take too long.'

'I've got plenty of time,' Maitland said. 'All the time in the world.'

'No, you haven't,' Woodend countered. 'You an' your lads must be worn down to a frazzle. Just listenin' to you, I can tell your judgement's almost gone. You'll make a mistake soon – and somebody will end up gettin' killed.'

'My team and I are just as much in control as we were at the start of this operation,' Maitland said.

'How do you expect me to believe that, when you don't even believe it yourself?' Woodend wondered. 'Besides, even if it were true, I don't know how much longer I can hold back Colonel Danvers an' his lads, who are just burstin' to come in here an' take a crack at you.' He paused for the merest moment. 'You've got everything you wanted, Major – or you will have soon, anyway. It's time to put an end to all this.'

Maitland hesitated. 'How do I know I can trust you?'

'You have no choice. Look, if all I'd wanted to do was con you, I could have done a better job than this. Say that, instead of comin' in alone, I'd brought some feller with me who confessed, in front of you, to havin' killed Clive Burroughs. Would that have made you any happier?'

'It might have,' Maitland said uncertainly.

'No, it bloody wouldn't! Because, for all you'd know, the man could be an actor from Whitebridge Rep. So ultimately, it's your decision, an' your judgement. Do you have faith in me, or don't you?'

Maitland's hesitation was longer – agonizingly longer – this time.

'I want to know *who* killed Burroughs,' he said finally.

'An' so you will.'

'There's more. I want to know *why* he killed him, and how you *know* he killed him.'

'That sounds fair enough,' Woodend said.

And told him.

Woodend stood in the bank doorway, painfully aware that he was right in the sights of a dozen sniper rifles.

'I need to speak to Colonel Danvers!' he shouted in the direction of the nearest armoured car. 'He can approach. He'll be quite safe. I've Major Maitland's word on that.'

Danvers appeared from behind the armour-plating, and walked quickly across the street.

'Are you all right?' he asked.

'No,' Woodend replied. 'I'm crappin' myself in case somethin' goes wrong – but I do have a deal.'

'What kind of deal?'

'You're to clear the High Street completely of both your men and the police. You can leave the normal street-lightin' on, but all the searchlights will have to be switched off. Once you've done those two things – an' Maitland's made sure you've done them – he'll let all the hostages out.'

'Why *should* he want the street cleared and the searchlights off?' Danvers asked suspiciously.

'He didn't say.'

'And you didn't *ask* him?'

'What the hell's the matter with you, Colonel?' Woodend demanded. 'You wanted the hostages released, an' he's releasin' the bloody hostages. Why are you quibblin' about the small print?'

'You have a point,' Danvers conceded. 'Anything else?'

'Maitland an' his men are prepared to surrender themselves to you, but not immediately.'

'Why *not* immediately? What's the point of a delay?'

'You're askin' questions that I don't know the answer to, again. But if you want my *opinion*, I think they're hopin' that by surrenderin' on their own terms, they'll manage to salvage a little of their dignity.'

'And they trust us to respect their terms?'

'No, of course they don't bloody trust you. Neither would I, in their place. But they're hopin' you won't endanger the life of a senior police officer unless you absolutely have to.'

'What?'

'I'm to stay in the bank with them until they surrender. So if I can make a personal plea here, I'd appreciate it if you didn't go in for any "death or glory" tactics even once the hostages are completely clear of the building.'

'Did you volunteer to stay with them?'

'Of course I didn't volunteer!' Woodend said. 'Nobody in his right mind would bloody volunteer. But,' he conceded, 'I did *agree* to it.'

'Aren't you concerned about your own safety?'

'No,' Woodend lied. 'Maitland wants me alive, if only because I'll be no bloody good to him dead.'

An' I hope those two lads he's got with him also take that view, he added silently.

Woodend had seen cowboy films in which cattle were herded into a corral, and the exit of the hostages reminded him very much of them. They came out of the back room in the twisted, disorganized caterpillar formation, which was all that the door-space allowed. They looked neither to the left nor right, but focused only on the front door and the freedom which lay beyond it. They were clumsy and confused. They stank – even from a distance – of sweat, fear and bowels which had not been able to quite contain themselves. They were an undignified stream of frightened humanity – and Woodend, who had sweated and worried enough himself – found it one of the most beautiful sights he had ever seen.

'What now?' he asked Major Maitland, once the hostages had cleared the building.

'I thought I'd already made that plain,' Maitland answered. 'We wait.'

'For how long?'

'Until I say we *stop* waiting.'

Minutes ticked by. Woodend's legs ached, and he was starting to develop a fiendish headache.

'Why haven't your lads joined us?' he asked.

'Why should they?' Maitland replied.

'Why *shouldn't* they?' Woodend countered. 'It's not exactly the Ritz in here, but I'm sure it's a bloody sight pleasanter than it is down in that vault. An' now the hostages have gone, an' there's nobody left to guard, there's no *reason* for them to stay down there, is there?'

'Perhaps they like it in the vault,' Major Maitland suggested.

'They've gone, haven't they?' Woodend said, with a sudden insight into Maitland's tactics. 'They put on civvies, and left with the hostages.'

'That's right,' Maitland agreed. 'When they volunteered for this mission, I promised I'd get them out in one piece if I possibly could – and that's just what I've done.'

'They'll be caught, you know.'

'I doubt it. In all the confusion out there, they'll have found it easy enough to slip away.'

'An' how will they get out of Whitebridge?'

'Transport has been waiting to whisk them away ever since we first entered the bank.'

'So *that's* why we're waitin'? To give them a chance to get away?'

'That's why we're waiting.'

'Even if they manage to get clear of Whitebridge, they can't run for ever,' Woodend pointed out.

'They won't need to. They both have alibis for at least a good part of this siege.'

'Alibis can be broken.'

'Not these alibis. They'll be provided by their comrades, and they'll *never* be broken. That's something you should realize about the professional army, Chief Inspector – we know how to look after our own.'

'An' what about you? You've no chance of gettin' away.'

'True,' Maitland agreed, 'but I've got what I wanted, and I'll take full responsibility for my actions.'

'You'll be in prison for a long time.'

'Better me than Judith. I'm a hard man, Mr Woodend.'

'An' *prison* is hard – even on hard men.'

Maitland laughed. 'Men's gaols aren't run by the authorities. You know that. *Real* control's in the hands of just a few prisoners, and I'm going to be one of them. Within six months, I'll be running whatever prison they put me in.'

'I wouldn't be surprised if you were,' Woodend admitted. 'Did you really have the hostages wired up to explosives?'

'The most important thing about wars – and this *was* a war of sorts – is what the people involved in them believe,' Maitland said. 'Clive of India defeated forces many times the size of his own, because the enemy *believed* he would defeat them. The armies opposing Napoleon knew they would lose *because* they were opposing Napoleon.'

'An' it wasn't necessary to wire up your hostages because the people outside believed you had?'

'Colonel Danvers might have been willing to take the chance that I hadn't – and stormed the place on that basis. But wiser heads than his, higher up the chain of command, would never have let him get away with it.'

'So the only real danger to the hostages was that they might get shot – either by your men, or by Colonel Danvers' lads?'

'They were in no danger from my men,' Maitland boasted. 'My men are well trained. They would never have done anything without a direct order from me – and I would never have given that order. I was always prepared to risk my own life, Chief Inspector, but never anyone else's.'

It was truly amazing just how arrogant the military mind could be, Woodend thought. It was almost *inconceivable* that anyone could be so sure he could maintain complete control over two armed men who were trapped in a fraught situation which might well cost them their lives.

'You don't believe me, do you?' Maitland asked. 'You think I'm just a bull-headed officer who has no idea what his men really think, or what they might really do.'

'My opinion doesn't actually matter, does it, Major?' Woodend said. 'Not any more.'

'I still wouldn't like you to go away with the wrong impression,' Maitland replied.

And Woodend realized that now it was all over – now he had got everything he wanted – the Major was actually starting to enjoy himself!

'Do you have a sense of humour, Mr Woodend?' Maitland asked. 'Is your mind finely tuned to the little ironies of life?'

'Depends who you talk to about me,' Woodend replied. 'Some of the people I work with think I'm a real comedian, but I don't think my Chief Constable finds me very funny. Why do you ask?'

'Just curious,' Maitland said.

He placed his submachine gun on the counter, and took his service revolver out of its holster.

He looked totally exhausted, Woodend thought. And much worse than that – he looked as if he were about to do something incredibly stupid.

'Listen, Major—' the Chief Inspector began.

'I've been thinking over what you said,' Maitland interrupted him. 'And perhaps you're right. Perhaps a long prison sentence is too much of an unbearable strain for *any* man to stand.'

They were roughly fifteen feet apart, and there was a counter and grille dividing them. True, there was a way under the counter. But using that would take time, and if Maitland tried what he seemed *about* to try, Woodend knew that however fast he moved, he would get there too late.

'I thought you said you'd be running any prison they sent you to within six months,' Woodend said desperately.

'I did, didn't I?' Maitland agreed. 'But that was mere bravado! The truth is much colder and much more depressing.'

Woodend shifted his weight on to his right foot. The odds

against reaching Maitland in time remained as astronomical as they'd ever been, but he was still prepared to give it a try.

'It would be very foolish of you to attempt any heroics at this stage of the game, especially with a man so obviously determined to kill *somebody*,' Maitland said. 'If I were in your position, my dear Chief Inspector, I'd just stand there and let it all happen.'

'Wait!' Woodend croaked.

Maitland put the barrel of his gun in his mouth, and pulled the trigger. There was a loud click, then the Major withdrew the pistol again.

'No bullets,' he said. He smiled. 'As I told you, it's what the enemy believes that really matters in warfare. We had guns, so it was assumed they were loaded. But they weren't. We didn't bring a single round of ammunition with us. And there was obviously no need to, was there?'

'You bastard!' Woodend said with feeling. 'You complete bloody bastard!'

Maitland's smile broadened. 'I thought you said you had a sense of humour, Mr Woodend. It's not much in evidence now, is it?'

Thirty-Two

Most of the Élite Catering building was in darkness, but a light was burning in the office, which meant that Stanley Keene was still hard at work.

Woodend parked his Wolseley next to the small fleet of white vans which belonged to the business. They were a good advertisement in themselves, he thought. They looked neat, they looked efficient, and – apart from their number plates – they were identical.

He walked along the row, checking the back doors of each one. They were all locked.

Well, that was only to be expected. Probably one of the first things that Élite Catering emphasized to its employees was that the vans must *always* be locked when they were left unattended, and – over a period of time – checking that they were would have become a habit with all the company's drivers.

A car appeared in the distance, and as it drew closer, Woodend could see that it belonged to one of the local taxi firms. When a light came on in the foyer of Élite Catering, the Chief Inspector supposed that it was in response to the taxi's imminent arrival, and then the vehicle signalled to pull in, and he knew he was right.

The main entrance door of the business opened, and two people stepped out. Woodend could see them quite clearly in the illumination which shone from the foyer, but – standing in the shadows as he was – he was not sure that they could see him.

One of the people was Keene himself, the other a woman who looked to be in her early seventies. The caterer led the woman slowly to the taxi, and opened the back door for her.

'Why don't you come home with me, Stanley?' the woman asked, in a thin, reedy voice.

'I can't, Mother,' Keene said regretfully. 'Not this close to Christmas. I've got far too much to do.'

'You work too hard,' his mother complained. 'You're never away from this place. That's the only reason I ever come here – because it's the one real chance I get to see you.'

'You know I wouldn't do it if I didn't have to,' Keene told her. 'You know I'd *much* rather spend my time with you. But now that Judith's not here any more, I'm having to do twice as much as I used to.'

'All work and no play make Jack a dull boy,' his mother said sternly.

Keene laughed. 'Do you think *I'm* dull, Mother?'

'No, no, of course not,' his mother said hastily. 'But I wish you had more time to enjoy yourself.' She paused. 'I wish you'd find yourself a nice girl.'

'Now, Mother . . .' Keene protested.

'It's not right that you're still not married at your age,' his mother told him. 'I want some grandchildren before it's too late.'

'Maybe once the Christmas rush is over, I'll find the girl of my dreams,' Keene said.

'Do you promise?' his mother demanded.

'I'll certainly try my best,' Keene said. 'Is that good enough for you?'

'It'll have to be, won't it?' his mother said sourly.

Keene bent down and kissed her gently on the cheek. 'I'll be home as soon as I can be,' he said. 'I love you, Mother.'

'And I love you, too,' his mother replied. 'That's why I want to see you happily settled down before I die.'

Keene helped the old woman into the taxi, and closed the door behind her. Once she was settled inside, the driver pulled away.

Woodend coughed.

'Who's there?' Keene asked, turning in his direction.

The Chief Inspector stepped out of the shadows. 'It's me.'

'Has something happened, Mr Woodend?' the caterer asked, looking worried.

'Aye,' Woodend replied. 'The siege is over. An' since you risked your neck by comin' into the bank with me, I thought it was only fair that you should be one of the first ones to know about it.'

'Over!' Keene repeated. 'It's over! But has it . . . was it . . .?'

'It all happened without a shot bein' fired,' Woodend reassured him. 'The hostages have been freed, an' Major Maitland's been taken into custody.'

Keene seemed to be temporarily frozen to the spot. 'I should feel elated,' he said. 'But I don't. I just feel sort of . . . numb.'

'Relief can do that to you,' Woodend reassured him. 'It's a perfectly normal reaction in the circumstances. So how about a drink?'

'What?'

'A drink. If anythin' was ever worth celebratin', then it's this, don't you think?'

'Of course,' Keene said, thawing a little. 'You're quite right. Come inside, Mr Woodend.'

He led Woodend through the foyer, and into his office. It struck Woodend, as it had the last time he'd been there, that the office was a perfect blend of functionality and taste – the functionality exemplified by the thoroughly businesslike desk and filing cabinet, the taste displayed in two fine easy chairs with an attractive glass coffee table between them.

203

'Take a seat,' Keene said, pointing to one of the easy chairs, then walking over to the rather twee cocktail cabinet which stood in one corner of the room. 'I don't have any beer, I'm afraid – I never touch the stuff myself – but I do have some rather fine French brandy, if you'd care to sample that.'

'Champion,' Woodend said.

Keene poured the drinks and sat down opposite Woodend. 'What finally convinced the Major to give up?' he asked. 'I assume that he *did* give up, didn't he?'

'Yes, he did,' Woodend agreed. 'It's hard to say at what point he was finally persuaded, but I think it may have been when I told him I think I can get Judith released.'

'You can? On what grounds?'

Woodend took a sip of the brandy. 'Very nice,' he pronounced. 'You'd think a man who'd supped as much ale as I have would have destroyed his taste for anythin' more refined, wouldn't you? But let me tell you now, I haven't. This stuff doesn't just stroke the palate – it makes love to it.'

'I asked you on what grounds you thought you could get Judith released,' Keene said impatiently.

'Oh that!' Woodend said. 'On the grounds that she didn't do what she was convicted of.'

'I always knew she was innocent,' Keene told him. 'But can you actually *prove* it now? Have you managed to come up with some new evidence which clears her name?'

'Not what you – as a layman who knows nothin' about the way the law an' the courts work – might think of as evidence,' Woodend admitted. 'But it's evidence of sorts.'

'Tell me more.'

'There's two basic kinds of evidence – hard evidence an' circumstantial evidence.'

'Yes, I *do* know that.'

'Now the case against Judith was entirely circumstantial. She'd been at the scene of the crime round about the time Burroughs was killed, she was presumed to be his lover, an' there was no sign of her caterin' overall which – everybody agrees – should have been in the back of the van. The prosecution thought it had an open an' shut case. An' it has to be said that the jury agreed with it. But the more you learn about *other* circumstances, the less convincin' the case looks. For example, Judith wasn't Burroughs' lover, was she?'

'No,' Keene agreed. 'She most certainly wasn't.'

'In fact, the only reason she was interested in him at all was because he could give her access to her child,' Woodend said.

Keene's jaw dropped. 'You . . . you know about that?'

'Aye,' Woodend said. 'Though I've only found out about it recently, whereas you've known all along.'

'I wanted to tell you. Truly I did. But Judith made me promise I'd never reveal the secret to anybody.'

'An' you kept your word,' Woodend said. 'But now it *is* all out in the open, you will admit that Judith would never have had anythin' to do with Burroughs if it hadn't been for Timothy?'

'Of course I'll admit it. She loves Thomas. She'd never have thought of looking at another man.'

'Just so,' Woodend said. 'But to get back to our friend, the late Clive Burroughs. He suckered her in beautifully, didn't he? There were no strings to her seeing Timothy at first, but once he'd got her so attached to the boy that she couldn't bear the thought of losing him again, he put the squeeze on her. Pay up, he said, or I'll take the kid to New Zealand.'

'It's hard to imagine a man being so cruel,' Stanley Keene said.

'Now, there are some people who would argue that this blackmail attempt was an even stronger motive for Judith to kill Burroughs than if he *had* actually been her lover. But I have to say that I'm not one of them.'

'Neither am I,' Keene said. 'I knew she could never have done it. I said it all along.'

'So you did,' Woodend agreed. 'But, with the greatest respect to you, Mr Keene, your argument for her innocence is based on emotion, whereas mine is based on logic.'

'Does that matter, as long as we've both reached the same conclusion?' Keene asked.

'Not to us, maybe,' Woodend said. 'But it will to the authorities. So this is the way I'll argue it with them: I'll say that the very *worst* thing Judith could have done in her situation was to kill Burroughs. An' why? Because that would be

205

tantamount to abandoning all hope of gettin' close to Timothy ever again. She was almost bound to be arrested, an' even when she eventually came out of prison, Timothy would never agree to see the woman who'd killed his father, would he?'

'Exactly,' Burroughs agreed.

'Anyway, she'd already solved her problem – at least temporarily,' Woodend continued. 'Burroughs wanted money, an' she was prepared to give it to him. So, while it was far from an ideal situation for her to find herself in, she could have kept on seein' her son. An' why should she want to jeopardize that?'

'You're right, of course,' Keene agreed.

'What I don't *quite* understand is why you, her friend and partner, didn't try to persuade her to use that same argument at her trial,' Woodend said.

'I did,' Keene told him. 'But she wasn't having any of it. She said the important thing was to protect Timothy. He must never know what had really happened.'

'What a woman!' Woodend said.

'What a woman!' Keene agreed.

'An' I suppose, given the sacrifices she was prepared to make to keep the secret to herself, we should respect her wishes in the matter,' Woodend said. 'I think, on balance, we have no choice but to continue to protect young Timothy from the terrible truth.'

Stanley Keene looked troubled, but said nothing.

'Is somethin' botherin' you, Mr Keene?' Woodend asked.

'Well, yes,' Keene admitted. 'Without Timothy, the whole argument you were going to use to get Judith released simply collapses.'

'You're quite right, Mr Keene,' Woodend agreed, frowning. 'That's a real problem, isn't it?'

'A real problem,' Keene echoed.

Woodend's frown melted away, and was replaced by a broad smile which suggested that a brilliant idea had just occurred to him.

'We'll just have to switch to Plan B, then, won't we?' he asked brightly.

'Plan B? What's Plan B?'

'Plan B is this,' Woodend said. He reached into his jacket

pocket, produced a single sheet of paper, and handed it across the coffee table to Keene. 'Read it.'

Keene scanned the page, and with each line he read, his expression grew more troubled. He reached the end, then read through it again, as though he couldn't quite believe what he had seen the first time through.

'But this is a statement to the police,' he said. 'Made by me!'

'The *draft* of a statement,' Woodend corrected him. 'Nothing but a bald outline. I'm sure it'll read so much better when you've got round to putting it in your own words.'

'You want me to say that I thought Clive Burroughs actually *was* Judith's lover?'

'That's right.'

'But I didn't! You *know* that.'

'Nobody else knows, though, do they? An' if you can lie convincingly – which should present you with absolutely no difficulty at all – the rest of the world will be completely taken in.'

'You also want me to say that I thought he was mistreating her?'

'Exactly. Again, we can work out the details later, but I suggest you say somethin' like you noticed there were bruises on her arms an' face after she'd been with him.'

'And . . . and . . . you want me to confess that because I thought he was mistreating her, I killed him?'

'Yes, that's about the gist of it.'

'Are you insane?' Keene demanded.

'No,' Woodend said calmly. 'An' neither are you. That's why you'll eventually agree to make the statement.'

'You're dreaming!' Keene told him.

'Just consider your options for a moment,' Woodend suggested. 'If you play it my way, you'll be standin' in the dock as a man who murdered through love. You did it for no other reason, you'll claim, than to protect Judith. You'll probably be a hero in the eyes of the jury. An' you'll *certainly* be a hero in your mother's eyes. You'll be sent down – there's no doubt about that – but you'll be very unlucky to be given a sentence as long as the one that was handed out to Judith.' He paused. 'Now consider the other possibility.'

'*What* other possibility?'

'You'll be standing in the dock as a man charged with one murder, an' one attempted murder – crimes motivated not by altruism, but by greed. And what will your mother think of that?'

'Leave my mother out of this, you bastard!' Keene said.

'There's no way you can also be charged with arrangin' for an innocent woman to be locked away for a crime she didn't commit, but you don't seriously believe the judge is goin' to forget that – even for a moment – do you?'

'Wait a minute!' Keene said. 'Did you say I'd be charged with one murder and one *attempted* murder?'

'That's right.'

'This is going even beyond the realms of fantasy. Just who am I supposed to have *attempted* to murder?'

'Judith, of course.'

Keene looked wildly about him, as if hoping that some escape route had magically opened in one of the walls.

'Judith?' he croaked. 'But why, in God's name, would I ever have tried to kill her?'

'For money. Or rather, for the lack of it.'

'For *money*?'

'It's the only motive that fits the circumstances,' Woodend said. 'The only one that makes any sense of this whole tragic mess.'

Keene raised his hand to his mouth, and bit into one of his immaculately manicured fingernails.

'Well, it certainly doesn't make any sense to me,' he said weakly.

'Of course it does,' said Woodend, brushing the denial aside. 'Judith wanted to withdraw money from the company to pay off Burroughs. But – though she didn't know it herself, because she trusted you to look after the books – there wasn't any money to withdraw.'

'You could never prove that!' Keene protested.

'No, not me personally,' Woodend agreed. 'I'm not much good with figures. But by the time the forensic accountants have been over your books, I should have all the evidence I need.'

'So I tried to kill Judith, did I?'

208

'Yes.'

'How?'

'By doctorin' the brakin' system of the van she was drivin'. At first I thought it might be somebody else. Sebastian Courtney-Jones, for example. He might have done it because he was enraged that she wouldn't go back to him when he wanted her to.'

'Yes, he certainly might—'

'Or Mrs Burroughs – who may have really believed Judith was havin' an affair with her husband.'

'She's also a poss—'

'But it couldn't have been either of them.'

'Why not? Both of them seem perfectly plausible to me.'

'I should have seen right away why they couldn't have done it,' Woodend said, shaking his head at his own slow thinking on the matter. 'But it wasn't until I was walkin' alongside your small fleet of identical white vans that the truth finally hit me.'

'What truth?'

'*Identical* white vans, Mr Keene. Not one kind of van for the bosses an' another kind for the ordinary workers. They all look exactly the same. So who'd know which particular one Judith would drive away in the followin' mornin'? You would, Mr Keene! An' *only* you.'

'If all this is true, how do you explain the fact that, having once tried and failed, I didn't make a second attempt?' Keene asked.

'Ah, because you'd thought through the implications of her death by then,' Woodend said. 'And you'd realized it wouldn't make things better for you. In fact, it would make things worse.'

'Insane!' Keene said. 'Totally insane.'

'Judith's husband would have inherited her half of the business, wouldn't he? An' he's a military man, with a very orderly mind. He'd have had his own accountants in here before you'd had time to turn around – an' they'd soon have discovered the huge hole in the accounts.' Woodend lit up a cigarette. 'Where did the money go, by the way?'

'I told you, I didn't—'

'You might as well tell the truth – on this matter at least – because it won't take the police accountants long to find the holes.'

209

'I had a friend,' Keene said sadly. 'A very dear friend – or so I thought. He told me about this wonderful business opportunity. All he needed was a little backing, to get it started.'

'An' then he vanished into thin air – an' the money with him,' Woodend guessed.

'That's right,' Keene agreed. 'But Élite's not bankrupt, you know. It's still a very profitable business, and I could have paid back all the money I'd borrowed, given time.'

'But Judith didn't give you the time, because she wanted money immediately,' Woodend said. 'You should have confided in her, you know. I'm sure she would have understood. She knew all about the kinds of things that people will do for love.'

'But just because I'm an embezzler, it still doesn't mean that I'm a murderer,' Keene said defiantly.

'No, it doesn't,' Woodend agreed. 'But I haven't finished paintin' the picture for you yet. This jury at your trial is goin' to be askin' itself several important questions. An' one of those questions is goin' to be, "Who knew that Judith was plannin' to meet Burroughs that night?" Well, it could only be somebody who shared with her the secret of *why* she was meetin' him. An' that somebody is you.'

'Dozens of people could have known that *Burroughs* was going to be there that night,' Keene said. 'Hundreds of them!'

'I don't think he would have told anybody at all about what he was doin',' Woodend said. 'It was as much in his interest as in Judith's to keep the reason for their meetin' a secret.'

'He could have been followed there. His wife could have followed him. Or anybody else, for that matter.'

'An' then there's the question of Judith's overall,' Woodend continued, unperturbed. 'That was a big black mark against her at her trial. The jury assumed that, because of the bloodstains it had acquired durin' the course of the murder, she'd thrown it away. But we know she didn't kill him, so it wouldn't be bloodstained at all. Besides, there was a witness to her leavin' the buildin' – a nightwatchman called Goodrich – an' he's convinced she didn't have it with her.' He paused. 'By the way, that nightwatchman didn't only see Judith – he also saw you.'

'You must think I'm a complete fool,' Keene said angrily.

210

'What makes you say that?'

'If the nightwatchman had seen me – which he couldn't have done, because I wasn't there – he would have told the police at the time.'

'Ah, but he didn't *know* he'd seen you,' Woodend said. 'He claims he saw Judith drive up. But he's wrong about that. What he *actually* saw was simply a white van with the words "Élite Catering" written on the side. Then he went off to have his brew, an' to listen to the radio for a few minutes. When he came back, he saw Judith drive away in what he thought was the *same* white van. That's how he was sure she'd been there for fifteen minutes. But she hadn't – and it wasn't. What he'd actually seen was two white vans from the same fleet – the first driven by you, an' the second driven by Judith.'

'You'll never be able to prove that,' Keene told him.

'Probably not,' Woodend said easily. 'But with all the other proof I've got, I won't need to, will I? Let's get back to the overall, shall we? What actually happened to it?'

'How can you possibly expect me to know that?'

'Judith said it was still in the back of the van when she entered the builders' merchant's. But the police didn't find it there when they looked there later. So it must have disappeared while she was inside the buildin'. An' who took it? Why, you did! After you'd killed Burroughs, you hid your van somewhere Judith wouldn't see it, then returned to the scene of the crime on foot. You must have been lurking in the shadows when Judith drove up.'

'Fantasy! Pure fantasy!'

'All right, let's assume for a second that somebody else took the overall,' Woodend said amiably. 'How would they have gone about it?'

'I'd imagine they'd simply have opened the back door of the van and removed it.'

'The van would have been locked – just like all the ones parked outside are. Judith's not the kind of woman to have one rule for her employees an' another for herself. Whatever her mental state at the time, she'd have instinctively made sure she'd locked her vehicle.'

'Then whoever took the overall must have forced the lock.'

'They couldn't have done that with leaving evidence of their

211

handiwork behind – an' accordin' to the police experts, there was none.'

'Then they picked the lock, for God's sake!'

'Even that would have left traces. Besides, they wouldn't have had long enough. Judith was in that office for a very short time indeed – you don't hang about when you discover a dead body – so whoever removed the overall would have had to be very quick. That suggests he had a key. An' who had a spare key to Judith's van, Mr Keene?'

'You're surely not suggesting—'

'You did! You killed Burroughs, and made sure Judith would be charged with it. Because even though she was in gaol, there was no reason why she still couldn't be a partner in your firm. An' as long as *she* was your partner, nobody else was goin' to ask to take a look at your accounts.'

'This is outrageous!'

'Were you wearin' gloves that night, Mr Keene?'

'I . . . I . . . I wasn't there, so it doesn't matter whether I was wearing gloves or not.'

'I'm guessin' that you were. But even gloves leave traces at the crime scene, you know. Minute threads that you don't even notice have gone. Then there's the other clothes you were wearin'. More minute threads left behind. The forensic boys will have bagged them all, you know. They'll still be there in the evidence store – just waitin' to be compared to what you've got in your wardrobe.'

'I've . . .'

'Got rid of all those clothes? Well, that doesn't matter. It was just an example of what we can do to pin the murder on you. There are a hundred other ways we can place you at the scene of the crime – ways you wouldn't even dream of – once we know where to look. An' now we do.'

'I want to see my lawyer!' Keene said.

'What for?' Woodend wondered. 'We're only chattin' here, Mr Keene, an' if you don't want to say anythin', then I'm certainly not goin' to make you.' He took another sip of the brandy, and smacked his lips in appreciation. 'Shall we talk about Major Maitland now?'

Keene folded his arms, and kept his mouth tightly shut.

'No?' Woodend asked. 'Then I'll just have to talk it through with myself, won't I? Let me see . . . what was I goin' to say about Major Maitland? Oh yes! Everythin' was goin' so well after the murder. Your scheme had worked out just perfectly. Then Maitland came along, took his hostages, an' forced us to re-open the case. You must have hated him for that. But then you persuaded yourself that once he was out of the way, the whole thing would soon blow over again. Any comment you'd care to make at this point?'

Keene shook his head.

'But you had to make sure he was *really* out of the way,' Woodend continued. 'That's why you came to me, and asked if you could talk to him. That's why – when you did get to talk to him – you reminded him of *just how long* his wife still had to serve of her sentence. Your objective was never to convince him to give up – it was to strengthen his resolve to stay in there. Because the longer he held out, the more chance there was of him gettin' killed. Of course, there was also the chance that some of the hostages would also get killed in the process, but that was a risk you were prepared to run, because you don't really care what happens to other people.'

'I care about my mother,' Keene said.

'That's true,' Woodend agreed.

'And I cared about Judith. You have to believe that.'

'Aye, you probably did,' Woodend conceded. 'But you were still willin' to destroy her if she got in your way. An' if that's what you do to people you care about, what lengths will you go to with people you don't give a toss for?'

During the course of the conversation, Keene's face had run through the whole gamut of expressions – from concern to mystification, from mystification to outrage, from outrage to self-justification. Now it had assumed the cunning look of an animal which finds itself trapped – but believes there might still be some way of escaping.

'If I'm as big a monster as you seem to think I am, why are you offering me an easy way out?' he wondered aloud. 'If I did what you say I did, why aren't you pushing for the maximum sentence?'

'I thought we'd already discussed that,' Woodend said. 'I'm doin' it for young Timothy's sake – so he'll never learn the truth about his father and Judith Maitland.'

Keene studied him carefully, for at least half a minute. 'I believe that *is* part of it,' he said finally. 'But there's something else, isn't there – something you're not telling me.'

'I give you my word that if you sign the confession I want you to sign, I'll back you to the hilt. After all, I've no choice, have I?'

'Haven't you?'

'None. Because if your story falls apart, then the career of the feller who came up with it – which is me – will go just the same way. So we both have an interest in hidin' the truth, don't we, Mr Keene?'

'You haven't answered my question,' Keene said accusingly. 'You're still holding something back.'

'Perhaps you're right,' Woodend conceded. 'But that's my business, isn't it? *Your* business is to decide whether you serve ten years or twenty-five. *Your* business is to work out whether you want your mum to go to her grave thinkin' of you as a cold-blooded murderer, or whether she dies believin' that you found Miss Right after all, an' killed to protect her. So which of the two is it goin' to be?'

'I don't seem to have much choice, do I?' Keene asked miserably.

'No, you don't,' Woodend agreed. He lifted his brandy glass, held it up to the light, then took another drink. 'Do you know, I thought this stuff was perfect when I had my first sip,' he said. 'But it tastes even better now.'

Thirty-Three

'There are some cases that are mainly down to the work done by one member of the team, an' when it's solved it's he or she who deserves most of the credit,' Woodend said, reaching for his freshly arrived pint. 'But I can honestly say that in this particular investigation, that's not true at all. If you, Monika, hadn't found out about Judith's baby, we'd have been stymied. An' if you, Beresford – Colin, I should say – hadn't come up with the information on Keene's attempt to kill her, we'd never have had the glue we needed to stick all the other pieces we'd collected together.' He raised his glass. 'So here's to us – a bloody good team.'

The others raised their drinks and clinked them against his pint pot, but not with the full enthusiasm he would have liked to see. Monika Paniatowski seemed strangely distracted. And young Beresford – who should have been over the moon that his first case had reached a successful conclusion – looked positively depressed.

Monika stood up. 'If you'll excuse me for a minute, I have to make a phone call,' she said.

'Just make sure you're not away too long,' Woodend told her. 'Because we've got some serious drinkin' to do tonight.'

Paniatowski dialled the Dunethorpe number, and the man at the other end picked up immediately, almost as if he'd been waiting for the call.

'It's me,' she said.

'I thought it might be,' Baxter replied. 'I've just seen the news on the television. Congratulations.'

'It was a team effort,' Monika said.

'And it certainly leaves me with a good deal of egg on my face, doesn't it?' Baxter asked.

'You were *part* of the team,' Monika told him. 'If you hadn't collected all that evidence, we'd never have got anywhere.'

'I might have collected it, but I certainly don't seem to have known what to do with it.'

'You just had a blind spot,' Monika said. 'Your gut was telling you all the right things, but you chose – on this occasion – not to listen to it. We're all guilty of that, from time to time.'

'That's more than generous of you,' Baxter told her.

'Bollocks!' Monika replied. 'Listen, I've a few loose ends still to tie up in Dunethorpe tomorrow, so maybe we'll finally get the lunch we've been promising ourselves.'

'That would be delightful,' Baxter said.

Constable Beresford had not said a word since Paniatowski had left the table to make her call. In fact, he was doing a fair

215

impersonation of a man who'd rather not be there in the pub at all.

'Are you goin' to sulk all evenin', lad?' Woodend asked. 'Or would you rather tell me what's on your mind?'

'I don't see why you let Stanley Keene off so easily, sir,' the constable said, the words bursting from his mouth as if he'd only been containing them with great effort.

'When I'd spelled out the alternatives to Keene, he was just about willin' to sign a confession which would earn him a ten- or twelve-year stretch,' Woodend said. 'But he'd never have signed one which would have put him away for a quarter of a century.'

'I know that, but—'

'An' while I managed to convince him that we could put together a case which we were bound to win, the truth is that it was a long way from a racin' certainty that we would. There was always the distinct possibility he might have been found not guilty.'

'It still doesn't seem right,' Beresford said. 'He didn't just murder Burroughs, did he? He destroyed other lives as well.'

'Aye, he did,' Woodend agreed. 'Major Maitland's for a start. Even though the guns he used in the siege weren't loaded, he'll still be goin' to gaol for a long, long time. An' then there's the rest of them. Judith – who's had enough tough times in her life already – has all but lost her husband. Timothy an' his sister, who *have* lost their father. It's a complete bloody mess, an' it's all Keene's doin'.'

'Then how could you even consider offering him the soft option?' Beresford asked, almost in anguish.

'Is that what you think it is? A soft option?'

'Don't you?'

'I had quite a little talk with Major Maitland before he finally gave himself up,' Woodend said. 'I asked him how he thought he'd get on in prison. He said that a hard man like him will be virtually runnin' the gaol within a year. An' I think he's probably right.'

'I don't see what that's got to do with Keene.'

'Then I'll explain it to you. Keene's *not* a hard man. He's cunnin' an' he's vicious, but he's not hard. I don't particu-larly want to go into the details of what the other prisoners

216

will do to him once he's inside – it'd give a lad like you night-mares just to think about it – but trust me, gaol will be hell on earth for him.'

'He'll be able to stand it though – because however bad it is, he'll know it won't be for ever,' Beresford said.

'That's where you're wrong,' Woodend contradicted him. 'He won't be able to stand it. I agreed to a short sentence because I knew it would have exactly the same effect as a long one.'

'How's that possible?'

'Because whether he's servin' ten years or twenty-five years, the only way he'll ever come out of that prison will be in a box,' Woodend said.